PENGUIN MODERN CLASSICS

Liveforever

Andrés Caicedo was born Luis Andrés Caicedo Estela in Cali, Colombia, on 29 September 1951. A precocious teenager, he was passionate about cinema, about the theatre and especially about literature. While still in his teens, Caicedo acted with the *Teatro Experimental de Cali*, founded the Cineclub de Cali and launched *Ojo al cine*, a short-lived but highly influential film magazine. And he wrote constantly. At thirteen, he had written his first short stories; by fifteen he had written a number of award-winning plays. During his life, he published only one novel, *¡Que viva la música! (Liveforever)*. Begun in the early '70s and completed in 1975, the novel was resolutely urban, at once a celebration of music and of the city that he loved, and a cry of despair and a conscious reaction against the magical realism in vogue at the time. *Liveforever* was published on 4 March 1977; on the same day Caicedo received the first printed copy. It was the day on which he took his life. He was twenty-five years old.

In the years since his death, Caicedo's fame and influence have steadily grown and he has been championed as one of the most original voices in Latin American literature. Much of his work was published posthumously, including collections of short stories and three unfinished novels. His plays continue to be performed today. *Liveforever* has recently been published in French, Italian and Dutch.

Frank Wynne is a literary translator from French and Spanish. He has translated some forty works of fiction and non-fiction, including books by Michel Houellebecq, Ahmadou Kourouma, Claude Lanzmann and Tómas Eloy Martínez. His translation of *Atomised* was awarded the 2002 IMPAC Prize, and he has also won the Independent Foreign Fiction Prize (2005) and the Scott Moncrieff Prize (2008). More recently his translation of *Kamchatka* by Marcelo Figueras garnered the 2012 Premio Valle Inclán, and that of *Alex* by Pierre Lemaitre won the 2013 CWA International Crime Dagger. He is an Honorary Member of the Irish Translators' and Interpreters' Association.

Born in Bogotá in 1973, Juan Gabriel Vásquez is considered one of the foremost Colombian novelists of his generation. His novels, which seek to explore 'dark corners of Colombian history that have made us what we are now', include *The Informers* (translated by Anne McClean and shortlisted for the Independent Foreign Fiction Prize), *The Secret History of Costaguana* and *The Sound of Things Falling*, which won the 2011 Alfaguara Prize. Having spent sixteen years living in France, Belgium and Spain, he has recently returned to Bogotá.

ANDRÉS CAICEDO

Liveforever

Translated by FRANK WYNNE
Introduced by JUAN GABRIEL VÁSQUEZ

PENGUIN BOOKS

PENGUIN CLASSICS

Published by the Penguin Group
Penguin Books Ltd, 80 Strand, London WC2R ORL, England
Penguin Group (USA) Inc., 375 Hudson Street, New York, New York 10014, USA
Penguin Group (Canada), 90 Eglinton Avenue East, Suite 700, Toronto, Ontario, Canada M4P 2Y3
(a division of Pearson Penguin Canada Inc.)
Penguin Ireland, 25 St Stephen's Green, Dublin 2, Ireland (a division of Penguin Books Ltd)
Penguin Group (Australia), 707 Collins Street, Melbourne, Victoria 3008, Australia
(a division of Pearson Australia Group Pty Ltd)
Penguin Books India Pvt. Ltd, 11 Community Centre, Panchsheel Park, New Delhi – 110 017, India
Penguin Group (NZ), 67 Apollo Drive, Rosedale, Auckland 0632, New Zealand
(a division of Pearson New Zealand Ltd)
Penguin Books (South Africa) (Pty) Ltd, Block D, Rosebank Office Park, 181 Jan Smuts Avenue,
Parktown North, Gauteng 2193, South Africa

Penguin Books Ltd, Registered Offices: 80 Strand, London WC2R ORL, England

www.penguin.com

First published in Spanish by Colcultura 1977
This translation first published in Great Britain by Penguin Classics 2014

004

Copyright © Andrés Caicedo, 1977
Translation © Frank Wynne, 2014
Introduction © Juan Gabriel Vásquez, 2014
Translation of the introduction © Rosalind Harvey, 2014

Excerpts from the following three songs are reprinted by kind permission of the copyright holders:
pp. 36–7, 'Moonlight Mile' Words and Music by Mick Jagger and Keith Richards © 1971
(Renewed) ABKCO Music, Inc., 85 Fifth Avenue, New York, NY 10003, All Rights Reserved
p. 64, 'The Last Time' Words and Music by Mick Jagger and Keith Richards © 1965 (Renewed)
ABKCO Music, Inc., 85 Fifth Avenue, New York, NY 10003, All Rights Reserved
p. 67, 'Doo Doo Doo Doo Doo (Heartbreaker)' Words and Music by Mick Jagger and Keith
Richards © 1973, Reproduced by kind permission of EMI Music Publishing Ltd, London W1F 9LD

Typeset in 10.5/13 pt Dante by Palimpsest Book Production Ltd, Falkirk, Stirlingshire
Printed and bound in Great Britain by Clays Ltd, Elcograf S.p.A.

ISBN: 978-0-141-19668-8

www.greenpenguin.co.uk

MIX
Paper | Supporting
responsible forestry
FSC® C018072
www.fsc.org

Penguin Books is committed to a sustainable
future for our business, our readers and our planet.
This book is made from Forest Stewardship
Council™ certified paper.

This book is no longer dedicated to Clarisolcita since, when she grew up, she became so much like my heroine that she no longer deserved it.

Andrés Caicedo

It's so sleazy but it's so good.
    Popular Song

I hang on with one hand to desk, write with other.
    Malcolm Lowry, *Through the Panama*

Contents

Introduction
Leave Work and Die Happy

I

On the day of his third suicide attempt, Andrés Caicedo dreamed that he was holding a gun and pointing it at his son's chest, but his mother woke him before he could shoot. In fact, Caicedo had no children: he was twenty-five years, five months and four days old and had long since realized that not only was he not cut out to have a family, he was not cut out for life as he knew it. It was 4 March 1977. At some point during the day, the first copy of *Live-forever* (*¡Que viva la música!* in the original Spanish) arrived by post; Caicedo showed it to a friend who dropped by his house, he spent some hours visiting various haunts in Cali looking for a woman, and he wrote two letters. To Patricia Restrepo (the woman he was searching for, the woman with whom he had argued, the woman he loved as only a suicide could love) he wrote: 'Don't think that my joy at receiving the first copy of my novel today can compare to my abject misery because of the contempt you have shown me.' In a line reminiscent of Cesare Pavese, he added: 'I don't think I will write any more. I've nothing left to say, except don't leave me.' To Miguel Marías, a Spanish film critic, he wrote that over the previous days, he had read the complete works of Witold Gombrowicz, four novels by Pío Baroja and three by Virginia Woolf and had watched several films, including *Dial M for Murder*,

Jules et Jim, An American in Paris and *Singin' in the Rain*. Later he wrote: 'I've just received the first copy of my novel. With luck, I hope to be sending you a copy in about a week.' He did not keep his promise. Shortly after writing these lines, he took sixty Seconal tablets and died, according to those who found him, slumped over his typewriter.

In the thirty-six years since then, Caicedo's reputation and his fame have continued to grow. *Liveforever*, published in the slim, 200-page volume he received just before he died, has become – at first in Colombia and later throughout Latin America – a genuine example of a much misunderstood and misused term: the cult novel. Caicedo's book provokes passions, heated arguments between friends, fierce loyalties; it is passed from hand to hand like the secret key to some Masonic lodge. For over a decade it could be read only in photocopied and pirated editions, until Caicedo's friends finally overcame their grief at his death and devoted themselves to promoting his work. There is a poetic justice of sorts in this, since it was in part for them that Caicedo wrote it. *Liveforever* is a novel about the last years of adolescence – or at least the last years of a certain type of adolescence: as aimless, frantic, furious and demented as an LP played at 45rpm. The adolescence portrayed in this novel is not the kind that naturally leads on to adult life; instead it is cut short – more or less like the novel itself, which ends with a list of songs and unidentified lyrics. An adolescence in which the world is sensed and understood through salsa, the music young people in Cali danced to then and still dance to today. For the characters of the novel salsa, a fusion of Caribbean rhythms and Afro-Cuban jazz, is not simply a musical style: it is a sentimental education. In *Liveforever* salsa lyrics are the closest thing the characters have to a philosophy of life. To quote María del Carmen Huerta, the blonde narrator of the novel:

I open my mouth to speak and no one stops me, and all that comes out are lyrics, because before me came a musician, someone infinitely more power-ful and more generous, someone happy to let people sing his lyrics without having to take responsibility, and so I wake up in the morning with a lyric that will run through my head, over and over all day long like a sort of talisman against every miserable moment . . . (p. 75)

Salsa is a way of being in the world. 'Music that knows me, music that inspires me, fans me or shelters me, the pact is sealed' (p. 117), as María del Carmen says. And the reader cannot help but wonder: what pact?

II

Like all Colombians, particularly those who gorged on novels since childhood, I first read this book when I was the same age as Caicedo's characters. Rereading it now, some twenty years later, I was a little apprehensive; I tiptoed through each page, each scene, terrified that at any moment the spell that had bewitched me in my youth might be broken, and I would be lying if I didn't admit that I was surprised to discover a novel as brash, as vivid and as relevant today as it was on the day it was published. In other words, Caicedo's novel has not remained fixed in the generation for which it was written – the *washed-up generation*, to paraphrase the author (p. 84), who were born in the middle of the last century. This is what María del Carmen means when she says: 'Oh, I had high hopes for my generation!' (p. 44).

The fate of *Liveforever* has not been to sit around waiting. Over the course of its history, Caicedo's novel has continued to speak to successive generations of young people, washed up or otherwise. With each generation its reputation has grown, and the novel has never been so avidly read outside Colombia as it is today. The Chilean writer Alberto Fuguet recently tried to explain the reason for the 'Caicedo phenomenon'. 'In an age of Twitter and iPhones, of chatrooms and Skype, WhatsApp and YouTube,' he wrote, 'Caicedo seems the obvious author to tell the story of this new generation: of people at once connected and disconnected, overdosing on information but experiencing emotions they don't fully understand or can't control.' But beyond such technological analysis, *Liveforever* is a whisper in the ear of every truly disillusioned soul. Though I have always mistrusted the modish rebelliousness of so many overly self-conscious writers, I feel there is an aching sincerity in the story of the *blondissima* María del Carmen Huerta, a palpable vulnerability that immediately makes her real and genuinely moving: a character we feel we could talk to, one we are fascinated to listen to. And the reasons for this are obvious: *Liveforever* is not a Bildungsroman, a sentimental education, but a sentimental *miseducation*. In these pages, we witness a frantic, inexorable quest whose weapons are salsa, cinema, (relatively) suppressed violence and (relatively) uninhibited sex. But it is a quest that leads not to enlightenment, not to insight, but to ever deeper levels of frustration and despair. The pages read like a riotous hymn to life, and yet the novel ends with a kind of manifesto that invokes violent death and even suicide. 'For the hatred instilled in you by the censor, there is no better cure than murder,' writes Caicedo. 'For shyness: self-destruction' (pp. 154–5).

Yet it is not this wilful iconoclasm, this marriage of James Dean and Janis Joplin, that has ensured *Liveforever* has remained forever young. There is a different, much more subtle rebelliousness at work here, one that lies not in what Caicedo's novel does, but in what – stubbornly, persistently – it *fails* to do. Let me try to explain.

III

In 1975, Caicedo wrote the only suicide note we are aware of. Though he did not commit suicide on that occasion, the document is one of the most revealing that we have. 'Please try to understand my death,' Caicedo wrote to his mother. 'I wasn't made to live any longer. I feel a terrible weariness, a disappointment and a sadness, and I know with every passing day, those feelings are slowly killing me. So I would rather get it over with now.' We can assume that this weariness was the product of his hypersensitivity, of the turmoil in his love life, his creative anxieties and his frequent clashes with a father whose views were utterly at odds with Caicedo's emotional world. But a few lines later we come across an agonizing sentence, a keyhole through which we can glimpse an entire world: 'I'm dying,' Caicedo writes, 'because I'm not yet twenty-four and already I'm an anachronism.'

An anachronism: the verdict is (painfully) accurate. In Latin America, particularly in the '70s, the lives and interests of young intellectuals – and though he despised them, Andrés Caicedo was a young intellectual – were inextricably linked to a certain kind of political engagement which, in turn, was inextricably bound up with left-wing politics in general and the Cuban Revolution in particular. In those days, the worlds of cinema and literature established rigid boundaries between the revolutionary and the counter-revolutionary, between avant-garde and bourgeois art. Something recently reaffirmed by the playwright Sandro Romero and the filmmaker Luis Ospina – two friends of Andrés Caicedo who were largely responsible for rescuing his work and for collecting and publishing his papers. 'If you were involved in the arts, you were expected to be militantly left wing,' Romero told me. 'Andrés was in sympathy with these ideas, but he also liked American cinema, rock music and salsa. The problem was that salsa was played by Puerto Rican musicians living in New York, musicians who were seen as being reactionary.' Caicedo did not share, and would never manage to share, the political passions of his contemporaries. The words 'revolution' and 'Cuba' appear only once or twice in this novel, and every time they drip with irony or caustic cynicism. 'This was not helped by the *coup d'état* in Chile in 1973,' Luis Ospina told me. 'For those of us who were politically involved, Pinochet's coup was the last nail in the coffin to our dreams of revolution.'

It was in March of that ill-fated year that Caicedo began writing the first pages that would grow initially to become a long story and, later, this novel; after Salvador Allende's death in September the novel lost any interest it had in politics, or rather confirmed it had never really had any. 'Our revolutionary hero wasn't Fidel Castro, it was Jean-Luc Godard,' Caicedo once wrote in a letter to the Colombian novelist Jaime Manrique. This was the kind of statement that could – and, in fact, did – turn him into a pariah, an outcast. To another friend he wrote: 'I know, I understand, I accept the fact that my presence doesn't always foster harmony, order or coherence, for the simple reason that the people I work with tend to be unambiguous.' Not so Caicedo, who was messy, incoherent, ambiguous. Andrés Caicedo: the anachronism.

Traits that are – unsurprisingly – shared by his novel. *Liveforever* was written during the reign – or perhaps we should say the imperium – of the Latin American Boom: the magisterial generation led by Gabriel García Márquez, Carlos Fuentes, Julio Cortázar and Mario Vargas Llosa that forever transformed Spanish-language literature and redefined for the whole world the meaning of 'Latin America'. The publication, during the prodigal 1960s, of novels such as *The Death of Artemio Cruz, Conversation in the Cathedral* and in particular *One Hundred Years of Solitude*, proposed a paradigm that was virtually impossible to oppose. The great Latin American novel was epic, it was political without being politicized and capable of moulding history into fiction. In *History of a Deicide*, his 600-page essay on García Márquez published in 1971, Vargas Llosa coined the phrase *novela total* – the 'total novel' – to refer to those fictions that aim to compete with reality in their richness and diversity. This ambition, this ethic of excess, went hand in hand with the ineluctable sense that Latin American history was one long string of lies and that, as Carlos Fuentes wrote, the novel had a duty to 'say all that history has hushed up'. *The Autumn of the Patriarch* by García Márquez and *Terra Nostra* by Carlos Fuentes embody this dictum, two major works published in 1975 even as Andrés Caicedo, a stuttering, introverted twentysomething (yes: shy and self-destructive), cowered in a dark corner of the literary world, writing a novel that was the polar opposite of what his elders were instructing him to write.

So it goes. *Liveforever*, this intimate, idiosyncratic and erratic monologue, rejects all the intricate obligations that the Latin American novel had taken upon itself. It is almost apolitical and certainly anti-historical: it flatly refuses to squeeze the whole world into fiction, content to be bounded by a few snatches of salsa, a few streets in Cali, the apartments of a few friends; the reader will search in vain for some eloquent pronouncement about historical tensions or the fate of the Latin American peoples, and will have to make do with the private angst of a teenage girl searching for a humble epiphany through dance and music, sex and drugs; and the voice of that young girl – oh, the voice of *la pelada*! – owes more to the *skaz* of Salinger's Holden Caulfield or of William Burroughs than to any narrators in her own language. The name García Márquez is not mentioned in Caicedo's letters; but Vargas Llosa's is, almost always referring to *The Time of the Hero* (1963), his novel describing the 'sentimental education' (or miseducation) of a group of teenage cadets at a military academy. But the fundamental issue remains. Compared with the great Latin American literature of its time, *Liveforever* is like Melville's Bartleby who goes through life saying: 'I would prefer not to.' Or, to put it another way, like Peter Pan: refusing to grow up, rejecting the social responsibilities, the political concerns of adulthood. '[P]retending not to grow up,' says María del Carmen, 'that's what nostalgia is' (p. 31).

The disgust Caicedo felt for the adult world is a thread that runs through his public works and his private writings. Neither he nor María del Carmen can understand other people's eagerness to grow up, to become part of a world full of hypocrites and (to use Holden Caulfield's word) *phonies*. It was a disgust Caicedo had been cultivating for several years before he started writing *Liveforever*. In fact, it is obvious in the dedication that holds open the door to the novel for us: 'This book is no longer dedicated to Clarisolcita since, when she grew up, she became so much like my heroine that she no longer deserved it.' No: in Caicedo's ethos, growing up is not acceptable. Clarisolcita was a twelve-year-old girl Caicedo met around 1972: Clarisol Lemos and her brother were, as he described them years later, two 'wildly precocious and deeply perverse' children. Caicedo joined their gang – or rather, he joined in order to become its leader, as though they were the Lost Boys – and with Clarisol he was able to 'create the appearance of a child who does not – or refuses to – grow up'. The two made an unholy pact: 'You pretend to be my age and I'll pretend to be yours.' It is hardly surprising, therefore, that in his dedication he castigates her for breaking her promise. Towards the end of

Liveforever their childhood pact becomes a philosophical maxim, an existential *mode d'emploi*:

Let no one turn you into a grown-up, a respectable man. Never stop being a child, even when you've got eyes in the back of your head and your teeth are starting to fall out. Your parents gave birth to you. Let them support you forever, and fob them off with empty promises. Who gives a fuck? Never save for the future. Never let yourself become someone serious. Make heedlessness and fickleness your rules of conduct. Refuse all truces, make your home amid ruins, excess and trembling. (p. 154)

For us as readers, these words come as a shock, as though we are watching an actor stepping out of his role. It is here, for the first time, that we realize it is not María del Carmen but Andrés Caicedo who is speaking to us; that the young man from Cali has peeled off his mask to reveal his face, his true face: the same troubled and tormented face he revealed in December 1974, a few short months before his first suicide attempt, when he finished writing this novel.

A couple of lines before this brief litany, María del Carmen says: 'Leave something of yourself behind and die in peace.'

In his 1975 suicide note, Andrés Caicedo says: 'Leave some work behind and die in peace.'

More than three decades on, his work is still with us.

Andrés Caicedo: you can rest in peace.

Juan Gabriel Vásquez

Translator's Note

'Translation,' Anthony Burgess once said, 'is not a matter of words only: it is a matter of making intelligible a whole culture.' It is a much quoted bromide but one that has never seemed more pertinent than in attempting to recreate the strange hermetic world of Andrés Caicedo.

All novels are distant from us in time or in place; they introduce us to worlds – whether real or imagined – that only the author truly inhabits. In one sense, *Liveforever* takes place in the real world, Cali, Colombia, circa 1977, and consequently I knew I would have to wrangle with the mysterious slang of the city at that time. But the novel also takes place inside the mind of its narrator, María del Carmen Huerta, whose thoughts are so suffused with the music she adores that as the book progresses, her voice and her tale become shot through with song titles and lyrics, especially from the classic salsa of the period by perhaps the most famous salsa duo, Richie Ray & Bobby Cruz. In the original, these musical references are not signalled to the reader in any way; they simply weave through the narrative as bizarre images and curious non-sequiturs. Using his narrator's unique voice, Caicedo creates a shimmering, shifting, increasingly hallucinatory pattern of words and images.

Few Colombian readers would recognize all or even most of these allusions since Caicedo wrote down lyrics as he heard them, often paraphrasing or misquoting them in the process. Salsa lyrics are not immediately comprehensible even to those who wrote them: in an interview with Sandro Romero, Ray and Cruz confessed that even *they* did not know precisely what they were singing, nor the exact meaning of their lyrics.* To further complicate matters, the lyrics combine Spanish with Yoruba and Ñáñiga dialects and are suffused with images of the gods and the myths of Santería. (Also known as *La Religión*, this is an amalgam of Afro-Cuban beliefs with Catholicism.) The hallucinatory style of Caicedo's novel and the fleeting nature of his allusions means it is almost inevitable that I will have missed some of the references.

Since few English-language readers are likely to have an in-depth knowledge of salsa and the many related styles of Afro-Cuban music (*cumbia, guaguancó, bembé, bugalú, salsa brava*), I have decided to italicize the musical allusions in the novel to highlight this thread that runs through its pages. I was keen to avoid annotation here, but those interested in following up references will find a 'List of Song Lyrics' at the end of the book, giving the song title in each case, and an alphabetical 'List of Songs', giving the singers too. Otherwise, I have done my best to preserve the curiously poetic voice of María del Carmen Huerta, drawing on '70s slang in the hope of conjuring the period, but electing to keep some Spanish words to preserve a sense of place (while *pelada* ('little girl') might be translated as 'chick', for instance, it sounds too 'California Girls'). I have done my utmost to follow Caicedo's sinuous, free-flowing sentence structure, the tumbling torrent of words that are María del Carmen's own song.

None of this would have been possible without the help of Luis Ospina and Sandro Romero, friends of the author whose films and books have been indispensable in teasing out the delicate harmonies of the novel. I would also like to express my gratitude to Bernard Cohen and Lulu Norman for their support and encouragement and to the Santa Maddalena Foundation, where I spent some time working on the translation.

Frank Wynne, 2014

---

* Sandro Romero, *Andrés Caicedo o la muerte sin sosiego* (Bogotá: Grupo Editorial Norma, 2007), p. 63.

Liveforever

I'm blonde. *Blondissima*. So blonde that guys say, 'Hey, angel, you only have to flick that lustrous mane of hair over my face to free me of the shadow hounding me.' It was no shadow on their faces but death. And I was scared to lose my sheen.

Anyone seeing my hair these days wouldn't really understand. You have to factor in the night as it draws in, bringing with it a strange mist. Plus, I'm talking about the old days and, well, good times and bad habits have robbed even my locks of their lustre.

But there was a time they'd say, 'Hey, *pelada*, I just gotta say, your hair's *dazzling*.' And some creepy, prematurely bald guy: 'Lillian Gish had hair like yours.' And I was thinking, 'Who's she? Some famous singer?' I recently found out she was a silent movie star. All this time, there was I imagining her with strings of necklaces, blonde to her fingertips, belting it out as the crowd went wild. It's amazing the stuff you don't know.

Everyone else knew all about music. Everyone except me. Because I had a thousand things going on in my head. I was a good girl. Okay, not exactly a good girl; I was always screaming and throwing tantrums and fighting with *mamá*. But I read my books, and I can still remember the three study sessions we arranged to read *Das Kapital*. Me, Armando 'the Cricket' (we called him the Cricket because of his baffled, bug eyes that were always checking out my knees) and Antonio Manríquez. Three mornings those study sessions lasted and I swear, I totally got it, every last word, the culture of my country. I don't want to start thinking about all that now: it's all very well remembering stuff, but wanting to remember such dedication and devotion is something else.

3

What I want is to start my story from the day I first missed the study session. Because that was the day I first slipped into the world of music, records and dancing. I plan to tell my tale in detail and I know my gentle reader won't be bored; I know I've already got you spellbound.

That morning I woke up so late that even with my eyes open I couldn't summon any energy. But I thought, 'Just put one foot on the cold tiles and you'll see, you'll get there on time.' I was kidding myself. The study sessions started at 9 a.m. and by now it was – what – noon? I set my small pale feet on the tiles and felt a shudder run through me as I realized I could walk, one tile at a time. So off I set, happily, taking baby steps, with no goal beyond making it as far as the window.

I drew the curtains and the sight of my outspread arms reminded me what a determined young woman I was. One of those women capable, as they say, of tilling the earth with their bare hands if they have a mind to. Not me. With the curtains open, I found myself staring at the venetian blinds. Is it true that Venice brings death? I only mention it because it's something I used to hear (not any more) in old songs. I could have pulled the cord, raised the venetian blinds like a sailor hoisting a sail and let the new day stream into the room in all its glory. I didn't. I leaned closer – only the slightest movement but one I knew was tainted – and I slatted the new day through the blinds and suddenly I longed for night. For the twilight, the colour of the sky, the wind in my face just the way I like it. It's the wind that gives my hair its strength, its perfume.

But not any more, not these days. Looking out I saw a curdled sky in thick brushstrokes and the Western Mountains that looked like a black man's knees. I snapped the blinds shut, feeling panicky and defeated. What was the point, it was too early. 'The mountains burned last night,' I thought, 'and all that's left are little frizzy hairs.'

My legs were very white, but an ugly, plebeian white with little blue veins behind the knees. Yesterday, the doctor told me the little blood vessels I was so proud of are just the beginning of varicose veins.

I went back to my bed wondering, 'How long before night comes?' No idea. I could have shouted down to the maid to ask what time it was. I didn't. I could have closed my eyes and drifted off. I didn't. I was already conflicted and I was angry. I don't deny I was getting to enjoy sleeping late, but how could I square that with my strict schedule?

So I called down to see if anyone had phoned and of course straight away they told me, 'Yes, *niña*, those boys called, the ones you study with.'

I buried my face in the pillow, wallowing in the dampness of the sheets – I don't know how clean they were – my body smooth and slippery as a fish with no scales. I felt a surge of shame, quickly followed by remorse.

This was the first day I missed the reading of *Das Kapital*, and I never went back. Since that day, morning shame has plagued me, trying to make me blot out and deny the great time I had the night before, all the new people . . . Well, that was only at first. These days, believe me, there's no one new; it's the same people, the same old faces, and there's only two I really fancy: one is a brilliant dancer with a macho Mexican moustache. I tell him, 'It makes you look old,' and he flashes his big, beautiful teeth and says, 'Why would I want to be young again? Like I didn't go through enough shit to get to the age I am. When I talk about life, I don't get hung up on passing fads. I deal in *concepts*, you dig? I'm pretty set in my ways these days, but I've got things sussed and the way I see it, there's no accounting for taste, yeah? Otherwise why would I come here every night to see you, *pelada*?' Because he always calls me *pelada* – little girl. And the other guy, the one I really fancy, well, the less said about him the better; he's trouble, one of those lanky thugs who still thinks it's cool to wear black T-shirts.

Sorry, I was talking about my shame. But I think, and I really believe this: 'I've got no reason to be ashamed.' So what if I grabbed the night by the balls, so what if I broke its spirit, wore it out and drained it dry? At least I was still standing: not like the men, who drop like flies. At worst I end up with my hair wild and dishevelled, looking all little-girl-lost as I wander the streets, heading home. But then, as I'm closing my eyes, I swear I think to myself, 'Now that's life.' And I sleep like a baby. But then morning comes around and says (I think it's something to do with the strange sunlight these past months): 'Change your life.'

What's the point of that? Why change my life just when I've finally got it together? But such is the weight of my conscience – I picture it in mourning black and wearing a veil – it almost has me confessing my sins and promising to make amends (amen). Not that that makes any difference: as soon as 6 p.m. rolls round, I'm done with praying. I really think it's something to do with the sun, it doesn't agree with me. I've tried not going out, I've tried sitting in my room thinking. *Nada*, zilch, nothing works. So I go out, dazed but utterly pure, filled with good intentions, meaning to melt into the crowd of shoppers, the elegant ladies and the foxy guys on their bicycles. Once I nearly found myself screaming, 'I love people!' But I didn't. Because just then the clock struck six and I surrendered to the night. *Babalú*[1] *walks with me.*

That was last week, probably last Saturday. But I don't want to get ahead of myself or I'll end up chasing my tail, which is hard to catch the way it whips and twists. Prithee, gentle reader, try to keep up; my pace is pretty brisk.

Let's get back to the day I broke with my routine. Why did I do it, when I'd seriously got into the Method? Especially in the last couple of years at school. I was a brilliant student and all set to study architecture at the Universidad del Valle: I came second in the entrance exam (some skinny, anaemic girl with glasses and wonky teeth from *Presentación del Aguacatal* convent came first). There were only two weeks left before lectures started and I know how the world works – I mean, hey, I was studying *Das Kapital* with my friends – it seemed obvious that I was going through a new phase, maybe the last phase of the life that people I run into these days say is sad, say is pallid. And as I wander the streets I run into the girls I knew at school and sooner or later, they're like 'you're *un-re-cog-nizable*'. And I say, 'Forget it.' I've already forgotten them, anyway. All it took was one study session for me to laugh in their faces when they called to suggest some pathetic trip to the pool: they didn't know that when I left my first study session, exhausted from the effort of understanding, I went down to the River with Misery Guts Ricardo (I call him that because he's constantly miserable, or at least that's what he'd say). For the first time in my life I discovered the River.

'How come I didn't know this was here before?' I asked Ricardo and he said, with the humility of someone speaking the truth, 'Because you were a stuck-up bourgeois prig.'

I glared at him, shocked by his bluntness, so to be nice (and because he loved me) he added, 'But now you've bathed in these waters, you're not like that any more. You're adorable.' And when I heard this I jumped into the River fully clothed, threw my arms wide, gazing at the lawn of spray thrown up by my frenzied splashing. This was the Río Pance in peaceful days.

So obviously when my old girlfriends phoned, I laughed in their faces. 'The swimming pool? Why would I want to go to the swimming pool when a stone's throw away is a gift of nature with glorious, crystal-clear waters, good for the nerves and the complexion?'

They didn't understand me then and they'll never understand me now. I see them sometimes with their little boyfriends who look so pale, so respectable (so perfect for me since I'm a strangling vine that haunts the nightclubs). And I know they're thinking, 'She's so *vulgar*. We're respectable girls, so how come we keep running into each other in the same places?' I wouldn't give them the satisfaction of an answer: let them work it out for themselves. Instead I think of that no-man's-land, that wisp of night entwined with the endless party that is the *rumba* where they'll never see anyone more entranced, more loved (superficial, I know, and frivolous, but that's my whole problem) or more desired, and as they're heading home early they'll be thinking, 'How late does she stay?' For the record, I'm always last to leave; I stay till I'm thrown out.

I've squashed the little bug called conscience but that's not the same *bicho* that bites the next day, the horrible morning-after guilt. Heaven forgive me but one morning, at some God-awful hour – nine o'clock maybe – I thought about calling them, well, about calling Lucía, who used to be a friend – bubbly and big-hearted, at least that's how I remember her – thought about calling her and telling her my story. Bad enough that I thought about it, what's worse is that I did it. I picked up the phone and when I heard her voice stammering on the other end of the line, I fell back on the bed and cried, all alone.

Now I realize it was a stupid idea to call her. There are better ways to tell this story, something my gentle reader, *mi papito lindo*, is beginning to realize. I still have life.

Anyway, to get back to the day I broke with my routine. Ricardito had called that morning early, even earlier than the Marxists. Why? Because he hadn't been with me the night before – a night that somehow perfectly sets the tone for the day on which my story begins. So he didn't know how wild the night had been, how it had been mine, all mine, how when the other 90 per cent were burned out, dead on their feet, I was resplendent, with my brightly coloured dress and my boundless energy. Trust me on this.

'I could call Ricardito, the River boy,' I thought. 'Today, I could go lie naked on the white-hot stones.' But the girl never phones the guy, I believed that then, I still believe it now; I'm very young, that's one of the things guys can't forgive me for. That and the fact that I never call them, obviously.

Standing in front of the mirror, I pulled my hair into two long tresses, opened my eyes so wide my eyelids disappeared, my fore-head shimmered and my cheeks dimpled. That's something else guys used to say: 'Wow, you've got amazing eyes!' And when they did, I'd look down, all coy. My eyes looked a little sunken that morning but that's only because back then I liked them like that; I wanted my eyes to look like Mariángela's, this girl I used to know who's dead now. I wanted the same edginess she had when she shot some guy a sidelong glance, those nights when she danced alone, when no one dared go near her. How could they when the fury steadily took possession of her until it wasn't her that was moving to the music? I'd see her completely unhinged, her eyes wild, jolted by some powerful force deep in her belly. It was the fury inside her respond-ing to the rhythm.

'Don't walk so fast,' she'd say to me if we were going to hook up with some guy who was waiting for us. 'Better to make him wait. Anyway, this way we get to meet people.'

She loved to be seen but she couldn't stand to be touched. As far as I know she was the first girl from *El Nortecito* – posh, bourgeois north Cali – to dive into this world, the first to try everything. I was the second.

Standing in front of the mirror, I was thinking, 'Take a shower, do my hair, get dressed: twenty minutes tops.' Problem was, I desperately needed to be out of here *now*, to be out there listening to music, meeting friends. 'What if I don't shower, don't wash, just head out and scandalize the neighbourhood?' Check it out: even then I realized the power of a weapon as revolutionary as scandal. 'Can't do it,' I thought. 'The club last night was cramped and smoky. If I'm going to get used to going clubbing every night [this was a private joke, an impossible possibility], I have to wash my hair at least every other day, just to get rid of the stink of smoke.'

Smoke doesn't suit hair as blonde as mine. Now, a girl with a shock of hair black as a raven's wing, that would be different. So I thought, 'I'll wash my hair: forty minutes.' Such a momentous decision called for a truce. I smoked a whole cigarette, pulling faces at myself in my mirror, which used to have – I guess it still does, whether they've sold it or not – a crack down the middle that swallowed my reflection, literally sucked it in. Not that I ever asked for a new one; given how obsessed *mamá* is with keeping up appearances, she'd have been quite capable of buying me a two-metre-square mirror with a gilt frame. I was fascinated by this cracked mirror, which is why I still remember it: I found one just like it in a junk shop, a mirror with a frame as white as bone and the same identical crack; it was like my old mirror had come back to me and time had narrowed and deepened the crack.

I thought about turning on the battered old transistor in my room, but then I remembered a friend of mine, Silvio, had given me some records and said, 'I'm lending you these so you can learn to really listen to music.' Given that I trusted him, because

I've known him since we were kids, I didn't call him on it, but if it had been anyone else, one of the parasites of the night, I'd have said, 'Go on, ask me a question; let's see if I flunk.' But Silvio was a good guy, he worried about me, about my lack of culture; besides, he was right: when it came to music I knew sweet-fucking-*nada*. Mariángela, now she knew everything there was to know; she was always dropping the names of singers and even song titles in English.

Up in the hay fever of my room, I thought, 'Why don't I go downstairs and learn music and English from Silvio's records?' But the minute I stood up, I sat down again. 'No, what would I want to go downstairs for?' I thought, sort of beweeping my outcast state. 'Why would I want to listen to music in front of everyone [though at this hour 'everyone' was three servants and our dopey mutt who I think is a 'lapdog' in more ways than one], why would I want to listen to music at a respectable volume when last night it was thumping? Besides, I'd only have to turn it down because the minute *papá* and *mamá* came home from lunch, they'd say, "Turn that thing down!"' So I thought, 'No, no I'm not going downstairs,' and walked over to the window. It was only two steps away. It took me three.

What I wanted was to close the curtains, maybe go back to sleep. But I didn't. I stared down the day (quite a healthy move), knowing it was going to be horrible, ringed by those black mountains with their frizzy little hairs. Was the black guy spreading his legs?

The reader might think that this thing of seeing knees where there are mountains is because the *pelada* has already been hitting her stash . . . Okay, let's talk about drugs: weed left me with a heavy feeling in my belly, rambling thoughts, nausea, spiky hair, lethargy, insomnia; next came the little rivers of fire like tiny caterpillars biting into my brain (at least I still realized I had a brain), a melancholy feeling in my mouth, a weakness in my legs and, sometimes, shooting pains in my crotch.

But, oh, what was any of that compared to the vast, eternally new, never-completely-explored terrain of hard black sand you discover as the music plays? Like I've said before, when it comes to culture I'm a total ignoramus, yet I could hear every sound, every constellation of wonders. Is that how other people do it?

I closed my eyes to the mountains. As for the park, forget about it; I couldn't drag myself down there yet, I'd get caught up in its embrace sooner or later when I went down to face the day. As I thought about this, I was distracted by what looked like tiny dragonflies. When I forced my eyes in opposite directions, they tripled; when I squinted I saw a swarm of them on the tip of my nose. This I didn't like. I squeezed my eyes tight shut to forget. Forgetting was good, I saw thousands of colours, then only two: green and the saddest grey in the whole world, forming cross-words, cartoon speech bubbles with no words, the green fragmenting to become a million tiny points like pins buried deep, then I opened my eyes again. I *overexposed* the mountains (I use that word because *papá* is a photographer), their frizzy hairs, the blue sky. Was it blue because I overexposed it or because the day really was improving? No, it was arid and anguished after a long year without a single drop of rain falling on this good earth. 'Who cares about the rain?' people would say. 'Just seeing you, that hair of yours, I feel refreshed.' And I looked down happily. But they also said, 'Has a plague fallen on this city?' And some guy answered, 'Let it come down,' hurling himself on to the dance floor, small and frenetic. And I danced too. I was the second-best dancer (Mariángela was always the best) and I don't remember anyone saying anything else. All the people who knew English sang along with the lyrics, beautiful lights flickered on and there were no sad thoughts, just pure frenzy. As they say.

So, anyway, I decided to head straight for the bathroom. I also decided to order a big breakfast (which was not straightforward, unfortunately) to be ready by the time I went downstairs. I yelled down my order and headed for the bathroom, pulling off my shirt and pants along the way.

I always took freezing-cold showers; I still do. I tried to take my time soaping myself. I counted to thousands and then, stepping out of the shower, I sang as I untangled my hair.

Outside the windows the day was hard and dry. I decided I

wouldn't go out after breakfast, not in that sunshine, and I thought gloomily, 'If only someone would come and claim me, whisk me off to some cold climate.' But if I didn't go out, then what? An hour later I'd have to have lunch with the whole family. Not that I'd have a problem eating again, I've got the appetite of a wild boar, but I hated the heavy silence at mealtimes, broken only by *mamá* singing snatches of Jeanette MacDonald and Nelson Eddy songs in her fal-setto voice. She couldn't stand any other kind of music; she used to lull me to sleep on summer holidays singing me songs from *Indian Love Call*.[2]

And after lunch, then what? Come back up to my room since the heat downstairs would be unbearable, lie on my bed brooding from 2 p.m. to 4 p.m., since on a day like today I wouldn't be able to read.

I had a thought: 'Wouldn't it be great if we could live by night, in the twilight hour, with the nine colours and the windmills. Wouldn't it be great if people worked at night, because if they didn't there'd be nothing to do but *rumba*.'

Suddenly, there was a knock at my door and I screamed furiously, 'Who is it?'

'Ricardito,' he said, with that helpless voice of his that drove every girl wild. Except me, never me.

'A visitor!' I thought cheerfully, wrapping a towel yellow as wheat around me as I opened the door.

He was smiling, the poor guy. I smiled too: the shirt he was wear-ing was spectacular! He stepped into my room, following the trail of my blouse and my white pants on the floor. And I knew the sight of them would cool him after the blistering heat he'd endured for hours, because Ricardito always went out straight after breakfast and wandered the streets aimlessly, without this trail my discarded clothes now marked out for him.

He pretended he wasn't looking at them, stopped dead in the mid-dle of the room. The light streaming through the open blinds gave a certain grandeur to his look of permanent anxiety, and I thought, 'He always looks his best here in my room. Then again, who wouldn't in that dark green and lilac shirt, it's totally *psychedelic*.' The word made

me think that if I wound down the blinds, the light would paint horizontal shadows across his body, that if I took off his shirt he'd look
like John Gavin,[3] only thirty kilos lighter, that together, in this room,
in this lonely house in this desolate, sweltering city, we were the
opening scene of *Psycho*, a film I never wanted to see again so I
wouldn't forget it.

'How's the water?' said Ricardito, in a wistful tone. You could see
from the slick of sweat on his forehead and his nose he'd been walking in the sun.

'The water's fine,' I said and laughed. 'Still up at the crack of
dawn?'

And suddenly he went dark, as though my words had enfolded
him in the night he so dreaded. In that sudden darkness, he stepped
closer and confessed, 'I haven't slept in ten months,' and I backed
away, protesting, 'Don't pull that face on me, Ricardito, don't do it,
the day's only just beginning.' Immediately I realized my mistake.
He'd have been perfectly entitled to say, 'For you, maybe . . . ' but he
said nothing, though I know that's what he was thinking, and I took
advantage of his silence to turn my back and put on a little show for
him: in a single movement I threw open the doors of the wardrobe,
whipped the towel from my body and let it drop somewhere near
him (I didn't realize how near, but I couldn't let him start on about
misery; he'd ruined too many parties, bored too many girls to death
with his melancholy moods) and, shielded by the wardrobe door, I
gave a quick *psssht! psssht!* under each pudgy armpit and tossed the
can of deodorant on to the bed so he'd see that the brand I always
use is called 'Polar Dawn'. I never thought about what pants to wear,
I just picked the first pair off the top of the pile: there were hundreds
of them.

'I brought you something,' he said, all serious, and since I wasn't
looking at him I asked vaguely, 'Something small?' twisting as I
pulled on an orange shirtdress just perfect for days like the one I'm
describing. And for a night as strange as this, I wear a black cape; it's
tattered and torn, but when I touch it, I touch everything around me
– such is the confidence it brings, this shroud of mine.

Dressed now, I turned back to him and thought, 'Caught you.'

He'd been staring at my ass the whole time. If you look sideways you can see my buttocks are covered with downy blonde hairs. He looked up, embarrassed, and stared at my tender cheekbones. He'd have stayed that way for hours, staring at me, already pulling his martyr face, if I hadn't made him snap him out of it.

'Something small?' I asked again and, quick as a flash, like he'd just had an inspiration, he said: 'Small . . . [I tensed] . . . but power-ful.' And giggled to himself: 'Ha, ha, ha.' I'd tensed because I thought he was going to quote the Bavaria Beer ad: 'Small, but satisfying'. I'd never have forgiven him for coming out with such typical macho bullshit, so now I smiled at him in slow motion, grateful he hadn't let me down. I moved closer to him and imme-diately he noticed my perfume. 'It's because I've just washed my hair,' I explained. And he said: 'I know. It looks great,' and I said thank you and fluttered my eyelashes in *close-up* (the reader will have realized *papá*'s profession extended to a passion for cinema, so I'm entitled to use the term). And I was thinking, 'I'm making him nervous, he could easily do a runner.' Instead he sort of ducked away and went and threw himself on my bed, but he couldn't get comfortable; he was twisting his spine and breathing like an asthmatic.

Then he took out a diary, from the diary he took a white wrap of paper, from the nightstand he took my copy of *The Underdogs*[4] and, forgetting all about me, he tipped powder on to the cover and stared at it. He'd brought cocaine. I shuddered, like I felt sick and nervous, but I thought, 'No, it's just the excitement of anything new.' I'd dreamed about this, about *shovelling snow* (words that sounded erotic, even though they referred to a weak interaction of forces) against a sky-blue background. Then I'd dreamed of the South Pole, of a ship full of corpses. Later I realized the dream was just the cover of a John Lennon album which in fact had powder in the bottom left corner.[5] 'Ha, ha, ha,' I laughed to myself, seeing Misery Guts Ricardito looking so serious, and I thought, 'He hasn't even asked if I want some. Do I really look like a complete junkie?' He'd taken a couple of little straws out of his diary and was offer-ing me the shorter one. As I took it, I said, 'Thank you,' and I really meant it because he'd salvaged this horrible day. And at this he lit up and then I gave him his kiss, spontaneous, sincere and entirely superficial.

His mouth tasted bitter. Had he already done a line? He never said, the traitor. Then he asked, 'It's not a problem, is it? Your folks aren't in?' It wasn't a problem, but just in case I turned on my old radio, turned it up full blast; it took a minute to warm up, then started crackling. Ricardito looked at me in disgust. 'The batteries are nearly dead,' I explained, giving him a big smile. At least it was a good song – *Vanity, because of you I lost . . .* – a song I'd had on the brain for two nights running, one that, when I hear it now, gives me that delicious, useless feeling of all sad things and so I stay in. And if I do go out, I keep my head down, I don't look at anyone till the city wind whips away my conviction that I'll never care for anyone, that I'll always be alone. And then I look up and see the little boys straddling their bikes and by then (at 6 p.m.) the mountains look so feminine, so sisterly, that, in a surge of pure emotion, I surrender to the call of the night, which doesn't swallow me but only shakes me and I go to bed covered in bruises. Like I said before: my good intentions always come the next morning. I never keep them. I'm crazy about the night, I'm its creature. Everything else is not for me.

'You go first,' said Ricardito and, I don't know, I must have hesitated, because he said, 'You know how?' Not mocking me, just being nice.

'Of course I do,' I said. 'What, you think I've never seen *The People Next Door*?'[6] I picked up the straw and snorted hard, twice in each nostril, then he leaned down and for a second I lost him, till I looked down and saw him, nose buried in coke.

'Keep the noise down,' I said gently.

'Sorry,' he said. 'I've got a deviated septum.'

And I said, 'Should we turn up the radio?'

'No,' he said firmly. 'I can't stand the crackling.'

As I bounced around the room, he was already folding away the wrap, the greedy bastard. I skipped out and went to get my parents' cool little transistor radio and when I came back

Ricardito was sprawled diagonally across my bed. On the way, quick as a flash, I'd tuned the radio so it was playing 'Vanidad' and I was singing along. I smiled at him and it was like a whistle because music didn't stop coming out of my mouth. But he looked like he was scared half witless and a greenish tinge had spread across his face.

So I tried coke, so what? The effects, which are fantastic, last about ten minutes. After that it leaves you bummed out. You don't want to move, you get a horrible taste in your mouth, burning pains in the folds of your brain, a fever; you pinch yourself and you don't feel a thing, you can't watch a movie because any movement freaks you out, you feel paranoid and helpless and you grind your teeth. But the *lucidity* you have when you talk would be brilliant for the first few minutes of a speech! And as long as you've got enough, you never feel tired: you could *rumba* non-stop for three days! After that comes the insomnia, the terrible complexion, the yellow bags under your eyes, the blocked, peeling pores. You don't want to eat. All you want is another hit of coke.

But right then I felt fabulous. I told Ricardito we had to go out, I even gave him a nudge to get him moving. 'How did you get here?' I asked.

'Me? I walked,' he said, struggling to his feet between the sighs and the creak of old bones and new clothes.

'What about the car?' I said, disappointed, because I was already imagining the warm wind in my face.

And he said, like it was no big deal, 'They don't lend me the car any more.'

I wasn't really surprised they didn't lend him the car any more given that the first time he borrowed it he couldn't tell the accelerator from the brake. Then they signed him up for this posh driving school, the Academia Bolívar; it took him five months to learn the rules of the road, but as soon as they let him loose in a car it was a total disaster. The way he told it, at first he panicked because he was afraid of muddling up all the rules he'd learned and neatly classified in his brain, then felt ashamed because he knew he was bound to make a mistake, and the shame meant he couldn't think straight so he ended up confusing the accelerator with the brake again and crashed straight into an African palm. He managed to extricate the car (a difficult manoeuvre, since he had to use reverse) and as soon as he was out of danger, safe and sound, he piled straight into the same tree.

I didn't want to turn off the big old radio when we left, but as we were going down the stairs, the song ended and some tacky brass-band *charanga*⁷ came on, so I flicked off the little transistor I was carrying *ipso facto*. Since it was still playing up in my room, however, we could still hear it sputter and crackle, and just then I caught a whiff of food that turned my stomach: my big breakfast.

'I don't want it now!' I yelled. 'I'm not hungry any more; you took too long making it!' No one answered, as usual. I prayed to God the maid was hungry and she'd eat it. Let's be honest, she needed it more than I did.

Anyway, we stepped out into the accursed sunshine and somewhere in the back of my skull I felt a bad vibe I didn't like one bit. I was about to say something to Ricardo but one look at him and I stopped dead: he was standing in the middle of the street, arms outstretched, the sun on his face; it looked like he was giving thanks. The shirt he was wearing really was groovy.

'A present from your *mamá*?' I asked.

'Yeah, she got back from the States yesterday.' (I hopped across the scorching paving stones towards him.) 'She brought me the coke too, which was pretty dumb since it's like a thousand times more expensive there. She said since I'm always on a downer I should try it. Said coke would either calm me down or blow my mind. I think she's hoping for option two. She's already sent off for a brochure for a mental hospital in England.'

'Poor Misery Guts Ricardo,' I said, touched yet desperate for another bump, and now I knew it was a present from his mother, I thought wryly, 'A mother's love is never toxic.'

His mother was a beautiful woman. 'Sculptural' might be a better word, always dressed in leather and sequins. All she had in the world was Ricardo and a peacock driven half mad by her son throwing stones at it. Worried at the poor grades her son was getting at school, she spent her evenings showing him slides of her trips abroad and visits to museums. 'The Acropolis in Athens was the worst,' Ricardo used to say. That was when he usually fell asleep and would be woken by a jugful of cold water. Eventually his mother got bored and decided to ignore him. Ricardo got up before everyone else and had breakfast alone; he'd have lunch out – a fifty-peso sandwich and a Coca-Cola – and come home late at night, terrified, to eat his dinner cold. 'She's the one who ignores me the most,' he complained.

We crossed the Parque Versalles in silence, not thinking about its scabby pine trees, not breathing too deeply, but even so they made me feel nostalgic for Christmas and summer holidays. When we came out on to the street, Ricardo decided he needed music. 'Hey, why don't you turn on your radio?' So I turned it on and it started blasting out this incredible hard rock. I looked at Ricardo excitedly. 'They're called Grand Funk Railroad,' he informed me. He knew stuff. I was in awe of him.

'Oh, this is going to be a great day,' I said, a little relieved to have made it through the park without any weird thoughts, and I threw up my arms. And as I did so, I heard our music multiplied on the next corner and the next, all the way to the parking lot at Sears Department Store.

Had someone turned a radio up full blast or was there dancing? 'Dancing? At this time of day?' asked Ricardo, but I didn't answer; I went wild, I rushed across the Avenida Estación and raced down to the right corner, my corner, convinced that when I got to Sears' parking lot I'd find they'd set up 'Centro a Go-Go' again, my absolute favourite '60s thing.

Just three or four more steps, and already I was imagining what it would be like to see that big canvas and nylon marquee again, thronged with people, sagging under the weight of so much music so early in the day. 'I can start all over,' I promised myself. 'Start what?' At the very least I'd get to relive two moments: first, I'd see *her*, the dancer in the black-and-white checked miniskirt – totally Op Art – watch her lithe, sure-footed style, her beautiful thighs, watch her win First Prize; second, I'd see *him* as he arrived, the boy in the pink shirt – shocking pink for the time – with hair down to his shoulders, my first long-haired guy. The crowds would part as everyone stared at him, watching him dance with the chick in the miniskirt, and he wasn't all that good but he wasn't embarrassed and I wasn't embarrassed for him. 'This is the dawn of a new era,' I thought in exhilaration. That same night he was gunned down by the El Águila gang. The bullet went straight through his nose, his whole face was a swollen ball of blood, a huge bubble floating in the spellbound gaze of boys who'd never seen a dead man before; it floated for a moment and then suddenly burst with no noise, no spatter. The three guys who killed him got the fuck out of town (a while later I met someone in a queue who knew them). They shut down the 'Centro a Go-Go' the next day.

As I took the last step, I thought, 'I have to choose, I can't get to see both moments again: I have to choose between the dancer and the bubble.' I made up my mind. 'The dead guy,' I thought, 'the dead guy.' And then I turned the corner.

There were only two people in the vast parking lot. No milling crowds, no dancing. Nobody but Bull and Tico, who were joined at the hip, passing between them a transistor that was even smaller than mine and blasted out music at a volume that, as Ricardito quickly pointed out, was 'Far out! I know that model, it's a new one from Japan.'

When they saw us and smiled, I thought, 'They were there that night, they remember it too.' And then I thought, 'But they don't remember it like I do. They've come here to soak up the sun on the only patch of open space in north Cali.' A space, I might say, that no longer exists. Colombina, the company that makes sweets for export, built a thirty-storey tower block there.

They were happy to see me. They didn't try to hide it, they bobbed straight over, whereas I'd have preferred to meet them in the middle. Bull hung back slightly, I noticed. Was he tired of seeing me so much? I'd been really close to him in the summer of '66 on the Carretera al Mar, then he joined forces with Tico and after that the truth is I never saw him hanging out with girls any more. Tico, yes.

'Hey, guys,' they said. 'Cool sounds . . . Great minds . . .'

'Why don't we chill together for a bit, yeah? How many *rumbas* are going down today?'

'Three,' they told me. 'One at Pretty Patricia's [who was a complete bitch when it came to guys], one over at Skinny Flores's – he's just come back from the States with a shitload of records; no one knows where the third one's going to be. Everyone's meeting up in the park by the Teatro Bolívar and we'll wing it from there.'

'The one at Flores's place sounds cool,' I said, and they thought so too. 'So, what are we waiting for? Let's go . . . ?' I said, all charm.

We headed off, but not before some snide compliments about Ricardo's shirt, who reacted viciously to their disparaging comments about the colour and fabric.

We walked slowly across the parking lot and I was sorry I hadn't worn thick-soled shoes. The ground was sizzling. At Avenida Sexta, we reached the mimosa trees and their fragrant pools of shadow.

At the time, I lived in the most representative, most riotous area of *El Nortecito*, the triangle defined by Avenida Squibb, Parque Versalles and Deiri Frost. This was true north, the place where people topped themselves. The rest – Viperas, La Flora, etc – are just grubby, vulgar suburbs. My north was tragic, cruel and depraved. My window overlooked the Parque Versalles. I was friends with the youngest of the Castro kids, the one who put a bullet through his head in shame, after being humiliated by some cop in Felidia. I was the only friend of the oldest boy in the Higgins clan, an enigmatic, asthmatic, English family. He died of insanity, starvation (he never felt hungry) and insomnia (he never felt tired); the other brothers – there were three of them – are still around somewhere; I think they grew up to be delinquents.

This was the north where twelve-year-old kids grew up learning the solitary vices eighteen-year-olds had only just discovered and were enthusiastically promoting; the north of magnificent dancers and airgun snipers. I don't go back much these days, but when I do

the people who know me are pleased to see me. Really I'm just waiting for them to come down to the corner of Calle Quince and
Avenida Quinta where I live now, to lose themselves, come slum it
with the sleazy plebs. And being a good comrade, I take good care
of them and send them stumbling home late, struggling to forget
me, swearing to themselves they won't be back, won't come back
next Saturday, because those who come do come back, never go
home again. And there's not one of them who has the strength, the
stamina, the wit and the know-how that I have when it comes to living this twilight existence.

On the corner of Sexta and Squibb we ran into Pedro Miguel
Fernández, the guy who would later poison his three sisters, Carlos
Phileas, an H. G. Wells fanatic, and Lucio del Balón, who I'm convinced will one day be a famous doctor. All three were carrying
stacks of books. They'd been revising for some exam or other, they
said, but needed a break, so they joined our gang and we headed
south.

The pavement wasn't wide enough for all of us, and Ricardito
had to walk on the verge. I walked in the middle and since they'd
all heard rumours about how I spent my nights these days, they
had questions and I didn't interrupt any of them; I answered
everyone slowly and succinctly – I remember how they craned
their necks, how their faces lit up with each flick of my hair,
because what people said was true, it was refreshing, it cooled
the day – and as we came closer to the south it was obvious from
the heads that popped out of bus windows, from the two guys
who tagged along with the group, that my reign had begun. And
how terrible for a queen, newly crowned by the sun, to find
there was already a hotbed of treason in the person of none
other than Ricardito Sevilla, Misery Guts, the Sempiternal Mal-
content. He hadn't said a word for a while now, just stared at the
ground, watching where he walked, as though expecting to fall
on his face at any moment.

I began to worry that he'd defect, which would have been terrible, first because his hallucinogenic shirt suited my colouring,
secondly because he translated beautiful English lyrics for me when

I asked and thirdly because for three or four blocks now I'd been *dying* to suggest we duck behind a tree – I didn't care if the others thought we were a couple – so he could give me another hit of coke.

When I saw that dark look on his face, saw he wasn't walking but dragging his feet and, worst of all, that he'd started glancing over his shoulder, I said, 'Are you feeling what I'm feeling?'

I swear he did a double take, he stopped dead in his tracks and the whole gang had to slow down to wait for him. This was my way of reminding him about the psychedelic connection between us, but he didn't get it, or if he did, the smug bastard just thought, 'Yeah, what the fuck do I care?'

But this setback couldn't quash the effect of my joyful mood or my smile. The fickle radio segued from hard rock into the cheesy ballad 'Llegó borracho el borracho', which I immediately nixed (as did Tico), setting off a symphony of static and squeals in search of the best station, of consensus. 'There's no music,' I thought in desperation. Tico looked to me for help but I couldn't find anything either so I handed the radio to Misery Guts Ricardito, tossing it to him like a hot brick.

'Found something,' said Tico and I stared at Misery Guts Ricardo, waiting to see if he'd agree. He vented his misery, his deep unhappiness, by tuning to a station and blasting out: '*In the faraway mountains there's a horseman who's riding; he's alone in this world and for death he is biding.*' You should have heard the racket. The glorious 'House of the Rising Sun' (an oldie but a classic) clashing with 'A Horseman', to say nothing of the fact that we were strolling beneath rain trees and ceibas at exactly the time of day the cicadas were chirping. Tico angrily cranked up the volume on his tiny, powerful transistor. I gave Ricardito a dirty look and said: 'Come on, *please*, tune to the same station, we're a gang.' By now at least one of the guys was itching to beat him up. 'Put on something English or I'll thump you.' He took the path of least resistance: he turned off the radio.

In the silence, Tico's transistor sounded magnificent, the lead guitar shrieked, the bass boomed and Eric Burdon's wail (I knew the Spanish cover version by Los Speakers, so I understood the lyrics) seemed to draw a blanket of shadow from the mountains, a square blanket that moved quickly towards the city, drawn by this purring, and for the first time that Saturday, we had complete shade. And with it came the sea breeze.

'Tico,' I said, 'that radio of yours is wild,' and he flicked up his collar as Bull gave a jealous cough. 'With music like this,' I said, looking at the boys, 'I'm all yours.'

I didn't really know what I was saying.

'But you're not mine,' protested Ricardito, and then said, 'I'm off, I'm out of here.' He looked daggers. I grabbed him by the shoulder. It wasn't a hug and he could feel that, but he just looked at me even more arrogantly. The other guys probably thought it was a lovers' tiff.

I took him aside leaving – God forgive me – a gaping hole in that group of gorgeous guys, who understood and waited. A Simca drove past and Pedro Miguel Fernández, the future poisoner, recognized two girls he knew waving to him and preening like peahens; the car pulled over.

'Why are you leaving?' I asked Ricardito.

'*Sorry*,' he said quickly, coldly. 'Too many people. It's making me jittery.'

'Yeah, I noticed.'

I made a decision; shelving those scruples that plague me these days, I said, 'Before you go, you couldn't . . . leave me a little something?' I looked him straight in the eye, he couldn't resist.

He didn't resist, but he got his own back: 'That's the only reason you like me. Here . . .'

He handed me the whole wrap. I was astonished by the whiteness of his hands, by his veins. To tell the truth, I didn't care if the gift was intended as an insult. I thought about Mariángela. I blessed him.

'You take care,' I said finally.

I enjoyed seeing him turn his back, hating me. It always freaked him out when people tell him to take care. 'It's like there's an ambush waiting down the road,' he'd say, 'and the person telling me to take care knows where and when it'll happen, but they won't tell me because they're too scared and too selfish.' I watched him as he quickly lolloped away. He'd never been a pack animal. He could never dig groups.

As I turned round, the Simca was just moving off and Pedro Miguel was running back to the group.

'Another *rumba*,' he announced. 'That makes four. A bonfire on a farm down by the River: toasted marshmallows and Latino rock.'

'Sounds shit,' I thought. 'Latino rock and no one with a word of English to understand it.'

Now that we had a bit of shade, we walked more slowly. I'm sure you, gentle reader, are familiar with the frantic scurrying of a man walking in the blazing sun, looking around for any wall that casts a two-inch strip of shadow where he can shelter, shivering, till night-fall.

Ricardito stalked off, convinced that everyone would be talking about him, asking me questions about him. He couldn't have been more wrong. Carlos Phileas talked about getting state funding to develop Cavorite[8] and a drug that would make it invisible. He came up with an apposite simile – 'Invisible as cicadas that die from too much singing' – because now we were in the shade, all the trees fell silent as we passed. Everyone knows sunshine irritates cicadas and they sing to forget. When they're not singing, they're fast asleep and when they sing too much, they explode.

I tried to describe melodically what the night might bring now that all of us were together, assigning each guy a role, an attitude; they would all share me. If they stuck around. As we passed Deiri Frost we were listening to Santana and two blocks later to a Beatles medley some imaginative presenter had put together.

Just then came the fateful meeting, though actually it was more of a damp squib. Distracted by the mountain peaks that were like mirrors, I was thinking, 'Here comes the sun,' steeling myself and reassuring myself 'my face will stay fresh', staring straight ahead, counting the number of blocks before we arrived at Oasis. As I finished counting, I noticed two guys in thick work boots carrying piles of books as high as their heads, trudging along exhausted, bow-legged and shy: Armando the Cricket and Antonio Manríquez.

'The Marxists,' I thought, feeling the urge to peel off from my gang of groovy youths and go over to them, because, like I said, I had – still have – a lot of respect for their minds.

But I did what I had to do. I thought, 'It's not like I'm going to run into these loners tonight or any other night, and anyway I don't fancy either of them. If I go over and explain, they won't believe my reasons for not showing up this morning and I'll just wind up offending the guys I'm with.' So I kept on walking, chatting to everyone, smiling at everyone. By now, we were two pavements wide; numerically speaking, we were a force to be reckoned with.

All the more intimidated, the Cricket and Manríquez ducked behind the stacks of books, flashing their titles. I stopped because we'd reached Oasis. They stopped to bitch at me.

'I'm so sorry,' I said. 'There was a problem, you know what my mother's like. Did you get much reading done?'

'I would have thought that was obvious,' said the Cricket.

'Oh my God, yes – unwashed, unshaven, bags under your eyes – I'm really sorry. You know how committed I am to the struggle. Why don't we meet up Monday?'

'Same time,' said the Cricket and they walked on, crushed by the sun as it flattened the world.

I turned away quickly so as not to get a downer. It was a brilliant move because leaning against the wall a block away, looking like she'd seen it all and didn't much care for any of it, stunningly beautiful and staring straight at me, was Mariángela. With her was Prometheus himself, flaming red hair and all, chained to a huge guitar case. 'She's brought music,' I thought, skipping over to them. And she rewarded me with a smile, which, I'm sure, was her first of the day.

'*Quiay, pelada,*' we greeted each other and she introduced me to her way-cool escort, Leopoldo Brook, who was just back from the USA and played rock. I thought, 'I need an interpreter,' and cursed Ricardito for abandoning me. 'I'll die of embarrassment tonight if this guy sees me getting all emotional over lyrics I don't even understand.'

They'd already heard about the four *rumbas*, and had decided to go to Flores's place.

I went back to round up my handsome boys, who, as soon as we arrived at Oasis, had scattered to the three corners of the block – but not the fourth, where Mariángela was; they were in awe of her but afraid of her too. So began the wait for night, but it was an enjoyable wait since there was no chance of being stood up; it was a date and everyone had turned up early. But it's never easy, spending the whole afternoon in south Cali: you had to constantly dodge the negative vibes of relatives and enemies; you had to deal with the fact that all these guys were psychedelic – some of them were coming down when they showed up, hoping that hanging out with a crowd of beautiful people would take the edge off the sudden slowness of things, the terrible weight in the stomach that somehow heaves into the throat . . . There were always long queues for the gents' toilet, guys trying to make themselves lighter and calmer by taking a shit after their trip.

Say a boy, some kid of fifteen, shows up with peeling skin, hair falling out, his balance shot to fuck? Doesn't matter. These guys had an energy (I don't know, maybe it was the fashionable threads) that turned this debauchery into an entertaining spec-tacle. They laughed warily, criss-crossing Avenida Sexta a dozen times, constantly on the alert to the slightest movement that spelled a new hook-up, a new beginning. It was like an athletics display by a team of scrawny gymnasts. Me, I enjoyed it. Every couple of hours a crowd of people would flood out of the cin-ema and we'd take up strategic positions; everyone knew who went to the afternoon screening and who went to the evening show, and had a different attitude, a different greeting for each. The way you greet a passing (alcoholic) nun – or some kid your own age who's a freak, or a Marxist professor who once told you that in life every action should be a blow against imperialism – is radically different from how you greet a laid-back junkie who shows up with good news and three lines of coke for his friends. These guys hung out here, they practically lived here and spent their days taking drugs – something that the nun, the freak and the Marxist had to know. So what did they do to dodge scorn, or lob it back like a volleyball?

To these solitary specimens of rectitude and reason, they opposed their unity, their numbers, their music (which wasn't theirs) and what remained of their beauty. Everyone passed this way, the whole world passed this way. Those with a social conscience negotiated the area by averting their gaze, heading home to read an improving book and get to bed early. For their part the guys would swarm and neutralize any insult, circling gently and constantly like flies. Some – the more nervous ones – would jeer at passers-by, lay into them for their failure to appreciate the night, to get their kicks, like we used to say, accuse them of being square; others – the more lucid – clung to the conviction that when the time came to pass judgement on this era, they – the junkies – would stand as witnesses, those entitled to speak. And not the others, the squares who all thought alike and knew nothing about life, not to mention the intellectuals who indulged in nights of alcohol and cocaine till they were raving, vomiting and green round the gills – as though this was just poetic licence, the ungrammatical syllable essential to burnish a line of poetry. No, we were impossible to ignore, we were the last wave, the most powerful wave, the one that sweeps you from the sea wall of the night.

When it came, it was magical. The sudden flare of car headlights, the purple mountains, the music of the boys clapping, skipping, shouting. I smiled and in the newborn darkness my teeth – like Mariángela's – gleamed like marble as if they'd never rot, never decay. I should point out that it's no easy matter, having to get used to night always arriving like this, always extraordinary. To become inured to such a thing would mean madness. That's why we are the way we are.

I'd completely charmed Leopoldo Brook, while Mariángela, who'd been watching and watching for the night to fall, took her time telling me about her woes, how the day had grated against her body, just like the cicadas. 'Don't worry,' I told her. 'You've got your darkness now and soon there'll be music.' She was really sad, because she'd found thousands of photos of her mother out in the country as a girl, holding Mariángela in her arms. She was tormented by the idea that she'd seen more of life at seventeen than her mother had at fifty (a disparity that's understandable, given how times have changed). 'The only sin she ever committed was when she met my father, a touring Belgian tennis pro, and they went off together and fucked like rabbits.' She stopped, utterly bewildered, then said pleadingly, 'I need music,' at which the red-haired guy said she only had to ask. He opened his guitar case, and started strumming chords and belting out his message 'in front of all these *losers*' – that was the word he used. 'No,' Mariángela said, 'let's walk around the block so I can chill,' and the redhead immediately jumped to it.

I took a minute to look for my friends, let them know it I'd only be gone for a while and would catch them at Flores's *rumba* later. Bull and Tico had spent the whole afternoon with the radio turned up full blast and more than one solid citizen had come up to bitch about it. But Tico could be a dangerous bastard and Bull, just by standing behind him and thus staring down anyone who came to complain, provided solid backup.

'Listen, if you need to chill out,' I said as we headed south, like it was the most natural thing in the world, 'I've got a gram of coke.'

The redhead nearly dropped his axe, and Mariángela immediately changed course – she grabbed me by the shoulder and all but frogmarched me across the street. She was completely fired up now, and invited us all back to her place in Granada, near the hill.

Her mother wasn't home and we had to turn on all the lights. It was one of those dark houses with yellow walls; out on the paved patio there was a cracked, empty swimming pool.

'Poor *mamá*,' Mariángela said mournfully. 'She's gone to Saturday mass at San Judas. Better work fast, we don't want her walking in on us.'

Aside from instantly making us all happy, the cocaine also inspired Leopoldo to play two hours of English songs, while I admired and adored him in worshipful silence; it also inspired Mariángela to say something I'll never forget. Eventually Leopoldo bowed his head, his mane of red hair completely concealing his guitar; he was done playing. He asked for a drink – water or a glass of wine – and Mariángela said I should come into the kitchen with her to get the wine and when we got there she stared at me, stared into my eyes for so long, and she was so beautiful, with her hair just like mine and a face that said she knew exactly what she was doing, that I let her unbutton my dress and cup my breasts with both hands and then she said it: 'Guys are jerks. You'd be better than them at handling the little dick they make such a big deal of putting in you.'

'I like guys,' I said, taking a step back (no reason for me to tell her no one had ever put it in me), 'and I really dig your friend the rocker.' So I went back out to him, bringing my wine and the conviction (which in a way I'd copied from Mariángela) that in my wine and my company he'd find his repose. He totally got it, so much so that in that fit of empathy and goodwill, I almost admitted that I'd understood fuck all of the lyrics he'd been singing. But I didn't. Once again I wished Misery Guts Ricardito was here; he would delicately and faithfully translate every line of a song for me.

'Let's go – you want to?' said Mariángela, her words, as always, polite orders.

The night was deepest blue, and Mariángela danced alone down the middle of the street as we set off for the *rumba* through the Parque Versalles, dark and circular as a ruined amphitheatre. I glanced up at my house and saw everyone was already asleep.

Every life hinges on the course we decide to take at one precise, privileged moment. On that Saturday in August I broke with my routine, and the same night I ended up at Skinny Flores's *rumba*. It was a simple decision, but one that would have extraordinary consequences. One of them is that I now find myself here, safe in this haven of night, telling my story, shorn of all social standing and the crass manners I was raised with. No doubt I'll be held up as an example. *Peace and goodwill over my land.*

I knock on the door and it's opened by a young shirtless guy, and without waiting for him to say, 'Come in,' I push past, because I'm frantic at still being on the outside of all this music. I remember hearing a man singing in a high voice with sparse accompaniment. I remember I crept in like a dog tracking a scent. The walls were utterly bare, not a single picture, and I immediately started dancing, eager to get caught up in something so as not to tumble into this glassy chasm, its walls like ice floes; my dance is a nocturnal creeper, simple and arching, a solitary act; and so I danced alone, since everyone else was sitting down – was it me or were they already nodding off?

I didn't say a word, didn't say hello to anyone (behind me, I heard a commotion as Mariángela made her entrance); I caressed myself, grateful for the music, heard whispers of appreciation and approval, and as I tossed my hair I was thinking, '*Pelada*, you're bringing this place to life.' How else could I explain the sudden blaze of strange brilliance, UV light, little cries and a shrill unintelligible falsetto, all merging into a chorus singing the glories of my hair. These were my friends, yes, my friends. I realize now that the song only lasted a moment, that I suddenly stopped, stumbled, opened my mouth and focused, only to find I was about to fall flat on my face in front of my adoring fans. 'Lose your balance,' I thought, 'and you lose it all.'

I tensed, gritted my teeth, my whole body aching for the rhythm which some guy, a tall dark shadow, rushed to pick up. I was just thinking, 'I have to ask who's singing this, it's amazing,' when there was a burst of applause and everyone got up and I found myself surrounded by Silvio, Tico and Bull, Carlos Phileas, the women didn't even look at me enviously, and I was all smiles, little glances over my shoulder (none of them realized that seconds earlier I'd almost fallen on my face like a fool), and wreathed in such praise, such adulation, such glory, I never did ask the name of the song or the singer. Another yawning gap in my education . . .

They picked me up, sat me down and I felt calmer. And as the music had started up again and I was totally into it, I thought: 'This is life.' Ever since that moment, my life has been a conscious, lucid (if I can use that weird word) acceptance-extension of that fleeting thought. Never again, I realized, never would I encounter such closeness, such harmony. I knew I had friends all around me though I didn't recognize them all, but still I somehow understood that I would never again be so protected.

'How you feeling?' a face asked, the face of poisoner-to-be Pedro Miguel Fernández snaking between all the shoulders, the tangles of hair and the half-light, giving me a glimpse of the firefly of madness already flitting in that shadow that was his face with its huge, prematurely rotten teeth. 'Better than I've ever felt, Pedrito,' I said, and this was enough for him to close his eyes in satisfaction and go back to his business, to his little corner. I felt exhausted and all emotional. Leopoldo Brook had already found a place for himself and his guitar. The only person I couldn't see was Mariángela. I moved only when I no longer had the sensation of being at the physical centre of the house, which was clearly very big because from upstairs came the distant sound of footsteps, doors closing, the creaking springs of someone bouncing on a bed. No parents around, obviously. Maybe it was the whiteness of the walls that made it seem as if spurts of blue were coming from the courtyard planted with fruit trees.

There was no furniture, I noticed, apart from the powerful high-tech hi-fi system on my right. People were dancing now and I heard someone say, 'As soon as she gets here, everything changes.'

I missed Mariángela. I got up, not to look for her but just to see if I could stand. I went to join the dancers, walking the way I always do, as though I'm marching – someone once told me I had a masculine gait, I guess it was meant to embarrass me – like someone carrying a heavy weight, a stately electric guitar, a steel guitar, a lead guitar; moving forward, legs and knees first, back straight, conquering all before me. A pity my mouth wasn't big enough to ferociously peck everyone around me.

Hands reached up, strung garlands of bells around my neck. I still wear them, they ring out like Christmas Eve, that sad pealing that makes people stupidly long to be young again. I don't believe in that kind of reactionary nostalgia; pretending not to grow up, that's what nostalgia is. I was growing up, and in public: praised, pampered and imitated.

Was it my overwrought excitement or could I hear a live guitar being played? Chords strummed by a real person? I turned this way and that until I saw the redhead: lips pursed, perfectly in sync, he was playing the modest role of another speaker: the fifth.

'Who is he playing along with?' I asked suddenly, manically, looking for anyone to comfort me.

'Eric Clapton,' said a voice through the tangle. 'Eric Clapton.'

'Oh,' I said, turning to find a strange boy with a white shirt, a headband and beautiful lips. 'Is he good?' I asked.

'Good?' He adopted a serious expression and told me, 'In my humble opinion, he's God!'

I stopped dancing and went over to the redhead. I adopted the karma or kata position – that Indian thing, whatever it's called – and I watched him as he went about his munificent work, bringing to our feeble nocturnal celebrations all the wisdom gleaned from the USA, teaching us discipline. He pulled faces, becoming paler with each one, shedding beads of sweat that I would happily have lapped up to turn into tears of emotion. He closed his eyes, but between each blink – I managed to blink in time with him – which was every time he played a low note he'd open his eyes and then I'd give him a huge smile; he would see me and I imagined how magnificent was this vision, me and my tinkling bells.

At the end of the song ('White Room', someone told me), he took a deep breath; I felt moved and wanted show him how much I wanted to protect him, to clear a path for him through the feral tropics he had willingly come to.

'Here on holiday?'

'No, not at all,' he told me.

'Oh God,' I thought, but what I said was, 'Oh, that's wild! You'll see, I'll find you stuff to do, there's always stuff going on.'

Legs approached. I looked up, in pained anticipation. It was the lofty form of Lanky Flores, come to pronounce the inevitable 'Everything cool?'

'Everything,' I said excitedly.

'Cool! I want you to open your mouth,' he ordered, effortlessly dropping down so he was crouching next to me. In this light, the bones in his face all looked like splinters. A sexy thought popped into my head when he said 'open your mouth', which sounded

like a proposition, but I dismissed the thought and did as he said
– I opened my mouth, even stuck out my pink and pointy tongue.
Then he showed me his hands, one a fist, the other holding a glass
of water.

'What are you giving me?' I said awkwardly, my mouth still wide
and probably drooling. Opening his fist, he showed me two purple
pills.

'Acid,' he said. 'Now, open your mouth.'

This was because I'd snapped my mouth shut – gulp – the minute
I saw the acid microdots, my face slashed along the horizontal by the
name he gave them.

'Don't be scared.'

I stopped messing around and licked my lips. After all, I had to try
it some day.

'One or both?' I asked.

'Just one!' said the redhead, helpfully. 'Jesus H. Christ!'

So I took one and popped it. The water tasted funny. The redhead
took the other microdot and went on strumming.

'Is he ignoring me?' I wondered, scrabbling to my feet defensively.

He stopped strumming for a minute to ask: 'You leaving?'

'No,' I said. 'Can you hear something? Sounds like people fighting
outside.' I was thinking – by now I was up and running, I stepped on
someone and they apologized – 'They're beating up Mariángela.
Where's Mariángela?'

There were eight or nine people crowded in the doorway;
Mariángela was nowhere to be seen but I could hear her, hear her
swearing.

'Let me through, let me through,' I screamed, trying to force my
way past, and when they didn't let me, I pinched one guy savagely,
kneed him where a knee was meant to go, with the classic cry: 'Man
down.' I couldn't stand by and do nothing while someone beat up
Mariángela. 'She's had enough hatred in her life,' I thought. Outside the fresh air left me suddenly dazed but eventually I managed
to see what was happening and retreated, feeling a sudden splitting
headache.

It was a pitiful sight: Mariángela was kicking the shit out of

Misery Guts Ricardo, and the poor guy didn't even try to apologize, the more she kicked the more the idiot screamed and insulted her. 'What can I do, I have to see both sides,' I thought and I waded in, grabbed Mariángela by the shoulders, spun her round and said, 'What's going on?'

The moment I touched her she calmed down, breathing into my face. Incredible: yet again (for perhaps the thousandth time) she was delighted to see me. She started breathing more slowly, attempting, with some effort, I think, to count to six. What she said was said without anger. The action was all over. All there was now was me.

'There I was,' she said, 'thinking beautiful thoughts out here, because I didn't feel like going in to join the *rumba*, when I see this guy roll up to the door shambling like a halfwit. And I was feeling so blissed out I felt moved by his never-ending misery. So I went over to him and I said, "Welcome." And you know what he said? He said, "No one welcomes me." He even dared to touch me. He shoved me and said: "Get away, curvaceous woman, guitar body." Well, as soon as he lays a hand on me, I grab his arm and shake him from his fingertips along his spine to the bone that supports the skull, to the coccyx and down to his heels. Then I knock him to the ground and start kicking him. I think that's when you showed up. He says he knows you.'

I looked at Misery Guts. His mouth was smeared with blood. He wasn't crying, he didn't seem to be in pain. Someone tried to brush the dirt from his shirt and he furiously pushed them off and got another kicking for his trouble.

He stood up, brushed away the grass, the blood, the twigs from his eyes and stood there, hands in pockets, glowering hatefully at everyone except me. Me he looked at with divine distance.

'Sure, I know him,' I said and walked over to him and he smiled. I took his hand. I said, 'Come on, come inside, it's really buzzing.'

He went limp and allowed me to lead him. As we got to the door he said, 'Just don't ever say "welcome" to me.'

'Whatever you like,' I agreed.

I led him into the middle of the crowd. Was something exploding inside me? I stroked Mariángela's waist and she took my hand and squeezed it, very briefly, as I passed. The night air wasn't good for me. Was the headache following me? A thrill ran all the way from the top of my head as I stepped inside and saw that all the people who'd been propping up the walls had come together to form a crown of thorns, all spellbound, their heads high, staring at the stereo. From his strategic vantage point, Leopoldo was no longer playing accompaniment but something like a counterpoint and I thought, 'That's so sad.'

Ricardito, who always understood me, finished the thought for me. 'It's the saddest sound in the world,' he said, staring in astonishment.

'Oh, Misery Guts,' I said, touched, 'everyone here understands English. Just look at how together they all are. Do you know this song?'

'Sure,' he said effortlessly. I took his hand.

'Come on, let's sit down. Not here where everyone can hear us. Whisper the lyrics in my ear. You're my interpreter.'

'Forever?'

'No, sorry, it wouldn't be fair to promise that. Just for tonight, but you know me, you know my nights are long. Ready?'

'Yeah. It's called "Milla de luz de luna" – "A Mile of Moonlight".'[9]

'"Mile"?'

'Yeah. That's the literal translation. You picked a difficult song.'

'You can do it. The band?'

'Rolling Stones.'

'They're playing it again. They can't get enough of it. Oh, I'm so happy! "A Mile of Moonlight" . . . ' I repeated, memorizing the title.

The same head with the precise gestures picked up the needle and, without a hiss, dropped it back into the groove at the start of the song.

'Here we go,' said Ricardito.

'Quietly. We don't want to disturb them.'

So he moved closer to me and whispered the song into my ear and his voice was soft. He was happy too, and after every line I felt a shudder of pleasure, a quiver of amazing feelings radiating from my ear.

> *'When the wind blows and the rain feels cold*
> *With a head full of snow*
> *With a head full of snow . . .'*

'Snow?' I said. 'Does he mean . . . ?'

'Yeah,' whispered Ricardo, 'it's a double meaning.'

'Far out!'

> *'In the window there's a face you know*
> *Don't the time pass slow*
> *Don't the nights pass slow . . .'*

'Can you do it faster? Translate at the same time as he's singing, please . . .'

'You picked a tough song.'

'Shhh . . . they're singing again.'

Ricardito took a deep breath and became very cool. His temples glistened.

> *'The sound of strangers sending nothing to my mind*
> *Just another mad, mad day on the road*
> *I am just living to be lying by your side*
> *But I'm just about a moonlight mile on down the road*
> *Yeah, yeah, yeah . . .'*

'You don't need to translate the *yeahs* and the *babies* for me,' I snapped.

> *'Made a rag pile of my shiny clothes*
> *Gonna warm my bones*
> *Gonna warm my bones . . .'*

'God,' I said, 'it's such a sad song. Where's Mariángela?'

> *'I got silence on my radio*
> *Let the air waves flow*
> *Let the air waves flow*
> *Oh, I'm sleeping under strange, strange skies . . . '*

'I caught up,' said Ricardito, happily, 'I caught up, my mind's working at the speed of light.'

> *'Just another mad, mad day on the road*
> *My dreams are fading down the railway line*
> *I'm just about a moonlight mile down the road*
> *I'm hiding, sister, and I'm dreaming*
> *I'm riding down your moonlight mile*
> *I'm hiding, baby, and I'm dreaming*
> *I'm riding down your moonlight mile*
> *I'm riding down your moonlight mile*
> *Let it go now, come on up, babe*
> *Yeah, let it go now*
> *Yeah, flow now, baby*
> *Yeah, move on now, yeah*
> *Yeah, I'm coming home*
> *'Cos I'm just about a moonlight mile on down the road*
> *Down the road, down the road . . . '*

'There's no lyrics after that,' he told me. 'Just this long guitar solo.'

'Well, then let me listen to him.'

'Him who?'

'The guitarist sitting behind you.'

Ricardito turned. 'That creep?'

'He's totally rock and roll,' I protested.

'Do what you like,' said Ricardito. 'I feel good because I did my job. There's not many people could translate off the cuff, and that fast.'

'It's a slow song,' I objected.

'Actually my version's better. My lyrics are better than the original by those assholes.'

'Whaaaaaat?' I raised my hand and tried to grab him by the scruff of the neck, but he had already gone to sniff out some other corner. I was sick at the thought that it was a complete con job. If he'd improved the lyrics, that meant he'd changed them. I felt so helpless not being able to understand English! 'Where's Mariángela?' I almost whimpered. She didn't appear. But some boy with stubby arms and glasses came right over to me.

'Keep calm and stay sane,' he said. 'You're not the only one tripping here. If you're going to pull a whitey, then go outside and die there, because if you ruin my friends' trip, *pelada*, I'll kick the shit out of you.' And with that he disappeared into the night.

'What?' I jumped to my feet, half woman half panther. 'Who are you to threaten me? Who?'

Ricardito appeared from nowhere and put his arms around me.

'Who?' he asked me. 'I'll defend you.'

I looked at him, completely stunned, then laughed in his face (I know the redhead was watching me).

'You? Don't even try, they'll batter you.'

'Let them batter me, I'll batter them right back,' he assured me. 'Where is this guy?'

'I don't know who it was,' I screamed. 'I don't know!'

'Hey!' the guitarist called over.

I whipped round. 'Yes?'

'Coming, yeah?'

I went.

'Don't go,' Ricardito begged me.

'I'm not going for good. I'll be back, I swear,' I said, because his gesture filled me with a surge of tenderness as he sank his head into his shoulders, stretching out his arms to me.

In careful, happy steps I walked over to where the guitarist was sitting and sat down next to him, ready to receive his message, which turned out to be a question: 'Is this your first time?'

Not really knowing what we were talking about, I said, 'Yeah. It's also the first time a song's ever moved me that way.'

'Whatever you do, don't panic,' he said. 'If you want, you can stay here with me.' And I closed my eyes; I could have curled up in his arms. 'Oh,' I said, 'I'm really sorry.' I pointed: 'There's someone waiting for me over there.'

'Who?' The chords – guitar and vocal – jangled. 'That little runt?'

'We've been friend since we were kids,' I explained. 'Besides, he gets depressed. See you.'

He didn't answer. I walked back to where Misery Guts was standing. A distance of nine steps. How many it took me I can't remember. It must be inside my head somewhere. Sometimes I feel like I've got golf balls banging around in there making a *glu, glu* noise and I can't help seeing the shocked face of that expert player, Jesus, and I ask for some 10mg Valium tablets which bring me better dreams.

I know everyone's always inventing new shit for people to try, but of all the things I've tried, acid is the worst. You should see what it does to your eyes, the things it makes you imagine people are doing; you don't need to be sick in the head to think that people who love you are doing everything they can to get rid of you – it's a simple fact. It fills you with hatred for your parents, murderous thoughts about servants, terror at the first light of day; you feel like you're made of plasticine. If you have spots, acid gets rid of them and leaves you with pockmarks, dry hair, loose teeth; you won't be able to run or eat because you ache all over, in your joints, your cartilage, your gums; you try to read a book and the words dance in front of your eyes; you try to sleep and not think about all the horrible things in your past, the things you're ashamed of . . . and I'd scream: 'But I haven't got a past! My past is what I'll do today!' I couldn't do a thing. When I could summon up the energy, I'd get off the sofa and go out but, having no past, I didn't recognize people, I blanked them when they said hello, and you should have seen their faces when the most gifted girl in Cali blanked them – they stared furiously at the pavement, at the roots of the African palms. In the end you wind up doubting the whole world, and how can a doubter find consolation if she can't read, can't have a simple conversation without finding something sinister in it, some misfortune destined to degrade her still further?

Gentle reader, my hair lost its brilliance, it turned from gold to ash. Not that anyone would notice it now as I tell my story, because this hair has history. My skin, always so smooth and tanned, became scabbed with bruises like scales. For at least three days I was in a terrible state, scampering around like an animal trying to get its strength back, accepting outlandish invitations in the hope of discovering some new possibility; I even agreed to attend a graduation dinner with my parents. The main course was pork ribs, which I ate out of politeness. (My culture forbids it. I'd always been intrigued by the Maccabeus brothers' blind refusal to eat pork, by Moses' unconditional prohibition, and as a little girl I'd been scared stiff by the story – which everyone knew but no one talked about – of an aunt who died from worms in her brain after eating undercooked pork. I never knew what she felt like towards the end; I know I always kissed her when she came to visit, a memory that infects me to this day.) That cursed meat tasted so sweet. For at least a month I was *convinced* I had larvae hatching in my brain. 'I'll die a miserable death,' I thought. 'No fate could be more symbolic for a child of the second half of the century.'

But, oh, I don't have the words to describe the joy I felt, the dimples that appeared in my cheeks as I walked back to poor Ricardito, who had spread his arms wide and was whispering comforting words to himself. I moved towards him wreathed in colours, in my favourite colours. Green: the colour of the world's envy at my happiness; black: the colour of the sea that scares me; yellow: the colour of summer in countries further north and which I'll never see because I belong to, I am bound by chains to, this land.

Ricardito suggested taking me up to the first floor, showing me rooms he'd already explored I don't know when but which he assured me were fascinating. I followed him and people saw him take my hand and again they thought, 'They're a tragic love story.' We climbed stairs which, as they rose, formed a perfect circle. What was he so eager to show me upstairs? A series of terribly empty rooms.

'I've been trying to get it on with you all day,' he complained as we started up the stairs. Then later: 'I knew this house would be the perfect place for my ravishment.'

'For your what?'

I stopped dead and turned to face him.

'For . . . for pulling the wings off a reckless butterfly,' he muttered, embarrassed.

'You don't know what you're talking about,' I said harshly and walked down the corridor, entranced now by these empty rooms. I thought, 'Have his parents fled the country?' And as I walked along the corridor I felt a thousand feathery touches on my shoulders, on my back. 'If he touches me any lower,' I thought, 'I'll turn round and deck him.'

In the last room there were mirrors strategically placed such that I could see myself from all four sides. I watched Ricardito step into each reflection, too shy to look at himself. Instead he stared at me, fascinated by my fascination.

In the middle of the room were large pieces of furniture covered in dust sheets – wardrobes or beds. 'Beds?' I thought. 'So this was where they were bouncing earlier.' And I decided it would be a fantastic idea to try it myself. 'Come on, let's bounce on the bed, I dare you,' I said, and he looked at me nervously. He didn't refuse, but I could see he was afraid, weak. I decided to go first, to prove to him how much stronger my sex can be. I jumped and let myself fall back on to the nearest bed, the biggest one. I remember Ricardito, his eyes on stalks, making a vague, desperate attempt to catch me as I sailed through the air. The bed I landed on wasn't very springy. I'd got used to bouncing, to the upward motion which should have followed my fall, forcing me to tense my neck, arch my whole body, and giving a gleam to my eyes, so that when I felt myself not bouncing, not rising, not even bumping but sinking into something soft, uneven and still warm, I was terrified, as though I was suddenly inside an aquarium and Ricardito was standing stunned on the other side of the glass, making no attempt to help me. I didn't move a muscle, quickly trying to identify the sensation. Just then I realized that, on each side of my legs, trunks of flesh as real as my own living flesh had parted to make room for me. A nose was pressed into the back of my neck, two enormous pairs of breasts pushed against my back.

My bellowing (which no one heard downstairs) was joined by an ecstatic wail from Ricardito. To get up, I grabbed one end of the sheet and in a clean jerk split it in two: the moment of revelation lasted as long as it took the sheet to fold in on itself and I let it fall to the floor. In the double bed were three bodies: those of Doctor and Señora Augusto Flores, whom I'd regularly seen taking a turn in the park at around seven o'clock, and the body of a girl who'd been Lanky Flores's nanny before becoming a general skivvy: an Indian girl from the mountains of Silvia I'd never said a word to – that would have been all I needed. I thought, then said aloud, 'You think he invited us here to see the corpses?'

'I don't think so,' said Ricardito. 'Otherwise he'd have had everyone up here, he'd have had us all file past. I think he's just forgotten.'

'So you've already seen them?' I asked, without reproach.

'Yes,' he admitted, gratefully.

'Then let's cover them up again,' I said, carefully moulding the sheet around each form. We rushed out of the room. At the end of the corridor, like another mirror, a huge window loomed. I went over to it and stared down at the Parque Versalles, perfectly asymmetrical, marked out in 1920 by some demented Italian architect.

'The garden of Marienbad,'[10] Ricardito, sounding like a professor. I glared at him in disgust. Something in his words (which I didn't understand, because I didn't get the reference) completely contradicted what I was thinking. He always was highbrow, Misery Guts Ricardo, to those who knew the difference.

He must have mistaken my anger for weakness or grief because he offered me his arm and I didn't push it away. To tell the truth, I was shaking a bit and, according to him, a pale mask crept over my face.

'Was he miserable with them?' I asked him, since he was the one up early every day sniffing around the morning arguments of the families in the Parque Versalles.

'I know for a fact he was,' he said gravely and that was our last word on the subject.

Flores never mentioned the bodies to anyone. They were discovered two days later by an aunt. The crime was all over the papers. The son refused to say anything. His relatives refused to support him and he spent a whole year in the asylum at San Isidro, where he shared a bunk with vicious lunatics and blacks, was completely neglected, fed on slops, plied with drugs and so much shock therapy that when the authorities closed San Isidro for lack of official funds, the cousin who took him in (a stuck-up *gringa* bitch who always dressed in checks) had to hold him up just so he could put one foot in front of the other along the path of life, man. Turns out the cousin was an okay woman; she took him to Dallas, Texas, and he lives there now surrounded by cats, cornbread and country music all day long, crooning drivel about the flowers of Cali and asking in vain for tropical fruit.

Yeah, the whole thing created a massive shitstorm. This was back when respectable pundits were beginning to diagnose a malaise in my generation – the generation that appeared with the Beatles' fourth LP, not the *Nadaístas*[11] or the middle-class boys withering in the ruins of the *Nadaísta* movement. I'm talking about the generation defined by *rumbas*, the beach, by the orgies at La Bocana during Holy Week. We weren't trailblazers, none of us claimed to be the first to wear a paisley shirt or grow their hair long. By the time we came along, everything had already been invented. It didn't take a genius to work out that our mission was never to return to the beaten track, never to refuse a challenge, so that, like ants, our burrowing would eventually undermine the very foundations of this society, including those being dug now by the people who prattle on about building a new society in the ruins we left behind.

But we had no intention of dying that quickly. None of us worried about passing on our wisdom, sharing our deepest thoughts.

Me, I always knew that I had a gift for *rumba* and nothing else, and I don't even know who I get that from. My remorseless energy doesn't frustrate the men who want me but can't have me, because the more they watch me, the more they realize why they don't deserve me. My talent's a force of nature, a gift from life, and it's also an acknowledgement. It annoys me when some prematurely fat, prematurely bald smartass pops up to inform us that all this confusion, all this waste has been in vain, that our social structure is ill-defined, and dismisses the whole tragic phenomenon as 'imported decadence'. Oh, the gentle reader of these words would pay good money to see how I laugh in their faces, and my laugh, like my mane of blonde hair, is petrifying. It doesn't bother me when people compare me to an octopus. I've met tons of fat bastards who write beautiful bullshit and people call them poets, but when they're face to face with me, oh, the terror they feel, the crassness of their drunken binges, not to mention the greenish tinge of the compulsive wanker, the sort of guy with a scaly claw inside that makes him incapable of relating to women. We girls are mysterious creatures, man. The only guys I've ever been able to relate to are the kids I don't see around much any more, the guys who spend their days scratching their brains. 'It doesn't hurt,' they say. 'It's like running a comb through your thoughts and untangling your ideas.'

Anyway, by this point I was heading back downstairs, having witnessed Flores's patricide, his matricide, his *nannycide*. I admit I was a little shocked, but I don't know why I suddenly thought, 'A bond of death unites us in this and every *rumba*. I wonder what the others are capable of?'

Oh, I had high hopes for my generation!

Lanky Flores was grooving with a girl dressed in vivid red, but in the end he looked alone and ridiculous in the middle of the dance floor. Misery Guts, convinced I was traumatized by what I'd seen, kept murmuring comforting little words.

'Can you shut up about it now,' I snapped, gazing at the serene guitarist on the far side of the dance floor. 'Do you mind? You're ruining the *rumba* for me.' Ricardito shrivelled with embarrassment and I thought, 'Why has it taken me so long to realize the only support I'm getting here tonight is from the only guy playing music?' I didn't think twice about leaving Ricardito to wallow in his guilt and strode over to the guitarist, feeling a prickle of passion in my hips. 'He's the most fascinating guy I've ever met,' I decided, and without a second thought I flung myself into his arms, not caring that I'd forced him to stop mid-song, determined to make him realize how fragile I was, how much in need of consolation. And oh, joy, the first word he spoke to me was in English. Then he stopped himself and apologized. 'No, no,' I said, 'I like it. If you'd speak to me in English all the time . . . if only you'd teach me . . . ' And then, my terrible confession. 'I'm so ignorant.'

He accepted this resignedly. Or was the trade-off he suggested just an act? 'In that case you can be my guide to the city,' he said, and I reminded him I'd already offered to help.

By the time we left the *rumba*, there were only two guys left standing: mine, and the host. After I had left him to his tragic fate, Ricardo behaved like such a prick that within half an hour everyone at the party hated his guts and wanted to punch him. Oblivious to his terrible shortcomings, he kept banging on about how he missed the old days, the proper parties, not this tedious shit, about how no one here, not a single person here, was worthy of him, what with him being – as he put it – a young man with an 'intellectual background', and at that point they finally gave him a good kicking while he whimpered about how he was a future poet, how he wished he'd been born back in the days when party guests were judged by their intelligence and not on their . . . Who knows what bullshit he would have come out with if someone hadn't knocked him out.

By the time I left, they'd dumped him outside and he was curled up asleep on the ground. 'He's probably resting,' I thought, then said: 'He hasn't had a decent night's sleep in ages.' Then out of sheer spite, I kicked him in the ribs. He didn't feel a thing. He protested or apologized to himself, huddling into the 'classic foetal position', to quote Mariángela, who'd been disappointed by the lack of charm and stamina displayed by the guys at the party. The girls were desperately trying to revive their boyfriends, fast asleep, their mouths hanging open, defending them by saying they were just big babies.

'Babies, my ass!' spat Mariángela. 'Don't watch over this sleep of fools. Kick them awake!'

It was a simple fact that, at the end of every *rumba*, the girls were the only ones left standing, the only ones who managed to stay sane.

And so we stepped out into the new day, the second day of my story. Leopoldo put his arms around me and shivered with cold. Perversely, I decided, 'There's no cold. What there is, is a vast immensity.' I wasn't wrong. Beyond the park, which like I said was angular (scattered pine trees fashioned into cubes and other geometric forms), stretched a perfect field of colour that began in the mountains, a reflection of the sun rising in the east – somewhere I never look because I know in that direction there's no end and that terrifies me. Grey as they were, the mountains rose up dark blue and deep red the colour of sapodilla fruit. It took some time to wade through this creeping swathe of colour, through the low mist exhaled by the damp earth, and Leopoldo said, 'It's the sort of scene you'd imagine leading into the House of Usher, not away from it.' Even without music, his words were beguiling. ('Corpses walled up behind mirrors,'[12] I thought). 'He's a poet,' I thought. 'He'll write brilliant lyrics.'

Mariángela loped along, bewildered, her hands buried in the pockets of her jacket; I think she felt the glimmering light of the mountains in every fibre of her being. The girl was *bizarro*. Admitting to being excited by music infuriated her. Recognizing she had more staying power than anyone at a *rumba* embarrassed her, like it was an unseemly occupation.

'I don't understand you any more,' I told her towards the end of the last days when, frankly, her apathy no longer annoyed me, it bored me, and I'd stopped joining in her insults when some boy insisted she dance with him.

She had a lovely way of walking and as I watched her, arms wrapped around my guitarist, perhaps I understood some small part of her pain: the same vast immensity that made me feel light and lissom completely engulfed her.

I should mention we were walking in the opposite direction from my house. I hadn't said anything, though I knew Mariángela wanted more music. But where could we go?

'I don't live far,' said Leopoldo. 'I'm from the heart of *El Nortecito*.' Which earned him a grateful smile from me (something that took some effort at this hour of the morning, when a thousand things were flitting through my head), because to me his words meant: 'He lives alone.'

I abandoned – my God – the idea of abandoning them and going home to my own bed. I don't know whether this was the moment I decided that never again would I greet the new day through the slats of my venetian blinds.

After the party, Leopoldo didn't smell of smoke, he smelled of grass from some cold climate. And I thought, 'He comes from far-off lands, from a northern country where he's been better fed.' A stupid thought which only made me hug him harder, behaving like this guy next to me really was my boyfriend.

He never actually invited anyone back to his place, but Mariángela knew the house and led us there. It was on the corner of Avenida Séptima and Veinticinco. As he deftly slipped the key in the lock and opened the door, I thought, 'His parents' old house, a Versalles house, but his parents are gone now; they've left it to him so he can live here alone. I bet the interior design is acrylic and ultra-modern.'

Just then we heard a terrible wail like the howl of a wounded wolf (who wouldn't think of a werewolf or a wolf cub as the dawn is breaking?) that came from deep inside the Parque Versalles, which was at least seven blocks away. It was Ricardito opening his eyes and venting his horror, sprawled on the ground, as he faced the new day.

These are just lies, I tell myself, but what if I say that at that moment it was as though dawn was interrupted, as though time ran backwards? My father loved to explain how soundtracks could be added to silent movies filmed in 16fps, by duplicating frames, which produced something like a panning shot, a 'pan', to use the technical term. Ricardito's distant howl of pain that morning produced the same effect. Pain, *pan*, one short step. The newspaper boy pedalling his bike froze; the baker stood transfixed, hand squeezing a loaf of bread, and later felt no shame about selling the squashed and mangled loaf; even the creeping mist congealed (we risked ending up embedded in glass or ice) and Leopoldo, who'd already waved us inside, turned and looked at me, bewildered, because it was obvious this bloodcurdling howl came from somewhere near the house we'd just left; I think maybe he thought, 'This city is dangerous, weird shit happens here.' I brayed and threw my head back as though someone had slapped me. 'Poor Ricardo,' I thought. 'If he'd woken up and found me beside him, he wouldn't have howled like that.'

And then time returned to normal, especially since, like I said, these are just lies I tell myself. No one else noticed this strange phenomenon; maybe I did only because I had a connection with Ricardito, something that didn't much matter to me otherwise. Anyway, the howl of some gloomy bastard can't bring the day to a standstill, not even for two frames, no matter how miserable he is. Mariángela was the only one who didn't react, for her there was no pause, which makes me think she was the first to hear the cry, she always had unusually keen senses. But maybe she lacked a sixth sense, the one that all women have. She lacked a sixth sense and that's why she killed herself.

Anyway, she sat back, buried her hands in her pockets right up to the elbows and simply listened to that long terrible wail. All she could think to say was: 'Well, that should wake up the other pinheads.'

And I said, 'Ricardito will be insufferable today. He'll shamble around town like a dead man and, since he always remembers everything, he'll come looking for us to apologize.'

'Apologize for what?'

'For behaving like a dickhead in front of everyone. For nearly shitting himself at the *rumba*.' I said this as we climbed stairs carpeted with flowers and little birds and stepped into a hall dominated by a huge poster of people being blown away by the vibes at some concert. While Mariángela, lost in thought, collapsed into the first available inflatable chair, I looked around hungrily. Everywhere there were pictures of idols, a photograph of Salvador Dalí standing next to Alice Cooper, walls painted in rippling waves of startling colours and I thought, maybe I even said aloud, 'Wow, this is some pad!'

Leopoldo, ever attentive, was already putting on music. A simple action whose effect, though I can explain it, I can't begin to measure. From the four corners of the vast living room and, as I later discovered, from every corner of the house, poured beauty, perfectly distilled, into precise doses, a guitar gently played, so high, so high. It was the most exquisitely recorded album I've ever heard, the most pristine and powerful sound, the most electrifying song, and I confess I didn't have the strength to give thanks for such exaltation. I stood in the middle of the room, a defenceless witness to this fantasy. I didn't need to formulate the words to know the tangled skein of music was my destiny.

Each of us is a trajectory, constantly changing course, trying to recover the crumbs of the strength that once was ours and has been shamefully discarded along the way or entrusted to (and never returned by) those who didn't deserve it. Music is the creation of a generous spirit that (with or without effort) gathers this primeval strength and restores it to us, not so that we might have it, but to prove that strength is still out there somewhere, that the poor thing misses me. I am fragmentation; music is each of the tiny splinters that once were part of me and which I randomly scattered. I can be standing before one thing and thinking of a thousand others. Music is the solution to the problem I cannot see while I'm wasting time looking at things: a book (these days I can't get beyond two pages), the line of a skirt, of a grille. But music is also time regained that I have wasted.

It's the musicians who tell me how much time, and how and where. Innocent and naked, I am but a simple, attentive ear. They hold out the reins of the universe. Politely, to me. A song that never grows old is a universal decree that my faults have been forgiven.

How then could I not be grateful for this grace? Confronted with this wonder, Mariángela stretched her whole body and breathed calmly and deeply. I went over to her, stroked her little head; we looked at each other, saw through each other, our eyes melting into one expression as Leopoldo announced, 'Quadraphonic sound, speakers in every room.'

I went over to him, to thank him in the name of technology. I kissed him and he wouldn't let me walk away, he kissed me on the mouth. I turned and looked at Mariángela: her eyes were closed. I turned back and kissed him on the lips.

Lips are flabby flesh, this I know. Sleek worms coiled about teeth which, I also know, are an error of nature. But this was the first kiss I ever enjoyed in my whole life. He hugged me and my hair twined with his hair, which was the colour of ripe hazel. When we tried to pull away so we could see ourselves in this moment of passion, we discovered we couldn't because our hair was knotted together, and that's not some kind of literary metaphor, I'm just faithfully describing the abundance of our strength. This mane of hair I flick today for the benefit of some unsuspecting passer-by is not even the shadow of what it once was. Or rather it's precisely that: a shadow. And yet with this hair I bring light to people in this inky night. What a drag – the moon is full tonight but it's hidden by treacherous clouds.

Mariángela could see our love, or she could sense it, I know that.

I thought, 'I'm going to be the first nice middle-class girl in Cali to leave home to go live with her boyfriend. People will realize that in the States everyone does it.'

I collected a couple of my favourite shirts from my house, some pants and nothing else. At first, I missed the mirror with the crack down the middle. I wore his clothes, which were all unisex, my size and my style.

I'd always thought that the sexual act was, how can I put it, a collaborative effort. At noon I always felt an absence, one half of a man out there searching for me, guided by the knowledge that he could not be sure I existed. The guitarist turned out to be that man, but I could not complete him. I've thought and thought about this and finally I decided men don't enjoy sex. In the end I was terrified at the thought that this thing of his, this thing he slipped inside me (if the reader will forgive me), was mine; that without seeing it, almost without touching it, I knew it better than he did. I taught him how to use it, how to let himself go deeper without hurting himself, because I never felt any pain, never felt tired, and they never managed to fill me, the poor guys, no matter how they emptied themselves. They seek us out, but for what? So they can cry afterwards the way he cried? He complained about the ache in his thighs, in his neck, in his head. I'd look at him coolly, bright-eyed as ever, waiting – though I never said this – for him to want to be drained again. Or sucked off? No, I'd never think such a thing. He couldn't get over the satisfaction of seeing me writhing and moaning and sighing under him or on top of him, but the pain would always curb his arrogance. It never stopped hurting him. I'd tried (a little snobbishly) to get him to explain exactly what sort of pain it was, but he'd just look at me, screw up his mouth and his eyes, then pull away and pick up the guitar. Watching him pull away, already whistling a song that wasn't his, I thought, 'It hurts because he knows I could rip his prick out by the roots if I wanted.' In the brutal moment of passion, obviously. In the end, love's not that important. Here I'm quoting Mariángela, who waited patiently, listening to heavenly music, while I was losing my virginity and he was whimpering at every vicious scratch, every cruel bite; at least that's what it felt like I was doing to him on the first waterbed (*Made in USA*) I'd ever seen in my life.

We listened to music for twelve hours straight, then all three of us went out; him and me with our arms wrapped around each other, Mariángela prodding people with a stick she found. It did not surprise me that when we got to Avenida Sexta, Misery Guts Ricardito arrived; eyes bulging with panic, he said, 'I'm going round talking to everyone to find out if they've forgiven me for my appalling behaviour last night. I need them to understand I wasn't myself; either that or there's one last hope: that no one remembers anything. You guys don't remember seeing me, do you? You've no idea what Misery Guts got up to last night, you don't remember?'

'We don't remember,' I said, just to keep the jerk happy. 'I don't remember what you did and I don't care where you ended up.'

'I ended up sleeping on the ground like a dog,' he whimpered as though he was criticizing our poor memories, to boot.

'Sorry,' I said. 'We don't all have your memory.'

'That's true,' he nodded, looking touched and quite proud. 'I have got an amazing memory.'

Mariángela burst out laughing and Ricardo was clearly hurt by this, but I think we'd managed to calm him down a bit and he told us he had to get going, his feet marking time. He headed off in search of more rumours of his disgrace, more witnesses to his humiliation. Since there were, like, thirty people at the party, it probably took him quite some time to track them all down and apologize.

At any rate, I never saw him again. I heard he started deliberately disturbing his parents' sleep, letting out bloodcurdling shrieks in the middle of the night, and in the end they had him sectioned. But not in England's green and pleasant land, as he would have liked. They had him committed to San Isidro; I mean, he was a local head-case. Other people say he didn't stay there long, but no one knows exactly where he is now. Nobody knows the whereabouts of poor Misery Guts. There were rumours he and his mother went on some trip incognito and she came back alone, more beautiful than ever. I'm sorry I didn't get to say goodbye to him. I don't know whether he lost it first or whether I closed myself off. But one morning, by registered post, I received a piece of paper with the following information:

Patient Questionnaire Number 02 x 26
San Isidro Psychiatric Hospital
Cali, Colombia

Questionnaire to be completed by the patient and/or the
accompanying person.

Patient History No. 1
Name, Surname:
Ricardo Sevilla, aka 'Misery Guts'

In respect of the reason for this visit to hospital, have
you previously consulted a:

1. Psychologist . . .   2. Healer . . .
3. Friend . . .   4. Doctor . . .
5. Pharmacist . . .   6. Priest . . .
7. Psychiatrist . . .   8. No one . . .

With an (X) mark YES to those that apply to you now or
have applied in the past 30 days. For those that do not
apply, mark (X) NO. Have you . . .

Felt happy	YES [X] NO [ ]
Participated in sporting or other recreational activities (football, cinema, swimming, walking, dancing, etc)	YES [X] NO [ ]
Listened to the radio or read newspapers daily	YES [X] NO [ ]
Had problems with work or studies	YES [X] NO [ ]
Had difficulty sleeping	YES [X] NO [ ]
Had frequent headaches	YES [X] NO [ ]
Experienced loss of appetite	YES [X] NO [ ]

Suffered weight loss   YES [X] NO [ ]

Suffered fits or convulsions which made
   you collapse, caused jerky arm or leg
   movements, made you bite your
   tongue or lose consciousness   YES [X] NO [ ]

Suffered from a dry mouth   YES [X] NO [ ]

Had tremors or twitching in
   the arms, hands or mouth   YES [X] NO [ ]

Suffered from dizziness   YES [X] NO [ ]

Felt restlessness, inability to
   remain still   YES [X] NO [ ]

Noticed your vision become
   cloudy or blurred   YES [X] NO [ ]

Noticed excessive salivation   YES [X] NO [ ]

Felt 'wound up' or 'stiff'   YES [X] NO [ ]

Noticed feelings of sadness,
   weakness or felt the urge to cry   YES [X] NO [ ]

Experienced feelings of nervousness,
   anxiety, fear or dread   YES [X] NO [ ]

Used cocaine/heroin   YES [X] NO [ ]

Smoked marijuana   YES [X] NO [ ]

Taken LSD (acid), mushrooms   YES [X] NO [ ]

Seriously contemplated killing
   yourself   YES [X] NO [ ]

Attempted suicide   YES [X] NO [ ]

Do you hear voices other people
   do not hear   YES [X] NO [ ]

See things others do not see   YES [X] NO [ ]

Have you seriously thought
   about killing someone else   YES [X] NO [ ]

Physically hurt someone else   YES [X] NO [ ]

Experienced sexual problems or
   difficulties   YES [X] NO [ ]

Had difficulty concentrating

  or thinking clearly   YES [X] NO [ ]

Suffered from paralysis in an arm

  or leg, been unable to speak   YES [X] NO [ ]

Feared losing your mind

  (going mad)   YES [X] NO [ ]

Have you felt others are criticizing

  or making fun of you   YES [X] NO [ ]

Felt that someone or something

  is magically controlling you   YES [X] NO [ ]

Felt someone is trying to kill

  or hurt you   YES [X] NO [ ]

Do you feel you are important or

  possess special powers   YES [ ] NO [ ]

Information supplied by:
1. Patient [ ]   2. Relative [ ]   3. Other [ ]

Oh, Misery Guts Ricardo, this was your downfall; you took upon yourself all the symptoms of my generation! Some people claim that marking YES to every question was Ricardo's attempt to dupe the doctors. Even in the depths of his torment, he still had gallows humour.

I wasn't going down to Avenida Sexta much any more. Leopoldo was always introducing me to his intriguing friends. They'd come down from the USA and we'd throw huge parties for them. We listened to music 24/7, because when you've got coke you don't need to sleep. I learned a lot of stuff about a lot of stuff. You can't tell me that Brian Jones died because he was rash, or lazy, or even that he died of a broken heart. It's not as simple as that. He died of disillusionment. Brian was the one who brought the band together, he was the one who could read music, the one who taught the others, the one who was photogenic; he was the one obsessed with weird instruments – zithers, harps, marimbas, strings and brass, Mellotrons and cellos – while that dickhead Keith Richard[13] was only interested in *chaka-chaka-chaka*. He wanted to sing, this beautiful nobody. It was Jagger who stopped him, Jagger the eternal exhibitionist. After that, he found it impossible, the writing of songs for some usurper to sing, the gruelling tours, the constant gigging because it's gigs that bring in the cash – Jagger spent a couple of years studying Economics, don't forget – and then the unkindest cut of all: one night Keith Richard hooked up with Anita Pallenberg, Brian's girl, the girl he loved. You know what she looks like, big white teeth and that expression like she's mocking everyone. I don't know what she saw in Richard with his rotten teeth, but, well, some women are really dumb. The next day the two of them went round to Brian's place to tell him that Anita was dumping him. Brian wasn't there. They looked for him in London, searched all over and finally caught up with him, in some forest on the outskirts of London playing the flute.

Anita said, 'Brian, I've come to tell you I'm moving in with Keith'; Keith just stared at him. Brian stood up and smiled, he didn't say anything. He hugged them lazily – that's the sort of guy he was –

but he didn't play the flute any more. He'd just dreamed up 'Ruby Tuesday' – not that he got any credit for it, because he didn't want to shatter the Jagger/Richard image. He got into drugs and partying in a big way, though he always had a minder to look out for him, but I think inside he was a broken man, always brooding over what had happened to him. Keith had been his best mate; they'd just rented a flat together, they'd get together to jam and they were always getting up to crazy shit: once they nearly electrocuted some guy – by stuffing amplifier plugs in his ears – some fat, faggoty guy from the same town as Brian who'd showed up looking for him; because Brian wasn't from London. People say that, being hypersensitive, he had a bit of a complex about that, he felt like a country boy, still felt like that when the Stones were the best rock band in London, the best band in the whole world, and Brian was the one who made sure no one missed rehearsals, the one who made the group look good, always wearing the latest threads – he was named 'Best Dressed Rock Star' two years running.

All this was way before Jagger came and said they'd decided to tour the States again and Brian apparently panicked and refused to go. He wasn't into it, he didn't dig the States the way they did, he hated the fact you couldn't even hear the music over a bunch of hysterical screaming girls. He picked the most obvious excuse, weakness, but he wasn't weak, he was playing more than ever. Richard was present at this conversation. Well, he might have been, I'm not sure, I don't know. Anyway, the stuff Keith came out with later was all lies, about Brian being sprawled on the floor during recording sessions and him having to play both guitar parts. That's the kind of thing fans notice, man, when one musician dubs another; you hear, like, a scratch and a pause, yes, that's it, a scratch and a gap. But whenever I listen to them, they're tight and loud and hardcore. So Jagger said to him, 'So what? Are you saying you're quitting the band?' And Brian, who didn't talk much and who by now was really intimidated by Jagger, said, 'Yeah, I'm quitting the band,' and then added sarcastically, 'Maybe you should look for a replacement.'

Before he left, Richard was all sweetness and light: 'I'll call you in a week to see what you've decided, okay?' 'Okay,' said Brian and sat down to think. He knew they wouldn't find anyone to replace him and even if they did, the guy would be useless; they'd have to beg him to come back and that way he'd be in control of the band again like he used to be. Because Jagger had lost faith in Brian's genius, and because Brian knew that, he couldn't find any way to relate to the group that wasn't pathetic or humiliating.

This was what happened at rehearsals: he'd go over to Jagger, trembling, look him in the eye and say, 'What should I play, Mick?'

And Jagger would reply, 'You're a member of the band, Brian, play whatever you like.'

So Brian would start playing something on the guitar and Jagger would stop him and say, 'No, Brian, that's no good.'

'So what do you want me to play, Mick?'

'Play what you feel like.'

And Brian would try again, and Jagger would stop him again. 'No, that's not working either, Brian.'

So the poor bastard would end up drunk in a corner, tapping the floor out of time, tongue bleeding from playing the harmonica, trapped and unable to change the situation. He couldn't have imagined what Jagger was plotting. For over a week Jagger had been having little talks with Mick Taylor, this teenage kid who was playing with John Mayall at the time: meetings in places that weren't too hip, long conversations, notes written on the back of napkins, arrows, guitar tabs, never calling Brian, never getting in touch; I fucking hate them. I wonder how Brian felt when he read about it in the papers? After all he'd been the first to tell everyone this Taylor kid was talented. 'He even does that *chaka-chaka* thing you do,' he told Keith, thumping him on the arm. It was his idea of a joke. All we know for sure is that he heard the news and five days later he was dead.

For the rest, who knows? Personally, I think someone murdered him, but who? It would have had to be someone in their circle. There was a party, things got a bit wild, Brian wandered off somewhere and then there he is: lying dead in the swimming pool, his face flushed and swollen as though letting out that note he'd never sung.

They sang and played like shit the day after. Brian's death made their music harder and I know they were going for a harder sound, because Taylor's all scowls and ginger hair and moody and silent, Jagger's mangling his voice more and more, Charlie Watts is spending most of his time biting his nails and Bill Wyman, that lanky streak of piss, doesn't even tune his axe, just comes out with this solid throbbing wall of bass. What with Keith Richard's increasingly shrieking guitar, their sound would have unlistenable if it hadn't been softened by the gentle breezes of Bobby Keys and Jim Price on sax and trumpet, and now here they are, an eight-piece band, with the otherworldly Nicky Hopkins on piano. Summer of '72, the summer of the heatwave.

I didn't go out, didn't go talking about this stuff with Leopoldo's friends, who were all a bit foreign. Or if I went out, it was at night; this was the only time I'd allow myself the necessary contact with this city's magical breeze, and I knew that with every step, in the way I tapped on walls and railings, in the tempo of my greetings, I was beating out the rhythm of 'Salt of the Earth' or 'She's a Rainbow' or the tricky beat to 'Loving Cup'. And on every corner people would offer me transistors and cassette players, but what use did I have for them when I'd just come from listening to quadraphonic music from thousand-watt speakers?

Tiquito and Bull would have to forgive me for constantly avoiding them, the two of them passing the transistor radio between them, pressing it to their ears as the batteries ran down, getting used to watching me from far away, but always saying how cool it would be to see me more often, never admitting that it just wasn't possible any more. I wanted music, and music only existed indoors, between the beautiful walls of that glorious air-conditioned hi-fi.

'Look after your hair,' Bull said one day, a black day for me. 'You need to get out in the sun more, your hair's starting to look lifeless.'

I trudged back to the house, completely devastated, I who was always so joyful, and Leopoldo was there taking to his guitar because the guitar never really took to him. In his whole life he never actually wrote a song. All he was good at was playing along to a record. We'd pop drugs like candy and rarely move from the apartment to go to a *rumba*, we'd make our own *rumbas*, and so long as no one hassled me, as long as they left me to my music, everything was cool, everything was bliss. Except that beneath this sweltering sky Leopoldo still longed for the USA, the land of his schooling and his youthful delights. Coming here he realized it took more than happiness to succeed in life: it took ambition and determination, whereas he spent his afternoons lulled by the pained resignation of the tropics. Slow-hand guitar, slow-burn guitar, livid guitar, plucked strings sinking into the unforgiving sky . . .

I did my best to follow Bull's advice, though not because my hair was getting lifeless; I tried to persuade Leopoldo to come out with me, but the minute he set foot on the pavement, he'd be bitching about how there were no beautiful or interesting people, criticizing everybody for their average height, the dark anonymity of their eyes. Whereas I had only to pass a group of guys I knew and I'd instantly be completely alive, blowing air kisses, talking about cool parties, strutting confidently, and the guys would look up and half smile as they recognized me again, an increasingly rare pleasure now that I'd begun to shut myself away.

But I was kidding myself when I suggested they try new things, because the signs that they were trying new things were all there, etched around those eyes that once sparkled with life, around their dry mouths, in the incriminating flecks of yellowish spittle at the corners of their lips. Yet somehow I didn't mind seeing them diminished, my darling boys – we'll all be running in the same race, so don't go hiding on me – and I never stopped showering them with affectionate gestures, though I never touched them, since that would have broken the spell which, by that point, gave me life: the brevity and the distance of these meetings. They knew I'd retreated from the world, that Leopoldo Brook was my whole world now. So I when I passed them on the street, I left them with a memory of me in instalments so that on perilous nights, tossing and turning, lying fully clothed on the bed, throat red raw, brain teeming like an ants' nest, when I wrestled with memories of my childhood, when I got six diplomas and everyone predicted I'd have a brilliant career, they could fuse that image of me with the vague resolution that, tomorrow morning, they'd give up all this shit, yes, cling to my beautiful image so they could to get to sleep.

They saw me appear and asked no questions. They went on their way and I said, 'See you, see you, guys!' and they'd all turn, the better to place me now that I'd allowed myself the joy of goodbyes, but by then I was gone: two steps earlier Leopoldo Brook with a look of disgust had forced me back up the steps, complaining about the sugar carried on the wind; then I would scrape together images of the past and wallow in nostalgia while those outside wandered another half a block till they came to the junction that marked the boundary. Then they'd turn back, retracing the same aimless path until the weight of their legs would no longer carry them and they went off to seek refuge in the house of whichever of them still had a spliff primed and ready.

Walking back up the steps with Leopoldo behind me, I flicked my hair, tossed and twirled it to create a cyclone of myriad delights in the narrow stairwell and at least he was capable of identifying them; he had to take a deep breath so as not to miss any as each strand of hair created a kaleidoscope of colours in the twilight; outside the crackle of dust on the trees, the spine of each leaf flashing as it was whipped by the wind. Tico would have grabbed a branch and swung from it 'Wahaaaa!', conjuring up his mother's former pride when she peered into his face, cradled him in her arms and told him he was the most beautiful boy in the world. Music from outside, the fluttering of my hair making the branches on the walls blossom. Oh, the birds pecked and trilled. It was a long, slow climb. And as the stereophonic music rolled out a carpet to welcome us for a long stay in the apartment, I'd be filled with such a feeling of calm; okay, so we couldn't go out, but as long as we could play 'On with the Show' I could bear it, I could even understand Leopoldo's lyrics: 'Didn't I tell you we can't go out? Doesn't that humid wind put your bones out of joint?' And he would open his mouth, heave a deep sigh, his lungs shot: 'Oh, I miss San Francisco.'

Would he take me, I wondered, if he went back to the USA? I

don't think he could have. His family had told him to come home to manage an estate they owned near Kalipuerto, but it didn't take them long to realize, in the confusion of his homecoming, that their son was no good at anything, not even at playing the guitar.

As soon as we got to the hall, he would grab my hair with both hands and press his face into that nest of infinite fragrances, kiss the nape of my neck where it made a knot with my cervical bone, the apex of my broad back, my muscles and my freckles; I'd go so far as to fake a flurry of shivers. He couldn't pull away, he stayed there, shipwrecked on the nape of my neck, there in the middle of the living room, while I meditated on the state of the toenails on my left foot. After a while, I'd get impatient and scratch my ears with both hands, a sign that I wanted to move on to other things, then I'd relax my back muscles, my freckles advancing in waves over my firm flesh and poor Leopoldo would find himself exiled from the conjunction of my harmonies.

I turned to face his confusion, his eyes, his bruised purple lips. He took three steps back, stumbling over his guitar with no consideration whatever for the instrument. And, not for the first time, the guitar turned against him, filling his soul with poison and pain and he furiously hurled it away from him. But what did that leave him? Music played softly, the world outside quivered with the last vibrations of the afternoon. Poor Leopoldo was considering coming back over to me, burying his face in my breast so I'd cradle his head in my arms, so long, so tender, but he hesitated, managed to shuffle three paces and tripped again, this time over his indecision and his pain. He roused himself from this inertia with a groan, collapsed on to the nearest beanbag and, quick as a flash, he skinned up a Bacillus[14] of respectable size, took three long tokes and instinctively a smile opened like a wound in his face. Then he summoned me, making little faces, and I, contrite and faithful, I went over to inhale the twistedness of life.

By now, smoking *La Pasionaria*[15] produced in me a passion for everything and an inability to grasp anything, an obliteration of any notion of choice, a blurring of my concentration to the point where I hardly remembered how to use a spoon. A general hilarity, a heightened ability to communicate, cracks and tar and burning in my throat, a *white* pain, a tightness and an emptiness in my heart, an inability to relax, prolonged indigestion, 'X's and 'Z's of shooting pains in my belly, lack of appetite followed by fits of gluttony – though every mouthful of food simply made the bellyful of indigestion bigger and all you could do was collapse on the floor again and writhe – a hypersensitivity to trivial things, a splintering, a flaking of the brain, pincers squeezing the bulb and the seat, bloody cobwebs in the eyes, outbreaks and eruptions on the skin, a constant haze of dreams.

But, oh, how to describe the daisies that blossomed within me, the fantastical flitting of fireflies I felt as I walked over and sparked up my ticket for this trip, slowly, slowly, so that I would be more receptive, more sensitive to his caresses, suddenly discovering the good life; I found it difficult to hold in the oily smoke, but I let it slide down my throat, let it fall and wreak havoc inside me, squirming with pleasure and displeasure as I passed him the Bombshell. He took three quick tokes and passed it back, flecked with saliva, and I ran my tongue around the ring of his spittle, the connection between us, sucked hard on it again, burning gall, an off-beat drum. His eyelids drooped a few millimetres now. He gestured for me to give back the Barramundi, we did a blowback, the blazing tip in his mouth, while I thought about the dark jungle and the cursed sea of Chocó. I shifted closer to him, let him grab me by the throat so he could blow thin wisps of smoke into my nostrils, which left me disoriented, a jet of smoke straight to the brain that suddenly exhumed memories of escapades and parades, of a whole afternoon spent shut up in a wardrobe reading Dickens to my parents' astonishment, the music of lost footsteps, of rustling pages, the feeling I was inhaling a pungent, fiery greenness producing mustard in my brain and as I looked up, thrashing and shuddering, the wonderful certainty that each memory unearthed by the smoke was gone forever and in its place an empty space, and I needed another blowback so that the smoke could fill the space. I didn't care. I lost *Pickwick*, but I gained 'Play with Fire'.

Now I could whisper, 'Hold me,' and Leopoldo would immediately obey and, with all the smoke inside me, I felt my brain turn a thousand somersaults, an urge to grasp his hard flesh, to seize it triumphantly and use it to rip open my twisted, slick entrails. Leopoldo let slip some strange word in English and I kissed him hard on the mouth, which was bitter and heavy with moisture. But I quickly corrected myself: 'No, gentle lightness. I renounce my revulsion. All things are mine, and all things please me.' Then I coiled my silken tongue around the stiff, greasy pores of his tongue, so thick and long, then, *bang*, I'd squeeze his cock criminally hard as it throbbed against me, and if he started to scream, I'd squeeze harder and he'd go quiet and my edges grew rounded as I plunged head first on to this body, my breath warm on his mountain, the sap from my hair raining down on his face; I'd taste it on my tongue, smacking my lips, and unbutton his exclusive designer flies.

And then bells rang out, the birds hopped to a different branch. Visitors. Leopoldo swore in English, but I didn't care. Visitors were always a distraction. I relinquished this body and went down the stairs. It might be someone bringing new records. I did a little dance, singing praises, and opened the door to find two gringos and Roberto Ross, thirteen, the youngest junkie in Colombia.

They tramped upstairs, all greetings and salutations, and since Leopoldo made no move to get up and welcome them (he was still thinking about my sails and my rigging), I redoubled my enthusiasm and Roberto was thinking, 'Always so cheerful, always so eager.'

They did a little dance – *this could be the last time* – as though to distract our attention from their true purpose, to make us think – at least for the three bitter high-kicks of the chorus – that they'd come with good intentions just to dig the music. But they quickly revealed their true purpose, took out two good metres of nose candy carefully wrapped in wax paper, and once again I saw the vision of the South Pole, the ship filled with corpses, and my temperature plummeted so sharply the whole house was suddenly cold.

Roberto made some comment about the sudden chill but I didn't listen; I went over to the window with the pink curtain, stared out at the grey dusk drawing in, at the children playing blind man's buff around a street lamp, the mango leaves falling: a horrible thought had made me turn away, I was afraid the music had frozen, the record player or the tape recorder were broken, that inside us was an eternal sickness dooming us to spend the rest of ours lives humming half-forgotten songs. The nostalgia of pain. Ugh. I shook off the dark abyss of my mood, shot myself a smile, ready for anything.

By now, Leopoldo had got up and was in a friendlier mood. Robertico couldn't stop smiling as he cut the coke, eyes on stalks, shuddering with singular joy as he tenderly chopped each grain, being an expert at wielding a Gillette.

'You've never used that in a fight?'

'Jesus! Never,' he said, looking astonished. 'This blade I only use for peace. Isn't that right, bro?'

Both of the gringos nodded, completely spellbound by the little show Robertico was putting on: he flicked a small rock of cocaine from one end of the mirror to the other, chopped it, then, *bang*, on to one shoulder and, flexing his bicep, flipped it back on to the glass like the ringmaster of a flea circus, all the while murmuring to himself, '*Nice cocaine, nice cocaine, nobly fry our little brain, through the straw we snort the grain, don't complain, don't complain,*' and, still smiling, he split the heap of coke into two, then three, then four perfectly equal lines all pointing towards the master of the house.

Leopoldo Brook took out the $20 bill he kept for such occasions. Elbowing everyone out of the way, he bent over the mirror and effortlessly hoovered up his lines. Then he gazed at us, utterly fulfilled, while Roberto Ross coughed and stifled a laugh.

'Bang up, isn't it?' he said, not looking at Leopoldo. 'Shame it doesn't last when you snort it. One day, you'll figure out the right way.'

The giant of a gringo – a lanky lardass with a pot belly and goofball eyes – produced a disposable syringe, some cotton wool and a spoon, all the gear immaculate, and Roberto picked up the mirror and with great precision tipped most of the coke into the spoon. I laughed; everyone turned to look and I laughed harder – I don't know what I was laughing at, maybe at Leopoldo, who was standing plastered against the wall, utterly calm and serene. They lit a candle and were now holding the spoon over the hottest part of the flame and it wouldn't be long before it started boiling.

Looking at Roberto Ross, at his hideous acne-encrusted skin, I got to thinking about Misery Guts Ricardo and that was enough to make me spiral into terrible sadness (outside the kids were playing blind man's buff), but I thought, 'No, I don't have time to sort out my problems now. That would mean abandoning my boys and they need me to be happy, my poor, handsome, motherless boys,' so to show willing I asked stupidly, 'Is it ready?' and Roberto Ross said yes, scratching his spots, scratching his head, rolling his eyes slowly to reveal pure-white eyeballs shot through with sickly brownish veins.

I asked the fat guy for the syringe and he handed it to me and I said decisively, 'Right then, who's first?'

'Me,' said the other guy, who was half bald with hair like thatch. 'It's my gear.'

'Roll up your sleeve, then,' I commanded, sucking some of the liquid from the spoon into the syringe. The gringo squeezed his left arm with his other hand, but Roberto, ever efficient, had brought a clean cloth from the kitchen and now tied it carefully round the arm, which he gently held up to my face. I could see blue rivers and mountain ranges, powerful veins.

'Okay, all set, Jim,' said Robertico, his mouth watering. 'Total trip.' Then, to me: 'Go on, stick him.'

I made a Nazi nurse face and inched the needle closer, sharp and glittering. I made two jabs and punctured, broke the skin, sliding it slowly into the patient little maggot, then pushed the plunger gently while Robertico said, 'Gently, gently,' and Jim said, 'More, more,' and I was thinking, 'You like that, *papito*?' Suddenly a bleating sound like a goat from behind me made me hesitate and the gringo whined. I pulled out the needle and turned to look. It was

Leopoldo taking another hit. The gringo slumped to the floor, hugging his pleasure and his pinprick, and as the next song came on he started bouncing around, happily singing, *'Heartbreaker! Painmaker!'*

'Help me with the other guy,' I ordered Roberto Ross and, high on life, he said, 'She's a hard worker, our little girl.'

The fat guy had practically no veins, I found myself lost on a pale barren plain. Robertico laughed: 'Better off shooting it into the muscle. It goes straight in, it feels amazing.' And I said, 'This is going to hurt, *papito.'*

But the fat guy shot me a scornful look and showed me his arm, which had no veins, but lots of track marks.

'Naughty boy,' said Robertico and I said, 'Okay then, get ready.' With his finger he pointed to the spot where he wanted me to stick the needle and I thought, 'What if I stuck it through his nail?' But he moved his finger out of my reach, tensed his arm as much as he could and I jabbed but couldn't find an in. He didn't complain, he stayed calm, staring at the yellowing liquid oozing from the hole.

'She hit the muscle,' said Roberto Ross.

The fat guy didn't say a word. He knitted his brows and I spiked him again and this time I felt the needle sink into soft, supple flesh.

'That's the way,' said Roberto like some master of ceremonies.

'Oww . . . slowly,' said the fat guy and we all laughed as his eyes started to dance.

Robertico Ross said he'd sort himself out. He whistled softly, a song I later found out was a bolero called 'Si te contaran', a curious counterpoint to 'It's Only Rock 'n' Roll', which was blaring from the speakers.

And as he injected the liquid, he said, 'Such a fucking shame there are still people who snort this shit when the effect lasts, like, two hours if you shoot it. You should see the state of their nostrils. I've known coke fiends who've had to have a gold septum inserted.' He moaned a little as he pulled out the needle. It looked to me like his spots were suppurating.

'You ever do anything about those spots?'

'Nah, you get spots when you're my age,' he explained.

Maybe the story of Roberto Ross summed up the vortex of the times. He'd first tried drugs on a one-year visit to the USA, courtesy of a scholarship from the American Field Service. Back in Cali, he suddenly found himself very popular because he was always talking about acid and later shunned because he sold the stuff. People blamed him for the madness and death of his twelve-year-old girlfriend Margarita Bilbao, but no one could ever pin anything on him. To deal with the terrible depression he got coming down from cocaine, he started shooting up. He was the self-professed prophet of the bad example, not the corrupter, but the victim. He'd acquired a certain status in the last wave of gringo junkies and delinquents. He had contacts and could even spot plain-clothes cops. He was doing well. 'I've never had any regrets about what I might have been if I hadn't turned out the way I did,' he said. 'These days there's not a lot of people who put up with me; I don't know what I'd do if I couldn't put up with myself. I figure change will come at some point. Not because I decide, but because my metabolism will change. Right, I've gotta go, I've got some business going down.'

Leopoldo Brook offered me a hit and I happily accepted. Get hooked on snorting blow and you'll find yourself with a bad taxi habit. Feet and buses are no good any more for dealing with distances and emergencies. But you'll also find yourself twisting on the dance floor and not caring what anyone says, surefooted, head high, an air of sophistication filling your chest, your every sense heightened; you'll feel a devouring passion, a serenity as instantaneous as it is illusory, your heart hammering like a horse that's bolted, an all-consuming anguish that – you believe – is worthy only of the great and the unforgettable. Suffering dignifies us, so let's have another hit. And another and another till we explode.

'What's going down today?'

'Nothing.'

'Okay, let's have a hit.'

Then the terrifying comedown: 10mg Valium to steady our souls, and if we couldn't shake off the dreams of that sky-blue drug, we'd do another line of coke and if there's no coke, cut up cheap Ritalin and stuff it in every hole in our heads and dance to get the drug pumping through our bodies, rather than sitting around frying our brains, and if it was time to sleep and we couldn't sleep, then a little Mandrax – mequelone – Apacil, Nembutal, a fistful of diazepam: you felt a terrible panic when you found out it was true what they said, this shit affected the brain, fried your neurones, that it was irreversible, a one-way trip, but you might as well do it because you're already done for. Then you stop feeling panicked, you just feel angry at these puny brain cells that are incapable of reproducing, the only ones, the genuine article, because they're not made for you to fuck with or wear out through experience or knowledge.

It goes without saying that by now I was starting to look like Mariángela. Not the dark circles under the eyes – those I had already – but that way she had of always dancing solo, always furious, glaring around so no one dared come near, keeping at bay these new friends who were older than me and not very chatty.

This was when I began to notice the terrible progression of decline or decay. At first, I was surprised to find people weren't dancing much any more, or not dancing at all. Then they stopped talking too. My dancing, my constant need to move, my singing (I'd started to memorize lyrics) had always been an act of defiance, now it was an affront. Just like Mariángela, I started to stammer at critical moments.

When we were out together we never talked, because we realized we were gradually becoming the same person. We had the same graceful walk, the same tactic of leading a guy on only to shoot him down in flames when he came over to dance or chat; the same tic of running our fingers through our hair to calm ourselves. Later I started sniffing my hand; she copied me and when I caught her doing it, she turned away, but still she didn't take her hand from her nose, she breathed in long spasms and confessed, 'It smells like when I was a little girl and I used to go bowling.' More than once people told me something really weird was happening to her, more than once I saw people staring at us in disbelief, trying to size up our individual Furies when there was no point since our Furies were the same. They sized us up, but always from a safe distance.

I'd always loved a green-and-red striped shirt she used to wear. The day I turned sixteen, she literally gave me the shirt off her back, leaving herself with nothing. I don't know whether this thing of becoming like someone else is a way of boosting a fascinating personality in the eyes of the world or whether it represents a desire to rid the world of that personality and replace them, though not with the same intensity, the same appeal, or maybe I mean not with the same success. What I do know is that people started telling us, 'You're so alike that going out with one of you is like going out with both.' Before, when I was just starting out, Mariángela was the one who knew most and gave least of herself. I never got to know more than she did, I just caught up with her; I learned that *rumbas* were happenings organized solely for my benefit and that I and I alone had the painful duty of understanding them completely and the right to enjoy them all. So it wasn't a pleasant sight, seeing two *peladas* dancing together, each one utterly alone; all the more so since their every gesture was not just similar, it was so indistinguishable that it was impossible to tell who was copying who, which girl had become so like the other that she was losing her identity and which – given they were so alike – was stealing the other's persona, because she improved on the original or copied it so faithfully that one or other, the original or the facsimile, would eventually be superfluous.

The thing is, this rock 'n' roll thing puts a whole bunch of crazy ideas in your head. A lot of shrieking, a lot of well-sung choruses, a lot of studio polish and then silence and solitary confinement . . . I went out so I could see Mariángela, but after a while, all I got were messages from her and in the end not even that. By now the guys were used to people disappearing. By now Pedro Miguel Fernández had poisoned his sisters, and it doesn't matter how young you are, that sort of shit leaves you believing in everything and worshipping nothing.

I'd call round to her house but no one would answer, knock at the door but no one would come. I assumed she was in the country since she'd talked to me about maybe taking a trip to the mountains: 'To see this city from above.' How was I supposed to know that her *mamá* took a massive overdose of 10mg Valium tablets one night and never woke up, that Mariángela decided from that day forward to live life to the hilt, that she asked around for me but no one would listen because, when she was standing there, they'd forget my fascinating personality! Later, when I asked after her, they'd stare at me gormlessly and say they hadn't seen her in ages, that I was the one they'd seen, they didn't remember her at all. It was fucking complicated!

She'd unplugged the phone. Every time I banged on the door, she'd bite down on her pillow. I don't know how long her solitary confinement lasted but when she finally re-emerged, the people who saw her didn't dare ask questions. 'She was really pale,' they told me. 'But everyone's so pale these days, you don't ask questions.'

She walked slowly to the centre of Cali, saying hi to everyone she passed. When she reached the Telecom building, she took the lift to the top (she was always terrified of lifts), and head first, cupping her hands over her ears, she plunged from the thirteenth floor.

Aaaah! Don't say anything! I'll keep quiet, I won't say another word. We're all part of the same thing, we've all had the same opportunities; it's not our fault if we were born into an era where we're constantly seduced and then abandoned, where flies don't settle on us because these days we've invented incense that smells like cherry, we've invented a thousand perfumes for *rumbas*. I don't like that we give the impression that we're losers, kids who have no fucking clue what we've got ourselves into. Thinking about it, I decided that what Mariángela did was not the act of a loser, that when she jumped, she knew she had every chance of winning. And then I wept tears of relief, because grief is soothing and it's pleasurable;

I spent the whole day listening to 'I Got the Blues' and thinking, 'Maybe she was trying to set an example, trying to make some sort of statement.' Whatever it was, like Mariángela the day her mother died, I never felt more alive.

Alive, alive! And to celebrate we went out for the night. I bid you, gentle reader, pay careful attention because that night was to herald a radical change. A friend of Leopoldo's, recently unpacked from the USA, was throwing what people were saying was going to be 'a cosmic *rumba*' in Miraflores.

I spent the day wandering around like some spoilt little rich girl, rummaging through piles of clothes, picking out the best items, predicting fabulous things for the night ahead, because the very idea of going out, of going to someone else's *rumba*, was a novelty, so I tousled Leopoldo's hair while he looked at me neurotically, awkwardly, stupidly, nervously, jealous of my boundless stamina.

I wore flowers. He wore stripes. I didn't exactly encourage the combo but I didn't object either, because every day his mood was worse, then he calmed down and was like an empty shell, a deflated balloon. In the car I made a racket, heading up Avenida Sexta, calling out to the poor friends who didn't go looking for new things to do these days, not even on Saturdays, making sure strangers noticed me, remembered my presence (to tide them through those sleepless nights).

Arriving at the *rumba*, I felt half dead but so young, hair washed and pristine, a total *rumbera*, tongue not too numb from the effects of the charlie, sweetened with strawberry syrup, ready to kiss someone new.

I had a thousand plans in my little head. I'd already decided to dump Leopoldo, though he'd be the last to know. I'd get a new boyfriend, someone who travelled, we'd go to La Guajira, to the Galapagos Islands and I wouldn't be too fussy about the sound system – an ordinary two-speaker stereo would do.

As we got out of the car, I realized I couldn't even hear the music. The door was opened by some tall, lanky guy I never saw again who, with an almost imperceptible wave, pointed the way. And so we found ourselves in the living room with people sprawled all over the place. Chicago was playing on the stereo, but so quietly you'd have been better off with a transistor radio clamped to your ear.

'I don't believe it,' I said to Leopoldo, but he was already waving to some guy he knew, some washed-out nobody who didn't even stop to say hi, then he looked round for somewhere to crash, somewhere he could lie back and close his eyes. Close them and listen to the sounds, but what sounds? From what I could hear there were no sounds. It was completely inaudible. My nostrils flaring with pure rage, I stomped over to the stereo, which looked to be state-of-the-art and seriously powerful. I crouched down, respectful but curious. I worked out the dials: reached out, grabbed the button marked *Volume* and cranked it up full blast.

I heard the roar of a vast brass section. Everyone else felt a thousand thorns prickle all over their bodies and there were outraged screams of 'Bitch!' while I twirled across the floor, ready to begin my dance; they pushed me aside and someone scuttled over to the stereo like his life depended on it and, in a flash, killed the volume.

I stared at Leopoldo, then I said, 'Music's supposed to be played loud, isn't it?' This was the first truth he'd taught me. He didn't get up, he beckoned and I went over.

'We're completely out of it,' he said. 'These people, they've been through a lot. A bit of quiet wouldn't do us any harm . . . '

'Okay then . . . Peace out, as they say.'

'Come lie on my shoulder,' he suggested through a moronic haze.

'And by peace you mean no volume. This is what we're reduced to.'

'Too much, too much volume, too much speed,' he said, struggling to get to his feet and moaning that every time he stood up his spine hurt. Barely moving away from the wall (I mean he was hugging the walls), he set off in search of our host; I don't know if this was to apologize for my appalling behaviour or to try and score some kind of stimulant. Whatever the deal, he got his stimulants. Everyone except me had slunk back to where they were before, and there I was standing in the middle of the room going crazy. All my brilliant plans were useless now. I wouldn't get to kiss somebody new; here was I, the flower of youth, in a world of withered people.

'Why not just turn it off? Why not just go to sleep?'

No one answered. I turned my head this way and that, convinced that checking out the house would ease my pain, because it was always good to see the blue of night glittering on a patio, the cemetery of unchanging walls, Dutch furniture, Chinese porcelain.

But nothing . . . There was nothing in that house, or if there was it didn't make me feel alive.

I spun around again, plagued by the thought that there was nothing for me to do now but slump down amid these ashes, forever a prisoner of the shifting shadows. I decided to walk right over to my tired lover and insist that he give me another English lesson.

But even as I thought this, I heard the sound of new chords, deep but distant. They weren't coming from inside this house, and you should have seen me, I was a sight, staggering and reeling, trying to get my bearings as I worked out it was coming from the south, this music that was music itself, and I walked – a long way, I think – trampling over knees and shins, mercilessly stepping on heads that didn't complain. Could they not hear it? Did they not realize as I drew near to the source, that just south of here someone was listening to music cranked up to a bestial volume? Ear-splitting brasses, strings, skins . . . yet it was the piano that guided my steps, exposing my smile tooth by tooth. I reached the front door, and as I flung it open, I heard lyrics.

Who knows who maps our path through this world or how they do so; here in beautiful Cali I am the queen of *guaguancó*.[16] I stepped out into the street, into a sky so clear! An enormous moon and a deep wind from the mountains bore witness to my devastating revelation in that moment: that everything in life is lyrics, is words. Maybe my words here are of a different order. Maybe the moment he stops reading, my gentle reader will head out for a drink, and instead of writing things down, maybe I'd have been better off speaking my story, because I love to talk, even if my words are just filaments in the air, hackneyed lines. It doesn't matter: I open my mouth to speak and no one stops me, and all that comes out are lyrics, because before me came a musician, someone infinitely more powerful and more generous, someone happy to let people sing his lyrics without having to take responsibility, and so I wake up in the morning with a lyric that will run through my head, over and over all day long like a sort of talisman against every miserable moment, on one of those days when I set out to do the most miserable thing of all: take the train to La Cumbre, a village that, like, a thousand years ago was the summer haunt of the bourgeoisie and is now a ghost town with a haunted house on the hill. The soil is not so red now, the air is less health-giving and less cool; meanwhile, slowly eroding, there are lyrics to love songs carved into the earth by boys and girls who now work for the tourist office or the town council and don't remember. If we manage not to miss the train, who will greet us at La Cumbre? The little nuns who, every day for a thousand years, have been waiting for the five o'clock train, grimy now, its green paint peeling, the wooden train that's still the main attraction here now that even the travelling Mexican cinema has gone. But I step down from the train, breathe in the village and find myself more alone than anyone in the world, so I wander aimlessly, singing that song going round in my head, going round in our heads, and when night comes we dream another song and tomorrow, for the first time, sing its lyrics, and so on, and so on.

The music I could hear was coming from a house, not some posh mansion, but a house on the far side of the street I was about to cross: the street where the district of Miraflores ends.

I don't know what they call the *barrio* on the other side; maybe it doesn't have a name, maybe the people there just call it Miraflores, but this is nothing like Miraflores. Little shacks scattered across the hillside, kids who don't go to school at San Juan Berchmans, who don't shut themselves away, and I was standing there thinking, 'Given what I can see, they've no reason to shut themselves away!' I could see two windows, an open door, glimpses of dresses ranging from vivid yellow to ochre, to sapodilla red, to purple, to lilac.

Already I'd set off, already I was crossing over. I swear *I can hear within me echoes of a cry.* And I didn't look back, not once. The lyrics of the song said, *'This little girl is so famous, they know her all over the world. She entraps men like a spider, they'll do anything for this girl.'*

I had only to surrender myself to the music, and so I flung my arms wide; everything was mine, everything was in my favour, 'Take It and Give Me'.[17] Some guys who'd stepped out in search of fresh air found me instead; one look and they were breathless: this was no street I was crossing, it was a river and how in this river sweeping me along could they get the air they needed? Half drowned, they stumbled back inside to the fiesta and, finding their voices, they spread the word: 'There's some weird chick heading this way.' After they came outside and saw me, I never saw them dance; they hugged the walls, watching the other dancers, as though panicked by the state of the world. Had I stripped them of music merely by my presence? If I had, it was a mortal sin, because without music they were motherless children . . . *that speak of pain and hope* . . . I tripped over a brick . . . *weep for my country* . . . then over a bottle, came to a patch of unkempt lawn. I thought, 'Inside this house are fabulous women. These guys are already suffering for them and I have yet to cross over.'

I became entangled in the long grass, tripped and landed in dogshit, struggled to my feet, a pilgrim; I didn't even bother to straighten my hair as I strode in to the *rumba* – the *rumba* I carry with me is for me and me alone.

I've no idea how many guys were staring at me. Confused, I watched the confusion of bodies shaking to the *bembé*:[18] one, two, three, hop, *butín, butero tabique y afuero*.[19] I must have had eyes like a fish as I stared: not a single person was sitting down; this was music to be danced to *on the tips of your toes, Teresa, on the tips of your toes*,[20] otherwise you can't hop and that little hop is crucial, or you might as well be yokels – *paisas* – dancing a quadrille or a waltz.

None of the chicks were jealous of how pretty I was, *let's go back to my place and crank up the bembé,* I took two quick steps and a couple accidentally elbowed me and I ended up, stunned, back where I was before, *Hey, Piraña, release me from your clutches, this woman she breaks everything she touches.* The *pelada* the song was dedicated to flushed bright red and turned away; she had beautiful hair, *guaguancó* pulsed, everyone whistled but I was whistling the melody – don't mock her, her name's Teresa, this *Piraña* – and she didn't stay embarrassed for long because look, *hear the trumpets ring, hear the congas sing,* she just threw herself back into the dance yelling these were her people, so she was changing partners, *saluting the great dancers of her youth;* she had blue jeans, a red cropped T-shirt and a beautiful belly button. Then there's the guy at the *rumba, stand back and make way, he ain't got much to say, just comes over to you and his hips, how they sway,* and then two guys came over shouting over the music how they'd seen me around a bunch of times; I didn't believe their bullshit – '*I'd swear I'd recognize you guys though you're wearing a disguise,*' is what I said, but I only said it to blend in, because I knew by now this was a battle of the sexes; the guys hassled *la Piraña,* I hassled the guys and they just laughed it off like always, and instead of asking for ID they asked me to dance and I was a bit flustered and I said, 'I'd like to be introduced to the lady of the house,' so they introduced me. She was busy with the hooch and the spicy meatballs, she was dressed all in white, which looked strange in this sea of sapodilla red. What was I planning to do, tell her I was a gatecrasher? *Sambumbia!* She didn't take much notice of me, I shook her hand, our hands were burning up. '*Mucho gusto,*' she said and disappeared, *play me, Richie, play me like an animal,* and as I saw her back suddenly arch and heard the joyous roar of the next song, I realized – quick on the uptake as ever – that I'd spent too long in the shade, that I bore the mark of it on my face, that this was why all the guys were sniffing around me, surrounding me. Another guy turned up and then there were three – José Hidalgo, Marcos Pérez, Manuelito Rodríguez – all begging to dance with me, *we know Tito's all the rage and when he plays he owns the stage,* so I danced with all three of them, each one a more delicious mystery, and it was my previous experience, my experience with death, that had me bending at the knees like this, giving them the slip, staring down at their shoes and at mine; at a *rumba* like this you come to dance and you've got to find ways to constantly be different, *who was it said I couldn't make it, who was it said I couldn't fake it*, it just poured out of me with astonishing intensity, with a shake of my hips, with a sway of my hips. Manuelito Rodríguez smelled of ink. 'I make the stuff,' he explained. 'I've got a secret packing plant and rolls of *INK* labels'; Marcos Pérez looked like López Tarso,[21] his face a mask of mute tragedy, and I clung to him during the boleros, *a piece of wood from a sinking ship.* 'You smell like expensive drugs to me,' he said. 'I bet you taste bitter all over.' And I clung harder to him, my *bomba rica, oh, I'm just a soul in pain on a lonely shore, a wandering soul who can cry no more.* 'What I can taste is the sea,' I whispered into both his ears like they were sea-shells and he went all quiet and breathed me in; I could have had him lie on his back on the waves of my waters. Most important of all was what José Hidalgo told me – I clung to him too, and I'll conquer him; he was the one who gave me the low-down, who told me the three of them were volleyball players, and I told him I was a huge fan, and they all went wild, shouting, *'Pelada! Pelada!'* and as they clapped, for no reason, I suddenly remembered the old days when Misery Guts Ricardito used to take me to watch the football on the pitch behind the Departmental Library, to watch some school grudge match between Liceo Benalcázar and Sagrado Corazon, and Ricardito would hold my hand; but this wasn't me feeling nostalgic, 'Get Sharp!',[22] this was me realizing I was still thinking on the level of the junkies crashed out across the road, whereas over here everyone was yelling for them to turn up the volume, turn up the beat. Someone shouted, 'Enough with the boleros!' and I glared at him and he skulked off into a corner with a face like a tango, *come on, Ray, what's coming next will blow your mind*, yeah, the song they put on next was hardcore, the sound of congas, nothing but congas, and people said my hair was *the wave that veiled the mystery of Guarataro*, which should make any reader who's been to a salsa smile. 'Changó, bestow on us your sword; I got myself half cut and they gave me more drink.'[23]

The first thing you feel is that you're not on the outside, that in trying to share it, true joy arrives; oh, and joy should never, ever be conveyed with words, but only with hugs, because with booze you become tongue-tied and you think to yourself, 'I just need to concentrate,' so you close your eyes to concentrate, and as soon as you close your eyes, your soul escapes. And what do you do then? Carry on, carry on drinking – let the whole world join us until we're all plastered – with that aimless, directionless look as though we're under the sea with our eyes open. And alcohol, now that *was* good for my hair – it may have made it a little lank, but at least it wasn't tangled – and my skin . . . well, it may have been a little greasy the morning after, but it wasn't the horrible greasiness and the terrible pallor you get with cocaine, just a watery film easily washed away with Luna soap to leave no dark circles, nothing but glowing skin, although the sockets seem to shrivel and the poor eyes start bulging as though someone's pulling your hair, your ponytail, the whole circle of skin on your face, everything except the eyes, which stay, as though pleading for an explanation, for mercy. If it were possible to rip off someone's scalp and all the skin on their face, my wild eyes would still be here pleading with the world for answers. The agonizing morning-after feeling, the migraines, the thirst, never bothered me: I learned to do headstands, I'd stand on my head for a couple of minutes and the headaches would vanish; and I never confused the heavy, burning feeling in my stomach with feeling sick; as far as I was concerned it was a healthy sign that I needed another drink. I prefer clear spirits: *aguardiente*, gin, vodka. Of the dark spirits, brandy is the only one I can stomach, rum is fatal. For a bottle of brandy, I gave my whole life – just imagine the lucky soul who got that – I kick and I quiver like a broody hen and the guy lets me go, convinced that I'm shattered. 'Two or three of those,' they tell me, 'and it'll leave you zonked.' 'You're right,' I tell them, but I'm talking to myself, trying to work out how many of them I've got inside me, how many bottles they'd fill; I could slap a label on it and sell it as essence of man transformed into nothing. I eat a big lunch and in the afternoon, as always, I sit and stare at mountains I'll never have the strength to climb.

All I hear is a voice inside me: 'You're having a blast, you should never doubt that,' and when night comes I don't miss a single drop; night fills me with such confidence that I flash murderous looks at anyone who leaves early.

Me and the volleyball players are the last to leave. I say goodbye to our hostess, and ever since she's been sending me letters, little messages awkwardly trying to explain how wonderful it was to have me at her *rumba*, how when she was on the bus today and saw me walking down the street, my step light, my head held high, she thought, 'I'd rather see her walking along the banks of the River against the current.' I never see her, not that she wants to see me either. I know that if we meet, the poor thing will just blush and nothing will come of it. In her last note she asked me to forgive her if one day I see her wearing the dress I'm wearing now, because she tells me she copies everything I do.

That night I confessed to her that I'd been a magnificent but solitary dancer until the revelation that was her wild fiesta, I told her she was magnificent, with that pale complexion I like so late at night, her perfect serenity, the way she preferred to watch rather than dance. If you ever run into her, her name's Manuela. *Sambumbia!*

Daybreak was implacable, the advancing morning as stealthy as Indians. 'Party-girl *pelada*, for you there's more,' the volleyball players said, as though this was a present, a gift in good faith when actually it was a promise I'd wrung from them with all my many charms. *The rumba, the rumba is calling me, dance it, dance it like me.*

They had an apartment further up the hill, and there the music would carry on, there I intended to do the deed with them, but first I needed to revisit my past. 'Follow me,' I ordered. 'We're crossing the street.'

The house, the gate, the front door were gaping wide and inside everyone was sprawled on the floor, a scratched record endlessly repeating a single line over and over, and my new friends said, 'We can't understand a fucking thing.' Leopoldo was the only one in any sort of shape, wrapped around his sad guitar, his dry, dishevelled hair plastered to his forehead.

I swelled with life and my eyes grew wide as I remembered how I'd totally understood the Spanish lyrics I'd just heard, *the culture of my land where deep inside a sun is born*, and I screamed at the top of my voice, 'Down with Yankee cultural imperialism!' and got the fuck out of there, with not a second to lose, dragging my new friends with me. Instead of the simple satisfaction of seeing everyone wake with a start, I had two:

1. the satisfaction of picturing them waking and finding no one there – which was better than the simple pleasure of just seeing it for real;
2. the satisfaction of seeing the expressions on the faces of the volleyball players who, once we got outside, asked no questions; they just kept shouting slogans in a daze of rage and stupefaction.

I became a river of insistent thoughts, every one of them happy, I scaled the hill with them. A block further on I felt hunger pangs, and they said, 'It'll be quicker if we cut through the empty plots.' I don't know whether I believed them but it didn't matter, the *rumba* calls to me and *guaguancó* has carried off thousands. We headed across the waste ground, I cut myself on the spiky grass, I had to lift my feet high to get anywhere and I was thinking about this, a little angrily, when I saw them stop and wait for me. I thought, 'Do they want to devour me here?' and just then, from one of the houses nearby, came the smell of breakfast, fried eggs and bacon. This gave substance to their desire, to devour me whole; it filled me with an even greater urgency, and one by one I put my arms around them, one by one I tenderly called each of them *papito*, unbuttoned his flies and lay down on a patch of bare ground with an expression like a mental retard. It's a pity José Hidalgo felt hardly any pain because he went last and by then I was wet. As he emptied his whole being into me, I stared at the houses ringing the sky and as I looked around I noticed a group of guys who'd spent the night up playing cards; they were leaning on a balcony wall, watching the whole thing and howling like demons.

Anyhow, *inside a sun is born and I don't find my love. Let's go back to my place and crank up the bembé.* The volleyballers lived in a one-room flat with a bathroom and a kitchenette. We took four *pépas* a day to ward off sleep and partied for seven days solid.

I learned everything there was to learn. Their record collection, which they'd bought as a collective, covered the whole period of pre-revolutionary Cuba, *pachanga* and *charanga*, the revolution, and then the rolling wave of salsa that calls and calls to me now, and I thought, 'Hang on. Learn to control the call, make it reciprocal. Make it wait.' No one knows who got here first, who was whiter or blacker than you, who first had the idea, the good sense to ditch the slowness and bring on the beat, to lose the drag and bring in the bounce to create hard, throbbing salsa, to protect us all with the handiwork of Babalú, *I call on Babalú and he comes to me, Babalú walks with me.*

By the beginning of the fourth day, I was complaining of a stitch in my side; we'd got to the hardcore salsa phase – they were playing the records to me in the order they were first released – the era of King (Richie) Ray,[24] who I've mentioned already, and Ray Barretto;[25] they taught how me to breathe, how to shift my weight, listen carefully, shift the whole weight of the dance from one foot to the other for those with no faith and no refuge, and then the soft counterpoint of the piano solos, the noodling of Larry Harlow,[26] the rocks of Ricardo Ray raining down as the river rises – *Sambumbia!* – and the boogaloo bursts its banks; then you have to hold tight because the salsa pounds hard and fast, lean on your partner's shoulders, a wave of mystery, and steel yourself – no, I'm not giving you my strength, partner, excuse me while I try to find some balance to my breathing, and in the meantime I breathe your breath and won't let you breathe – and the guys and me, we like the way I sweat; I sweat like a horse. Everything's so alive, and now when I dance I never leave the dance floor; it takes incredible concentration, and these days I hate *cumbia* and *paso dobles*, and fuck Los Graduados.

But the golden rule in life is that every *rumba* comes to an end, *that's the rhythm of Guarataro.* And now my perfect apprenticeship was coming to an end. Whenever they fell asleep, I swore at them. Their reaction was harsh: Hidalgo got up and turned off the stereo and I was left with no music, alone and bereft, the space of a thousand tiny stars, like ants, against a white backdrop, and my body was so weak I needed someone to hold me up. But no one did and I collapsed in a heap on the floor.

There I slowly turned and turned in this silence – let no one take anything from me, let them leave me; the floor was wide and I scuttled around on all fours, flopped around, and it took them a long time to realize someone would have to get up if only to give me an explanation, to take away my pain, man. I'm grateful to Marcos Pérez that he got up. He told me, *'Pelada*, we've got college tomorrow. It's time for bed. Everyone's completely beat.'

'I'm not beat,' I said, pushing him away and starting to leave. I couldn't really judge the steps but I somehow made it out to the street, to the air; I don't know what the fuck they were doing giving pointless explanations that did nothing to relieve my pain, which already seemed far away.

By now, it was morning. There are people who claim the day is the perfect unit and the human body is the mechanism that proves this. Because the body can cope with working or studying for just over twelve hours, after that, it sleeps. My body was devised for a more perfect mechanism: I didn't feel sleepy that morning, I felt like visiting people and, more importantly, I realized I now knew, knew by heart, what English music was and what Spanish music was – I had achieved what they call 'informed political awareness'. I skipped through the streets of this area that was in fact Miraflores. In the first corner shop with a telephone, I bought a beer and phoned the Marxists.

The Cricket answered with a sigh. 'Just woken up?' I said, and then, 'Lazy bastard. The early bird catches the worm.'

'Who's this?' he said.

'Me, you idiot. I've just discovered mind-blowing salsa. We have to destroy Rock to stay alive.'

I demanded he meet me that day but eventually we agreed to

hook up the following Friday. Neither of us showed up. Me, because I was at a *rumba*. He – and it pains me to admit this – because those fucking theoreticians had decided to blank me.

That Friday, I was invited to a *rumba* by my cousin Amanda Pinzón in the very heart of *El Nortecito*. I arrived immaculately dressed so no one could make any comments . . . I wore jeans, obviously, but all the other girls were wearing skirts. I arrived in fine spirits: the place was heaving, the lighting was amazing, though there were too many people talking. I sauntered in, hands in pockets, smiling and waving at all my old friends. I wandered over to them, all excited; they were the only ones who responded when I said, Hi, What's up, What's going on, What's the score, What's going down, my darling boys, and just seeing me they got all emotional, some reacted with tears, some with the same laugh they had two years ago, some with that serious directness of precocious, dead young men who were all washed up, as they say. And God, how they acted, they all seemed so different, all staring into the distance at some point far beyond the dance floor, the patio, the house, beyond the whole block; it was like they were flying around in circles all over the *barrio* in the middle of the night. And their thoughts tended towards other kinds of music, towards the wild drumming of the distance.

'You look like you've crossed mountains,' I told them, and they said, 'Exactly. We crossed them and we came back. We went as far as the sea. It was weird being so far away and hearing the call of the city.'

'An abortive escape,' I said, but I thought, 'Some day, carefully accompanied and triumphant, I will plunge into the dark heart of those enchanting mountains.'

I was wrong, but just then the music started up. There was a band. Alirio and His Rhythm Boys[27] started playing something terrible and that set off laughter and lurching steps converging on me from all directions, and from the hideous expressions on their faces I was convinced everyone was attacking me and it took me a minute to realize that they were dancing.

And without a single exception they were shit. I thought to

myself, 'Go easy, if you're going for "El Guarataro",' so I started off softly: '*I once knew a brave mulatto, who died up there in Guarataro,*' but by now I wasn't singing, I was screaming: '*This fear that says to me: get sharp, they're shooting at you, but Babalú is with me too and I've brought saoco,*'[28] *fear and dread. Obatala, Obatala who owns all heads!*'[29] and by that point things were getting really awkward. None of my friends wanted to join in – I don't blame them, they had their own shit to deal with; but I kept going, kept screaming all this stuff – '*If I don't raise no objection, I can't get no satisfaction*' – right in front of the musicians so no one could say Ricardo was prompting me; laughing confusion on the face of the trumpeter – '*Monguito,*'[30] *where you at?*' – on the face of the guy playing electric guitar and the one with the fucking organ; it was the reactionary redneck sound. Just seeing these people dancing the waltz and the chicks all acting like they were wearing crinolines. *Because it's hard to die when you're still alive,* I forced the band to take more breaks and every time they shut up I'd yell, '*The Abakuá, when they come from the cumbá, waiting for the signal,*'[31] until four little guys came over to me, '*and the Enkame*[32] *of Moruá,*' with some girl who wasn't actually my cousin, though she was obviously posh, '*saluting everything that is Abakuá,*' and physically dragged me out of the place, and I told them calmly, '*Because the saints deliver me from everything,*' and as I was being frogmarched out, I looked over at my old friends, Bull, little Tico, the boys (who, over time, what with all the *rumbas* they had to go to, were edging closer and closer to the door so actually they were never even at the party), and they stretched their arms out towards me and I let them touch the dazzling strands of my hair and everyone knew they were on my side, that they loved me but wouldn't leave with me, and it was at this point they finally realized that they could never come with me (no one was prepared to take the risk); none of them ever found a woman, none of them ever got married.

I got out of there, I left; I was out on my ass but with such a glorious sadness (the news would certainly have reached my parents by now) and an overwhelming urge to *rumba*! I realized I'd been wasting my time retracing a path I'd already conquered just by crossing a single street. I felt lost, disillusioned with this north I trudged out of sheer boredom. *My love for Adasa still burned in my heart.* Feverishly, I headed towards the savage south, where people hear my song.

Ever since, the north has been a polluted wasteland to me. I explored other territories. My *papá* kept up my monthly payments and I lived in hotels or garages or on the street with friends indeed in my hour of need. And I hung out at the Universidad del Valle, making like I was a student or just some passing *pelada*, with blue jeans and boots made for kicking or for jumping puddles, depending on how I felt. But it wasn't easy getting along with people; nobody else seemed to live for music the way I did. And when they started trying to rope me into some movement to get the rector fired, I'd say something like, '*Beat out the rhythm, 'cos I don't plan on stopping,*' and I'd jump to my feet, become hateful and threatening: '*Give me salsa, 'cos salsa gets me hopping.*' I just turned on my heel and hit the pavement.

The volleyballers went crazy when they saw me, but as soon as I'd turned my back on them, they were all: 'That chick? Total middle-class prig, forget her.' Until I told them, 'Yeah that's cool, soon as you get politics you start giving people the brush off.' And I stalked off, feeling sad and confused.

I spent hours sitting on the little wall outside an old house under the venerable towering kapok trees, and thinking about how old the building was had me imagining better times in this world: watching the last of the king's emissaries stopping here around five o'clock to be served a mug of chocolate, some cheese and fine tobacco before going on his way, heading down into a valley where the only houses built since the Indians had died of grief when the Thugs arrived were the mansion at Cañaveralejo that belonged to Doña Amalia Palacios and the Cañasgordas house. I stared at the ruins of the mansion and imagined myself living there: utterly free, a family of lunatics, a twelve-year-old girl losing her mind in the attempt to prove Lovecraft's writings are based in fact; incest, a possessive mother struggling against the onslaught of the years; possible witchcraft, walled-up rooms, footsteps in the night, the wail of some imprisoned creature; but, oh, never were my fantasies more cruelly disappointed – the house was inhabited by an ordinary family, the Capurros, whose offspring had no vices other than a genuine interest in engineering. I saw them show up at precisely the time the king's emissary was due to arrive, trailing a cloud of dusk, their coarse features anointed with engine oil. I sighed to myself, sighed for the dead. I wandered off whistling 'Trumpet Man II' and, laden with sorrows, I slowly crossed Avenida Quita, deliberately holding up traffic.

I had various routes that would take me to the Parque Panameriquenque.³³ As I tramped through it, I allowed myself a flick of the hair, something that on more than one occasion caused accidents: drivers could not remain impervious in the face of this golden mayhem in such an open space, especially during daylight. Any man walking within a metre of me was caught up in the whirlwind and could hardly shout, 'Hey, watch out!' since I hadn't hit him with a belt or a strap or some such, but with a harsh and loving caress, and few men deserve such a glorious settling of scores. I lay down on the vast, soft lawn, staring towards the northeast, longing for two, three sips of beer, my solitudes. The place was full of footballers, but if any of them came near me I was like a wild animal: I'd rear up, glare at them and mutter, 'Leave me alone.' Cyclists passed unchained. No one could trouble my anxious indolence.

Gazing at the mountains, I marshalled facts. 'One day I'll look down from there,' I promised myself, feeling the grass creeping over my body as I counted acacias, rain trees and flowering logwood, six different palms and thinking that perhaps Mariángela was the only person who might have made the journey with me, then, cruelly, adding: 'To inhabit my body, not overstep by a millimetre my boundaries in the world, the borders of my flesh.' I closed my eyes and in my head fashioned a crown from the varieties of green. The air annihilated the vegetation at the back of my neck, creating little eddies; I brought my hands together, lost in my fleeting contentment as though in prayer, you might say. Guys stared at me, incapable of recovering from the wound inflicted by my hair, not rushing to anoint it with butter: a wound that throbbed and blazed, and burned, and prickled, but it was good and I knew that it would last long after they'd eaten, that this wound would make it impossible for them to study, to sleep, in their agonies, enfolding the wound, being enfolded by it, their dreams a thousand fractured images of me, a necessary presence from the beyond. Oh, the times I've felt grateful to have admirers! This is why I go out, why I stop in the street somewhere, or do a little dance, because in a blinding flash I've remembered the song of the day, and a crowd begins to form: ten guys wounded by my hair at one time or another; they compare notes, they meet up and gaze at me, they see me again and, *basta*, I avert my eyes as though in pain and I flee with my hair like a protective curtain, giving substance to the dark, sweltering afternoon. Oh, my suns, my loves, so many shifting greens for public illumination. I tell all those people who are listening to me, I open my eyes, *good as you are, come dance with me*, I stand up, give the park a quick 360-degree sweep – easy does it, the key ritual[34] – I pause my fantasies so I can walk to the far steps, run down them, feeling happy and excited, waving my arms, laughing to myself; already the bubbling twilight has begun to appear – now is the perfect time to retrace my steps and this time confront the stairs, slowly, one by one, climb the twenty-three steps to find myself suddenly faced by a great vista, an immensity, the open space, lights from the cars tracing lines from one end to the other, the grid of people, the restless smell of the tropics, a sky red as sapodilla, black mountains, delicious bongos: climbing those steps is the most faithful simulation of what's called the 'crane shot' (that you see in movies).

Thoughts like this were what made me go to the Cine Club in San Fercho. But if some totally rococo guy said, 'Mankiewicz,' I'd come back with: '*Che che colé, who led him astray.*' I'm not easy to get along with, I don't deny it. Death and laughter.

Besides, it made me more and more depressed, coming out of the cinema into the sunlight, having to close my eyes, cursing the end of the movie. No, I like the things that shackle me to this harsh reality, not the ones that take me out of it and toss me into a different hole.

Last time I came out tap dancing, stamping hard and moving fast, halfway up the block, little hop, tips of my toes, thinking about the *jala jala*,[35] *come and bring Richie, let's boogie*. And longing, oh longing, for a huge *rumba*, or if not that at least a little dance, a couple of songs, a couple of beers. But if no one invited me, I'd have to sneak back to my parents' place: visit, eat, leave, *jala, driver, take me there*. I wasn't getting far walking and the song ran through my head and I marked time with my feet, and just as I'm crossing at a junction, I hear a beat and a crash and *Caína, come on, come on*, but I didn't turn round – it couldn't be my illusions, a deeper desire for misunderstood solitude. But I no longer chased the illusions; once I'd have sought them out, but this time I turned away, and stared down at my feet, clenched my jaw and did a little twirl. A little pirouette above five holes bored into the concrete so that kids could play a coin game, the click of a heel and a little rush, and then I hear whispering, the purr of quick feet running towards me, *the jala jala, let's do the jala jala here*; lifting my left knee, I imagine a fifty-peso coin on the tip of my shoe, *and I brought it for you*, I look at it, spellbound; meanwhile, with my other little foot I manage to keep my balance, and nearby I hear a shuffle of feet that aren't mine, someone lifting the other knee, a clean well-aimed thrust, and I step backwards, sticking out my ass, to see if I'd bump into the Stalker, hoping to make him stumble so I could flash him a dirty look and he'd give up the game, and that's that. But I kept zigzagging backwards perfectly; dogs and cats barked and bristled as I felt precisely the same movements being repeated behind me. Agreement, mutual understanding, polar cunning. People were staring now, and a bead of sweat appeared on my forehead; I moved forwards, bent my knees, *the jala jala just for fun*, shook like a leaf, saw a commotion in the trees, a windstorm, the heavens breaking, the flash of a hard knee moving behind me, the guy behind me bending, and, *bam*, knee to the ground. I couldn't stand it any longer, I turned round.

The little guy was about my height, all eyebrows and buck teeth, a handsome face, long legs; we stared at each other, revelling in the celebration: his bony hand barely touching my waist; my strong, calloused hand barely touching his shoulder, on which I could have lain my head. We gave a quick jump, perfectly in sync with the memory of the song in our heads, knowing we were coming to the last twirl. Seven straight lines and no release of tension, three hours of endless afternoon in the last blast of trumpets and runaway chords on the piano, the part everyone likes best. Utterly delicious, but best to have something in reserve. We don't move apart, our shoulders, our hips barely brushing – is this it? Come on, let's end it now. Around us, people waving or clapping or hurling abuse, I don't know; the keenest observers making an effort to work out the name of the song playing in our heads, something of Richie's. I squeezed his shoulder a little harder, stared into his face, which was difficult because with that sudden drop your eyes get blurred, a little hop, in that look I offered him my gratitude and my undying loyalty; I winked, I started to count back from ten to one and *Caína, come on, come on, God, you'll see it's good, jala like you've never done before*; I counted down each number with a shake of my index finger, he with his left knee, pounding the thick sole of his right foot, beating out the rhythm, and *haaaaaaaay!*

The precision of the finish, joyful and sensual, can I hear a roar of approval? I'll tell the truth: I ended up done in. And you have to remember the song only lasts five minutes. This is why after a dance people ask for horse, gimme a horse, saddle up a horse: the urge you feel to ride across mountains and prairies, pushing your entrails, your heart, the whole orchestra up into your head, and breathing in the pines and the pine cones, the guava trees. Riding horseback is the only *pachanga* that doesn't tire you.

We hugged, mingling our sweat, reinforcing each other. He told me he'd seen me around a couple of times before, but this time he'd just come out of the cinema down on life and with the *jala jala* running through his head, and when he saw me, man, he might have been shy but the show I was putting on was too hot for him to handle. We walked along together for a bit. Who existed, who was around us? In that moment, absolutely no one. He gave me the low-down on his life: his name was Rubén Paces, and I said, 'Like a whole bunch of peace?'[36] 'Yeah, but I'm about hardcore violence. When it comes to music, I mean.' He was the manager and DJ of Transatlantic Rhythms, playing gigs and parties. My bouquet of breezes blew, my early August blossomed. I gave him two kisses.

He lived by the white wall at the Institute for the Blind and the Deaf Mute in the coolest, shadiest, quietest street in all of San Fercho. He lived in a garage with a bathroom and a tiny kitchen: there was no sign on the door ('just in case of burglars') and nothing indicated anyone lived there but for the fact that it was painted a gaudy orange; inside, the place was a mess, a jumble of bedlinen and men's clothes. He got totally flustered (assuming I must be pulling a sour face) and started tidying up, folding sheets, stuffing underwear into a bag, and I went round looking at the posters of Richie Ray, Bobby Cruz, Miki Vimari, Mike Collazos, Russell Farnsworth and Pancho Cristal[37] and the vast collection of LPs – there had to be at least 250 – a box of tapes, a box of cassettes and a huge hi-fi system with room for every possible technical innovation.

He rushed to press the button closest to hand. And as he did, there came the soft rumble of piano and cymbals, *I'm happy to be in Colombia, I'm planning to dance me some cumbia.* We were still in the same groove as our *jala jala*, and I pointed this out and he said, 'What did you expect? I got it going on!' *Go ask anyone who's got a clue: Colombia's got its own boogaloo.* Now that there was music, the tidying speeded up a little, *boogaloo, aaaaaaaaay!* The situation started to become clear; there was a huge bed. 'The volume's not a problem is it?' I solemnly asked the crucial question. He looked at me as if to say, 'As if!' and then said, 'In case you hadn't noticed, we're surrounded by deaf mutes.' He finished tidying and threw his arms wide, not at me, but like he wanted to hug himself, like he was weighing himself up before puffing himself up, offering himself, the salsa of generosity. 'This is my crib,' he said. 'You won't be short of music from now till breakfast.' Oh, I ran to him even though his stance with his arms flung wide seemed to repel all caresses. He took me in his arms, he stroked my head and I squeezed my eyes shut, then opened them and I lifted my head, searching for his mouth, but he pulled away, looking worried and sad. 'That's not my thing,' he said.

And he lay down on the bed and covered his face with his pyjamas. From under them, he told me to wake him at 7 p.m.: 'When Don Rufían[38] gets here.' That was his boss, a cantankerous old cripple who didn't give a shit about music: he'd inherited the equipment and the records and encouraged Rubén to practise petty larceny and hypocrisy at the gigs they played. That way, if some unsuspecting guest didn't tip or wasn't paying attention, he'd swipe their records. Rubén would go to every *rumba* weighing up the possibility of making off with a handful of records and cassettes; it was one of the few things he was proud of. At almost every party they made a killing. And since the victims were kids, some of them not even fifteen, there was never any comeback. Besides, Don Rufían had spread rumours about his (non-existent) mafia connections. I stared at this headless body for a while and then let my mind move to the rhythm of the throbbing beat. He didn't say anything about the volume, so I didn't turn it down. But he seemed to sleep like a baby anyway.

The reader might think that given my beloved was a recordfiend, party animal and salsa-freak, I couldn't ask for anything more. In theory, that's true. But no salsa gets you completely; in the end you're plagued by tears, broken by fears, engulfed in inexplicable sadness. I knew: I had waded through the tide, crossed the black sands, the difficult harmonies of melodies, in the early hours.

Don Rufían would swing by at seven o'clock precisely. I'd help Rubén with everything. I'd have two or three frenzied dances; the rest of the time I was all ears, primed to tell him when some kid was totally wasted and started scattering records all over the place, or stopping some of the kids from fighting, and keeping an eye on the best dancers, memorizing complicated steps and – I have to mention this – waiting for the moment when Rubén would start to throw up. It happened at every party, without exception. A discreet black spray of vomit like molasses. He'd go off and look for a wall and I'd cover for him so no one – especially not the parents – would see that the guy spinning the decks was completely plastered. No, Rubén would always let me know when the moment came, he'd leave me at the decks and head out, stone-faced, groping his way along the walls, disappearing deep into the night to relieve himself. It wasn't because he drank too much, I thought, so why did he have to throw up? This is something the reader will shortly discover.

At first he told me it had something to do with his liver, and I accepted that; eight out of ten Colombians have livers that are shot to shit. But he was the one who made himself vomit; he had to have his reasons – did it give him some kind of relief? Rubén was a weird guy: he'd spend all week doing nothing but talking about salsa, about power chords, but come Friday his face would grow dark and he'd stop laughing, which was strange because he laughed all the time.

As soon as he started spinning his first record – '¡Ay compay!' or 'Seis tumbao', his trademark song – he'd start mumbling stuff about shame, biting his lip and slapping himself on the cheek. 'What's with you?' He'd say, 'Nothing, just my personality is as difficult as a Ricardo Ray chord change. Come on, listen to this record, I'm dedicating it to you.' *Guaguancó bizarro*,[39] the weird workings of the world of eavesdropping, the torturous steps and the words; midnight would come and go, and in the early hours Rubén would crank up the volume on his thoughts, and I'd do my best to catch everything: it was like he wasn't even aware I was there, like he didn't realize he wasn't just talking to himself. 'More people than at Jonás's 14,000 *rumbas*,' he'd say (which ones?). 'And Ricardo playing his heart out. I'd ask him to play "Que se rían", and I'd fight for him, I'd fight it out with all the drug-free troglodytes; if you hang around I can play whatever you like, if you carry on with the show no one can accuse you of being a coke fiend or some degenerate freak; the dance floor is half full of people who reject the liberation of dance through the careful observation of bestial rhythms.' This is the kind of stuff he came out with, though it only came out at *rumbas*, and I thought, 'It's some kind of suppressed guilt. Some kind of compulsory purge,' and I left him in peace; we've all got a petty thief inside us. Come here, it's good to suffer, it's good to party, but there's no need to suffer all the time: because after every *rumba* he'd have a couple of terrible nights; I say nights but actually it was all day, the terrible Saturdays and the Sunday mornings where he'd be screaming and muttering to himself and waking up: 'I got to the stage just as they started playing "Colorao". The fat guy on the drums dedicated the song to me.'

And he'd look at me, sweating bullets, eyes and mouth wide open, eyes and mouth a rictus of sheer terror. 'It's okay, *mi amor*, go back to sleep,' I'd say, stroking him. 'Forget about those bad dreams.'

'They're not bad,' he'd say. 'They're memories. It's worse when you don't remember anything.'

I was puzzled. How was I supposed to sleep now? I pressed the button by the bed, normal volume; this way he'd sleep better, repeating, deeply asleep, smiling, 'I'm going to sing you a *guaguancó* with feeling, a mambo, a bolero, because it comes from my heart.' He'd repeat it sometimes three times and drift off into a sleep with no peace, with no beaches in view. I think he wanted another *rumba* to draw back the bow of his suffering.

There was no doubt this had something to do with his conscience, but what? There was a date carved into the wall next to the bed: 26 December 1969. And all the posters were of people associated with Ricardo Ray's Big Band, there were no posters of Ray Barretto, Larrycito, Celia Cruz, Tito Puente, nothing. Richie's public love was his profane love. But how come Rubén had never talked to me about the momentous occasion that was the series of concerts they played in Cali? This was how I started my investigation. As soon as he woke up, he found me sprawled across his chest asking him questions: 'What did they wear? What song did they end the night with? How did they agree on the choruses? Who signalled the key changes?' When he heard me, he turned up the volume and started rummaging through his dirty clothes. He took out a small yellow glass bottle, clasped it in both hands, showed it to me, his eyes like a madman's, tipped out two red pills and, *bang*, popped them and burbled a big smile.

And I said, 'What are they? You going to give me one or what?'

'You're the queen, serve yourself, help yourself, find out for yourself how shit life is.'

'I'm going to get you to tell me.' And I popped two pills. Boogaloo, he laughed, my little *papito*, and he danced with me right there and then, don't cripple yourself, and I pressed my face to his ear – 'Tell me your darkest secrets' – like in a love story where the hero's suffering the horrors of war. 'Tell me everything.' And he laughed: 'This one's for you, because it comes from my heart,' and he started telling me as I felt my legs buckle for some reason – I cling to you, you fill me with your rhythm, random, drunken escapades.

On 26 December 1969, he'd left his parents' house early. He loved December afternoons because he'd go to a cinema, which was empty because everyone was at the bullfights, and come out around 6 p.m. feeling deliciously sad, with the crushing feeling that he was growing up: ten days from now he'd be going to secondary school. He'd arranged to meet up at La Papiruza with Flaco Tuercas, his best friend. They had a special bond. Just six days earlier, Flaco had introduced him to what they call Cannabinol. It had blown his mind. They made a pact. The first day of the holidays, they smoked a fat Buenaventuro and while Rubén lost himself in infinite perspectives, the convergence of every possible colour, Flaco Tuercas's head lolled, he let his mouth drop open and lost the use of his eyes, drooling blissful threads of saliva. Rubén said, 'Flaco, Flaco, what are you feeling? I need you to tell me what's happening to me, I'm all squishy and I can't breathe properly,' but it was useless, Flaco had pulled a whitey. He mumbled an apology for not to being able to join Rubén on his first trip, but he was completely off his face; he told Rubén to go get some strong coffee or take a cold shower if he needed to come down, but to leave him in peace and not move him even a millimetre because he was busy throwing up. But Rubén said no, he couldn't just leave him here, so he picked Flaco up, threw him over his shoulder and, ducking through deserted sidestreets, left Flaco on the doorstep of his house.

After that, Rubén wandered along an Avenida Roosevelt that was deeper and yellower than it had ever been, the avenue looked like it stretched off forever, but an eternity later he arrived at the other end – the weight in his head was probably a good thing; six times he traipsed from one end to the other and stood for twenty minutes like a statue, seeing people as vacuoles, translucent shapes, thinking about the route he was about to take again, travel-ling and re-travelling the length of this avenue of subaquatic shapes until he could organize his thoughts.

By 9 p.m., his thoughts were fewer and further between, but that too was a good thing; fortunately he felt suddenly exhausted, his legs ached. He did not remember how he got home. The next day, as soon as he woke up, he swore never to smoke that shit again.

Around noon, he and Tuercas met up and the two of them laughed about it. 'Crucial experience, hardcore, yeah?'

Tuercas gave him grief for dumping him on his own doorstep in the state he was in: 'Just as well it was my brother who found me and he was stoned as a bagful of fish hooks.'

And they laughed, and Tuercas casually took out a huge spliff: 'You fancy a toke?'

'In the middle of the day?' Rubén said, shocked.

'It's completely different, just try it.'

He couldn't bring himself to say no.

The sun was like a truncheon beating on his head, but the pain was good; the two of them had a wild time and, Holy Mary Mother of God, Rubén even managed to talk to girls in a way he'd never done before. 'Didn't I tell you? This is good shit, it gets rid of your inhibitions,' and Rubén thought yeah, it was. He took a deep breath and deep inside himself he smelled the eddying perfume of Martica, the girl he really fancied at the time.

So, anyway, on 26 December, he met up with Flaco Tuercas on what he thought of as the corner that synchronized the shifting forms of this twilight of rich magentas. El Tuercas said, like it was no big thing, that they were waiting here to hook up with Salvador, an older friend who was already at university, and the three of them were going to see Richie Ray. Rubén agreed, though actually he didn't care much either way, thinking it would just be one more December gig, never for a moment imagining that the music would be so sharp, nor that it would forever mark every night and every cursed day of his existence.

Salvador showed up, a handsome, dark-skinned guy, hair carefully groomed, scarf sprinkled with cologne, dressed all in white – a colour that showed up the fact he was shit-faced. He'd just been to the bullfights, witnessed the grandeur of El Viti,[40] the rudeness of El Cordobés,[41] and was loudly proclaiming the glories and the colours of his people, tonight's going to be some night, and he did a little dance step; he'd brought along some Marracachafa,[42] good shit too, so he took them round on to the Calle Orquetona so they could see and smell this mind-blowing gear, pure Colombian *mango biche*[43] with a twist of *punto rojo*[44] that'll blow your head off, then said why talk about it when they could try it, so he got out some soursop-flavoured skins, handed Tuercas an eyebrow of weed to comb through and, one, two, three, as he was walking along, completely laid-back, he managed to skin up a huge Baboon.

'I can tell little Rubén here is nervous, he doesn't realize I'm the sort of guy who can spark up a fuck-off spliff in a force-nine gale with a couple of Feds half a block away and disappear before they can lay their hands on me. Just do like I do, Rubén.'

Rubén hesitated, then sparked up the fat doobie that tasted of *guanábana*. Fuck. It had a vicious kick to it.

'Sure it does, that's 'cos they grow it up in the north of the valley, the most vicious part of the country.' Then: 'Wow, your eyes, man!'

And they still hadn't finished smoking the Bandero when Salvador suddenly said, 'You know what, guys? You know what would be crucial, bestial, essential for tonight? Something *primo*, bang-up, first-class, guaranteed no bad trips, all chilled, no hassle? A couple of Red Birds[45] each.' A pause then he said: 'So, whaddya say?'

'Yeaaaah,' said Tuercas. 'Never tried Seconal, have you Rubén?'

'No, never,' Rubén replied, choking and coughing, listening to one or other of them talking.

'In that case, you've never had the best.'

Which was exactly how I felt, pressed up against Rubén, clinging to his body as he prattled on; he couldn't stop talking. 'Don't give up on me now, we're just getting to the salsas; you're the one got me to spill my guts so don't bail on me now.' Problem was I couldn't dance, I could barely stand without wanting to do anything but suck out all the insides from this body that was somehow holding me up. '*Pelada, pelada,* keep your head up, hold it together for me', *sacatión manantión ilé sacatión manantión jesua, sacatión manantión mojé.*[46] I felt so tired, but now he'd started tickling me and jabbing me in the ribs, the belly button, his fingers like spiders spreading pins and needles along my hips, and suddenly I wasn't tired, I was laughing like an idiot, *don't conk out now, keep pumping to the rhythm, Miki,* and now he was laughing too, laughing as he kept telling me his story. I had my eyes closed, then I opened them, thinking that if I stopped laughing I'd fall down, and he said, 'I Invite You to Get Down and Boogaloo,'[47] and then, *wham,* we hit the floor. 'Don't stop, don't even think about it, just open your eyes and listen to me, feel how cool we are, pie-eyed and pilled up – c'mon, enjoy life.' Oh, those were the days.

Anyway, Salvador paid for a taxi to the place they were going to score, some sleazy dive on the corner of Novena and Catorceavo, behind Fray Damián College – the asshole of the universe. They agreed Salvador and El Tuercas would go in, pop a couple of Seconal and bring Rubén's out, one in each hand. No payment necessary, it was all on Salvador.

That's how it went down. Rubén hardly even had to wait, though he really didn't dig the cold sweat he could feel trickling down his forehead.

'Hang loose, kid, we're back, it's all under control: now I'm going to make like I'm sparking up a cigarette; you make like you're shielding the lighter from the wind, and you pop the pills, cool?'

'Right here?'

'Absolutely, round here you can't be going round carrying; you're better going round loaded.'

Rubén just had time to think: 'I'll stash one down my jockeys.' But they were new and very tight and he had to be careful not to accidentally shove it up his ass.

'Ready?'

'Yeah.' *Boom*, he felt himself surrounded, felt trapped.

'Swallow hard.'

He built up some saliva, swallowed hard and down it went.

'Thaaaaat's it.'

So cool, all these strange new pleasures, new feelings, it was choice.

After that, they had to put on some speed to get to where the salsa was; it wouldn't be cool to show up late, there'd be no tickets and that would be a real bummer. They caught another taxi. This was motorvation. Rubén looked out at the passing streets, wide-eyed, waiting for the effects to kick in. He didn't want to ask, he didn't want to be told what they were. He'd read an article about psychedelia in a Spanish edition of *Life* and was waiting for the whispered murmur of hallucinations in his brain: 'I'd like to see a burning bush.' He would have been better off asking. He couldn't have been more wrong about what he'd just taken. It didn't produce any of the effects he was expecting. The only thing that happened was that as they were driving past San Fercho, he felt blissed out, like he needed to close his eyes and he found himself daydreaming about getting expelled, then someone thumped him on the shoulder – 'Heeey!' – then in the chest; he opened his eyes, expecting to find himself face to face with his teachers.

'You can't crash now, it's dangerous.'

'He's right,' Tuercas agreed.

'You got to learn to control it; you feel sleepy at first and it's nice, but then later you feel cool and fresh.'

'Bring on the crowds,' he thought, 'bring on the buzz.' Was someone repeating his thoughts?

And El Tuercas said, 'I'd love to see you in there, with all those *peladas*, with no bad vibes, no fear.'

They got to the Caseta Panamericana on the site of the old hippodrome. The bleachers from the old stadium were still there, and there were crowds, the place was heaving, but our three were lost souls so they'd find room, there were still tickets. The moon was swollen like a pus-filled sore in the sky and Rubén didn't think twice, he dived head first into the queue, because from inside he could hear music, the soaring trumpets, the tap of shoes, the glorious noise, but 'Don't be crazy,' Salvador said, tugging on his arm. 'Before we go in we're going to blaze up a Barbecue – look,' he opened his hand. 'It's already skinned up; come on, we'll go round the back (better keep an eye on this kid, he's out of his tree).'

'Chill,' said El Tuercas. 'I know the kid – isn't that right, Rubén? You mellow?'

'Mellow!' said Rubén.

'Way mellow?'

'Hundred per cent mellow!'

'Psyched!'

'Totally psyched!'

'Good gear?'

'The fucking best!'

So they dodged round the entrance, the blaze of light, in search of some shadow. Rubén stumbled along, propping himself up against the rough, badly plastered wall. He pictured a guy wandering through the city like this, hugging the walls and the trees to hold himself up. Eventually they ran into a gang of stoned heads who shot them a conspiratorial look in the darkness and smiled and Salvador sparked up the Baro and pulled on it hard, sucking it down in a long, deep toke. 'You get a better hit this way, smoke goes straight to your brain,' he said, the champion of dope-head purism. Rubén was really getting to like the taste of this smoke; he exhaled deeply so his lungs would be empty when the spliff reached him. The wall they were leaning against backed on to the stage. 'Listen to the salsa and tell me this isn't a fucking branch office of heaven.' They stubbed out the roach (it was brutal what a dope head he'd become these past few days) and hurried back round to the front.

'We're heading in,' they said to the guys next to them. 'Get Sharp!' *boom, boom.*

When they got back round to the entrance it was like a miracle, the heaving crowds had disappeared. 'See that? Nothing like a blast to clear things out – come, get in the queue.' They each bought a ticket but Rubén didn't feel like he was in the queue; he felt like he'd slipped into a parallel universe where the laws of cause and effect were different, mystifying, so he allowed himself to close his eyes for a split second longer and he *imagined* the band. It's one of his most lasting memories, and one he's tried to superimpose on the images of what happened later, because from this moment on, Rubén starts to forget.

There was a lot of pushing and shoving and Salvador ended up trading insults with some kid in a red shirt but they wound up shaking hands.

'We cool?'

'Sure, we're cool.'

Peace and harmony. A cop frisked them for weapons, then a security guard frisked them for illicit substances, they passed the ticket inspector – Rubén swears he had ticket number 1,001 – and then, *bang*, they were staring at the band across a sea of heads bobbing and bouncing to the sound of the hills. This first, sudden flash was enough to know he was now a part of a throbbing sea of colour, of the vibrant, pulsing side of a world that had only just unfurled before him. Wondrous, his every sense was heightened, bursting into bloom with every blast of the trumpets. Wondrous, this drowsy numbness, the limp, exhausting wait before he stepped in here, to this confluence of lights and voices telling him: '*Get sharp, people, because they're watching you.*' Wondrous, the taste: he opened his mouth, wreathed himself in its perfume, the scent of primal happiness and of the deepest depths of dreams. Wondrous, the pounding pulse of the thousands of feet that threatened at any moment to make the floor give way, bring the roof crashing down – divine retribution for so much joy. Wondrous, being elastic boy, taut and snappy as a voice sang, '*You've got to be a fly everywhere,*' and obedient to the power of frenzy with the seven powers behind him. Wondrous (though less so) being unable to bear the idea of being so far away from the band, *the congas, congas move to the rhythm.* Wondrous, the kaleidoscopic rainbow of shirts, colours kindled by soul sweat as he made his way alone through the crowd of couples. Some trod on his foot, but most simply moved out of the way, so clear and firm was his intent; he moved faster, getting steadily closer to the stage, Moses parting the waters, a blur of faces thirsty for sugar-cane firewater, for a kiss stolen in a flash of wild abandonment, pimped out and later conceived in double sweetness, because with this music no one could stop, *sambumbia*, frenzied spirits of every possible race, Chinese, Indian, Castilian, glorious Negritude, where is mine? Plumes of smoke, the pent-up aggression in every body, the intoxication of the drums, one vast eruption of joy and still Rubén crept forward, *I feel so close to you, I want you to know it,* and he peeled his eyes, clapping and waving his hands, and for the first time he recognized the expressions of bliss-ful exhaustion brought on by expending every ounce of energy and joy on a shifting wind, on a melody that was interrupted only for another song to begin, greeted by an explosion of applause. What do you want, blood? Fine, you got it – one false dance move and you could end up with a couple of broken ribs; total illumin-ation, ache for the rhythm, feel the pulsing force, jump and for what you are about to receive, be truly thankful. *I keep on moving; I don't stop like any decent person.* The trickling torrent of the piano helps him, gives him momentum, makes his body leaner so he can slip through the crowd, moving faster and faster, *hey, these people don't know but I've got a saint . . .* and his name's Richie, *I hear a voice keeps saying get sharp.* To the pounding of the drumskins he kept bounding ahead – the couples on the dance floor take him for some frenzied dancer – moved more by the fury than the rhythm, and then up on stage the *maestro supremo* gave the signal to finish; Rubén made one last leap and landed with a *booooom!* in the deafen-ing silence left when the music stopped. The dipshit looked around him wildly, trying to get his bearings, dazed and jostled by couples leaving the dance floor, needing a break, by the giggles of a hand-ful of girls staring at him. But now, miraculously, in front stretched twenty metres of empty space, and Bobby Cruz looked at him and opened his mouth, and Héctor Cubero blasted a conga riff into his face. Rubén wouldn't have said anything if Bobby Cruz hadn't been giving him clear signals to keep coming, to keep on running. And like the fruit loop that he was in that moment, he obeyed, but he'd waited too long, the congas were already pounding again and he was caught halfway by a new tide of dancers surging on to the floor. The problem was he'd hesitated, he'd frozen in the spotlights; he cursed himself, but he summoned his reserves, his stamina: screaming insults and shattering shinbones, he cleared a path and came to a line of kids hopped up on pills and dope like him, worshipping their idol and snorting in total agreement at every note, at every cryptic lyric, because the most wasted among them – the ones who've really lived – are busy deciphering what they mean. Now, with every grudging ''Scuse me', Rubén was getting closer. Surrounding the stage was a crowd of about thirty people and Rubén knew every one of them: these were the guys who hung out in the park in Barona, in Las Piedras, in Marque, Colseguros, Santa Elena, Fercho Viejo – 'Hey, there's Rubén, let him through' – and just like three years later, at the Fania All-Stars gig in 1973, the song 'Ahora vengo yo' by R. Ray and B. Cruz marked the start of his adventure:

'Get Rubén up so he can dance, where is he, where's Rubén, where is he, where's Rubén, where is he, where's Rubén, where is he, where's Rubén, where is he, where's Rubén, where is he, where's Rubén, where is he, where's Rubén, there he is, here's Rubén! Here's Rubén! Everyone agreed? Rubén's here, *si señor*, everyone agreed? *Si señor*, here's Rubén! *Si señor*, everyone agreed? Here's Rubén! *Si señor*, here's Rubén! Everyone agreed? Here we go . . .'

Hello, hello – okay – everybody happy?[48]
Yeah!!
Everybody hot?
Yeah!!
So now take off my clothes!!
Okay, we need a bottle, we got a bottle.

Right, we wanna welcome and compliment Okey que para Changó.

Right, now I want to introduce a man who made a real hit right here in New York, right from Brooklyn . . . we'd like to welcome [dark vibe of indecision of someone *who has no faith and no shelter*] . . . *direct from Puerto Rico . . .* [uuuuuuuuh, there's a heavy rumour, someone says Ricardo didn't want to come out on stage] . . . *direct from Puerto Rico, how about a very, very good man in the past: Bobby Cruz and Ricardo Ray on piano – gimme heeeeeeey!!*

The fact he didn't hear the chord, didn't matter: Bobby Cruz still hadn't taken his eyes off him – who wouldn't have jumped at the chance? – the crowd had cleared to give him a respectable space, the breadth of the pulsing rhythm until – *Jesus!* – until Rubén touched wood and Bobby Cruz's patent leather shoe. *Right here where you see me.* And Bobby Cruz bent down and shook his hand. This is the way I pound out the beat, this is the way I land on my feet. And before he touched the singer's yellowish hand, Rubén managed to recover some of his composure: he felt a thin strand of calm and remembered his friends – where were they? Or did he? Maybe he didn't have it with him, the key to the key change to the memory, the Red Bird, the second Seconal. Would that heighten his pleasure? Slowly, surely, he slid a hand into his underpants and found the pill nestling in his pubes, and under the watchful eye of Bobby Cruz who lazily watched his every move, Rubén popped the pill.

Are you starting to dig me? Who could have imagined he wouldn't remember a single thing. I made it all up. Like I said earlier: standing in the queue outside, Rubén closed his eyes and imagined the band, and all the stuff I've just told you is what he imagined in that moment. What actually happened, he never knew. Oh, his friends kept telling him stories about what a wild night it had been, stories that dovetailed with this rubble of memory learned by heart. 'Bobby Cruz dedicated a song to you,' they tell him to this day. But he can't remember and he can't forgive himself. That's why I'm saying that this guy don't know what he's got himself into.

What happened next is the most open to conjecture, to speculations that try to fit the facts, given that this was a public concert everybody knows about, and I have to say that Rubencito's experience doesn't exactly measure up.

Richie Ray was apparently alternating with the laid-back sounds of Nelson y sus Estrellas and Gustavo Quintero's pitiful combo Los Graduados. He was hardly likely to feel right playing alongside such rank amateurs. The way people tell it, Gustavo Quimba Quintero, the scrawny trumpet player, stepped up to the microphone and played a rising series of notes, then the piano comes in softly, then the keyboard and Bobby Cruz's distorted voice in the background, subverting Quintero's dumb bullshit, then the whole group joins in, Nelson (whose sound was a lot more salsa back then) helping out with the rhythm, with the backbeat – Nelson and Richie were forcing Los Graduados to jam! People talk about how that bunch of *paisas* were publicly humiliated, they didn't stand a chance, they couldn't hack the rhythm, *go back to your school, little girl, because you can't handle me*; the poor bastards were forced to leave the stage broken-assed by the mellow sweetness of the piano, and their departure was greeted by whoops and cheering and foot-stamping above the thunderous throb of the salsa. 'Have I got your permission,' screamed Richie and three times the crowed roared, 'Yes!' You've got it, soul brother, give it to us, give us the taste of salsa and the rippling wave of relief, the excitement we feel when you sing, when we celebrate you.

'That was the moment this city came into its own,' Rubén used to say bitterly. 'Ricardo Ray invented the myth.'

But they were still there, the fat bastards, the pigs, the censors; they hadn't missed a trick and they didn't like the idea of the half-assed group from Medellín being ejected from the stage, because they believed in the old slogan *'Co-lom-bia, this is your music!'* – they were happy to listen to miserable drivel as long as it was Colombian. They didn't take kindly to Bobby pulling out a hand-kerchief and – *sniff! atchoo!* – *saluting everything that is, Abakuá*, while the kids cheered his contempt, thinking, 'What *cojones*, what a vibe; maybe they'll pass round the coke at the end of the gig?' Fantasies like that, Bobby loved them; he loved their innocence about this strange *guaguancó*. These people accepted him, whereas in New York, with all the nasty rumours doing the rounds, who knew if he'd ever be accepted? Here, they celebrated his peculiar ways if he chose to flaunt them. 'When will it happen in New York, *machos*?' Then he said to Richie, 'These songs bring back memories, memories of the remote beaches of Puerto Rico we used to dream about under the bridges and in the subways of grey New York while we pictured the sunshine back home on the island we call Borinquen, while we were laying down new beats – remember? We'd imagine the wind in the canebrakes, in the palm trees, because we missed it – remember, Riquito? We've gotta go on living.'

And a memory came to them, a memory of New York at six in the afternoon, something that scared them and brought them closer together. 'Hey, go easy with the rabble-rousing,' Richie jokes like he's playing devil's advocate. 'Hey, if that's what the audience wants, that's what I'll give them,' says Bobby. 'And anyone who doesn't like it, fuck 'em.' And boy did he fuck 'em and that's the truth. There was a mass exodus of angry ladies and furious gentle-men, the promoters: 'To think we were bringing a group of homo-sexuals and drug addicts, we'd have been better off playing records'; and the promoters' daughters: '*Mamá*, what's boogaloo? You can't dance to it, it's so vulgar, I'm so sad for poor Pablo, you brought him all the way from Bogotá and Los Graduados didn't even get to play a second set. Gustavito? Why don't we go to a *grill* and listen to "El galiván pollero"?'[49] And out they trooped, leaving the VIP tables deserted. This *rumba* has stirred up the common people and it's going to go on till morning; you can hear the call: '*You want more boogaloo? Who says no, who? Chow down on that piano, Richie.*'[50] Round here they say someone broke a table over the head of an official from the city council.

Where the fuck were his friends? Where were El Tuercas and Salvador?

'Rubén, Rubéncito, there you are, we've been looking every-where, yeah; we thought maybe the salsa had got to you – wow, the face on you, you've got eyes like saucers, you feeling okay? How did you get to the stage so quick? It's taken us all night to get this far; obviously early on we had a table. Some mate of Salvador's was ordering bottles of gin like it was going out of style: cost him an arm and a fucking leg. I've got half a bottle here – go on, have a little swig. God, this is good – the salsa's fucking bestial, isn't it? No better way to listen to this than being hopped up on pills. The rest of us have just smoked another Balino; we looked for you all over but no dice – you want another slug? Thaaaaat's it, might as well enjoy life while we're young and we've got time because pretty soon we'll be dead: that's the law of existence, no one can do fuck all about it . . . what's the matter with you? Get off me, you've gone all pale, come on shape up, stand up, what's with you? Hang on to my shoulder – too much excitement, that's what it is, and you were there in the thick of the free-for-all – have another drink, take a deep breath and a long swig, thaaaat's it, a little swig, see if that brings some colour to your cheeks. Jesus fuck! Your eyes! If your *mamá* could see you, the people you've been hanging out with; I tell you, this is a *rumba* I'll never forget, best fucking salsa band in the world. Someone over there told me that Bobby Cruz was making eyes at you; hey, maybe we can hook up with them after the show and they'll take us back to the Grade-A Coke Hotel. Hey, quit leaning on me – you really feeling that bad? You need to throw up?'

But by this stage, Rubén couldn't even answer. Boils had sprouted all over his face, like noxious gases causing a commotion in his left cheek. Somewhere inside a crushing shame welled up as he nodded at Tuercas's question, squeezing his lips tight as he felt himself starting to swell. Before El Tuercas's horrified gaze, Rubén's boils began to bloat with viscous liquid, filling up his whole face so that his eyes were swimming in a sweltering ball of uncontrollable nausea.

'You can't upchuck here!' Rubén pressed his lips together harder, his throat was already flooded with vomit searching for a way out; he looked down and thought, 'All those cool shoes. I can't throw up here.' He imagined the yellow spatter, the flecks of green, the rising murmur of protest – that that would be the end of everything. He doubled over, almost touching the ground; what he wanted was to rub his skin against something, against the most delicious salsa. 'Better get you out of here.' El Tuercas glanced around but could see no way out: they were right in the middle of the crowd, getting out would take as long as getting in; the best thing he could do was to get gone – ditch Rubéncito, it was every man for himself, no point playing the hero – to Guarandaria with Suma and to Yemaya,[51] the furious *guaguancó*. How long had it been since he opened his eyes? When he opened them, he found himself knee high to his peers, that subsection of humanity most responsive, most sensitive to the rhythms – was it an illusion or could he just make out a tunnel, between the swaying and the wild leaps, an empty space through which it might be possible to scramble on all fours through to the other side? Yes, the thousands of knees and thighs formed a sort of passageway of bones and fleshy pads. The explosion of a whisky-coloured trumpet solo set him off on his new mission: he scuttled into the tunnel carved out by the salsa, looking for a place he could throw up in peace. With the permission of the singers, he took up the position of a quadruped and, like a wild boar, like a hog, he trotted along and he never had a more perverse vision of the rhythm as it twitched through thighs and asses, through the kneecaps of these people. 'Buried Alive by SALSA,' he must have thought. There was a damp, acrid smell, and he could hear someone – was it Tuercas urging him on, shouting words of encouragement even as he abandoned him? Here he had hit on the truth, as long as the boils on his face didn't explode, and then suddenly there was light, the light at the end of the tunnel, *'cos I'll bring you a little of everything*, but there was still some distance to go: the exit was a rhombus that expanded and contracted to chaotic rhythms, to the breath of the salsa, the jagged knees. Rubén scuttled faster: someone – with no malice intended – kicked him in the neck, someone stamped on his poor little fingers. 'But I can't complain,' he thought. 'All that matters is that this lung I'm crawling through expands enough for me to stick my head out.' Because what would happened if it closed around his neck? What if the salsa got more bestial, and the melody suddenly shifted? 'Decapitated by salsa,' he thought and focused the last shreds of his consciousness on begging Richie to keep on playing, to unleash the pounding beat with no rhythm change, no false ending, as he crept closer and the edge of the lung seemed to heave a sigh of pleasure, a circular pleasure, a glorious commotion, the tiniest shift; there was no clamour, no shudder, and now it was opening, this glorious mouth, the last two dancers in the crowd withstanding the vibrations of a whole people, preserving the boundaries and sustaining the reason for the rhythm.

Rubén poked his head between the last two pairs of knees, thighs, buttocks; and in that moment the pure feeling of the *rumba*, the homesickness, was transmitted to him by simple contact. He imagined burning sensations that could be felt miles from here, days from now, dancing in the sun, the tang of beer and fried food, children of the future dancing next to their fat-bellied mothers, the clicking fingers, the pounding music, the sun flaying flesh all the way from the mountains, the salsa that could be whistled by anyone on earth, the choirs of ten kids gathering on a Sunday afternoon in front of a recently repaired stereo whistling along with feeling to the aching sadness, the lacerating lamentation of a high melody that speaks of a language invented in far-off Africa, of a man who's not strong, of a man who falls but carries on . . . while all around stretches the city eaten away by the desolation of Sunday, and Rubén, I think, revelled for a moment in the limits of the spirit of music, waited for a moment before poking out his aching shoulders, and suddenly he was expelled with the cry and the sigh of a womb closing, because the song was over.

After that he would have realized that his body was drenched in some liquid other than the one he was holding inside, the bile that was still struggling to get out but hadn't found a way. It was the slaver of the salsa. He stopped when he found himself in a world of people calmly sitting at tables and drinking. He glanced around, stood up, clamped a hand over his mouth and squeezed hard, telling himself he would just go away, throw up and come back to face the music. But where? A vast expanse of walls, a sea of heads, a haze where the darkness and the ghostly spotlights clashed. He ran

around the tables, closed his eyes as he ran, didn't trip. Behind the
bleachers were some weeds, nettles and wild tomatoes. This patch
of greenery, he decided, would bring him relief and he buried his
head in it.

The boils began to pucker, his whole body made a noise like a
drain emptying, like pipes recently unblocked; the muscles in his
throat began a frenzied dance as vomit rose from his stomach like
a tidal wave. His body went so limp that nettles brushed against
his face. He squinted and focused on the wonders of nature and
the colour of his vomit: yellow as the fruits and the treasures of
our country, blue as her distant mountains and red as the blood of
her fallen heroes. All this effluent was forming a hard shell over
the plants, or, he thought, 'In my head?' He tried to think back, to
recreate the sequence of events leading to the present, lamentable
situation. He succeeding in calling up the image, only to forget it,
faced with the resultant vomit. *Comfort me, Adasa, give me your
blessing.* Then he slipped into deep but fleeting sleep, and he forgot Richie Ray's satisfied smile as he performed, forgot about the
wild gestures of Cándido[52] as he played the congas – three verses
of 'Babalú', the song he loved best. A girl had knelt in front of
him and, with her body, gave him the perfect pick-up with which
to sound the entrails of the blistering music – for a brief moment
the shrubs and nettles were like the burning bush: he forgot
Bobby Cruz with his arms flung wide, demanding greater adulation, he even forgot where, as, almost without realizing, he
grieved the loss of the most significant experience on his life – *pass
me the cauldron, Macoró.*[53]

From that moment on – to quote a particularly piss-poor bolero
– Rubén was *a rolling stone, flotsam from a shipwreck, a suffering soul
wandering alone.* He couldn't commit himself to anything except his
research, his investigation, until he'd recreated a more or less faithful picture (from what people said) of what happened to him that
night. He made a few fleeting friendships with other salsamaniacs,
and pimped the different forms of aggression caused by different
tastes. He became a citizen of the night and a tormented thinker on
Sundays: a suspicious, mistrustful character, destructively intro-

spective, asthmatic and, to this day (as the reader has witnessed), prone to vomiting. He waited in vain for Richie Ray to come back, figured out the class prejudices that had led to the group being banned. He'd say, 'And in New York he was attacked by Jews and Tito Puente fans, for his musical quality and his sexual peculiarity. And since he and Bobby Cruz never gave up on their in-your-face way of being and of dealing with others, and since Cruz was already getting tired of having to knock people on their asses, they decided to step aside, to shut themselves away, to become self-reliant. Later they made a genuine effort to adapt socially, introducing a female presence between singer and pianist – Miki Vimari – who could break the short circuit, allow their music to broaden to take on the viewpoint of the other sex. But did they get any credit for it? No.' And Rubén would wail, '*Ay, move like you, Ay, move like you, Ay, move like you. Viva Ricardo!* He never forgot me,' and shut himself away with his grief. But he would emerge every December and have a bunch of posters printed that read:

THE CITY OF CALI REJECTS
Los Graduados, Los Hispanos
and the various exponents of
Sonido Paisa made to measure
for the bourgeois
in all their boorish brashness.
Because it's not about
'Suffering is My Lot in Life'.[54]
It's about '*Get sharp, people, because they're watching you.*'
Long live the Afro-Cuban feeling!!
¡¡Viva Puerto Rico libre!!
WE MISS RICHIE RAY

But there was nothing to be done. Richie Ray never did come back, and in his absence an emptiness grew in Rubén's soul, one that consumed him, ate away at his most genuine, most vital emotions. But none of this could compare to the fact that he had lost his head just when he most needed it. And so he was forever marked by a terrible feeling of loss. Listening to music, getting people to dance was the fire that fuelled his damnation.

It goes without saying he flunked out of school halfway through the fifth year. One of his uncles got him a job in a record shop called Paz Hermanos – Peace Brothers – where he proved to be a brilliant salesman, but every now and then he would suddenly freeze and stand stock-still in front of some astonished customer, his index finger hovering over the record like a shooting star as some fragment of memory returned to him: a red rag waving in the spotlight, calling for another song.

He squandered all his wages on records (he got discount rates), bought a high-tech hi-fi and spent his Saturday nights holed up, irritable and unable to sleep. He never expected *rumbas* to bring him salvation, and as soon as he hooked up with Don Rufián, he refashioned himself as an angel of misrule and miscalculation, someone who brought music into people's homes, there to sow discord and division. He was never friendly to the kids who danced to his music. 'Just wait till they're a bit older,' he'd say. 'I've been groping my way through life without light or happiness since I was fourteen.' He constantly popped *pépas* as a way of staying loose-limbed for those (very rare) occasions when he felt like dancing, and as an effective means of revisiting those *already recovered* memories (of which there were no more than four), but he was kidding himself, going around thinking that at any moment he might manage to reconstruct his little story. His shtick of vomiting all the time was because he thought he could retch up memories to burn his throat, a miserable trickle of misspent time. But it never produced any results.

I yawned, end of story, and he pushed me away from him. Stumbled a few steps and lay face down on the floor. I came behind, following his zigzag movements, and kissed the back of his neck. Hungry for his skin, I licked around his ears *in the modern style*. He purred something in protest, but I marshalled all my forces – this was not some kids' party; I climbed on top of him and he rubbed himself against my hard, punishing protrusions, scraped himself off the floor with a dumb grin on his face and I goaded him, grabbed him by the scruff of the neck – get up, come on, *get hard, bongo* – and clutching each other we slammed into the back wall. We had to work quickly, to fight against the sleep that stalked us. I de-jeaned myself, popped my buttons and stood there facing him, pants flying, *pum catapum viva Changó;*[55] he tried to lean back, to get away from me, to get comfortable maybe, but I was having none of that, I knew all about his past and now I intended to carve on to his heart one more detail for his martyrdom, hee hee; I shinned up him like a greasy pole, ripped open his fly as best I could, pursed my lips into a trumpet and stared at him, mouth gaping – I wonder if the sight of my tonsils was erotic? It must have been because he was hard as a nail and I wanted to slip down the whole length, all the way to the bottom, leaving only his two aching pendulous *cojones*; then, without closing my mouth, I hitched my ankles around his neck, and, leaning down, pumped him with my fist – oh, the look on his face when I slipped him inside me: he didn't want any more memories, didn't want anything to do with love until he'd revived his memories; and I said: 'Shut up, rookie.' All he wanted was my rhythm, my hands crushing his head and I was the one doing the pumping – he was in no position, he was my prisoner, my little pissant, offering up his strength to my cavernous cunt, my echoing interiors. He tried to slide down the wall but he couldn't – I opened myself wider and swallowed him whole, he couldn't hold out any longer, it was impossible, car horns, the *poc-poc* of a ping-pong ball, kids playing outside: as he came inside me, I rode him brutally and almost snapped his cock in two. I thought of the old joke 'I wrung the duck's neck, broke its eggs and burned its nest'. What would that have been like . . . To drive out this thought, I unscrewed myself from him. He whined but I said, 'It's cool, we're done.' I looked down, and it looked like a long drop, but I jumped, lithe as a length of bamboo, and landed on tiptoe.

He slumped down and found himself on the floor, sat there with his thousand-yard stare like he was dead, like he'd been bled dry. After that he just whined and snivelled for his *mamá*.

'Doesn't a guy's stuff ever run out?' I asked once, back in primary school.

'It runs out, but it lasts a long time,' someone whispered to me in the playground. 'They've got like a one-litre keg of the stuff just above the bladder.'

Smiling, thinking back over my sins, I fell asleep but couldn't seem to dream. It was like some dull doze, my muscles and my brain felt all weak. It wasn't sleep at all, just a desire not to sit up. I never did like pills, though I have to say that when it comes to dancing and to sex, they make a perfect sieve for preconceptions, gazelles running amok across a field of giant reeds, *the Christmas bomba*.[56]

When Rubén wanted to shoot off at three o'clock, I went with him. I learned a lot about his misery. He revealed to me the glorious mystery of playing 33rpm LPs at 45rpm, a Cali innovation which creates the distinctive frenzy of the dancers here. I wonder who first decided to find out what '¿Qué bella es la Navidad?' would sound like at 45rpm, or 'Micaela se botó'? When he heard the results, whoever came up with the idea must have thought he was a genius, a Walter Carlos, a composer. Playing a 33rpm at 45rpm is like being whipped as you dance; you feel the need to say everything, because you've got to say it sixteen times more, and let's just see who can hold out, who can dance like us. It means unlocking the mind rather than the voice, or rather that darkness that rages deep inside us, the primal need to get off your ass and seek out the light, the song. It makes every trivial thing necessary and painful, *because, mamá, we got salsa*. It means squeezing notes together, snarling pianos riffs that started out as straight lines, shunting dancers into a parallel universe where the men singing have changed sex or turned into eunuchs; it means dancing the delusion, flogging wild horses, stoking the fever of the whirling trumpets, hacking off hunks of hot spicy music like meat, turning a singer's languid sigh into an order, stockpiling energy, *Tulia Fonseca, Tulia Fonseca*, and the dancer's thinking, 'Jesus, this is hard and I've only been dancing for two minutes. How am I going to hold up after half an hour?' Music that feeds on live flesh, music that leaves you with nothing but blisters, music hot off the wax, that's what I want, that's what I live for; bring it on, sap my energy if you can, turn my values on their head, let me founder, abandon me to criminality, because I don't know anything any more, I can't be sure of anything, I can't hear the instruments now, only a torrent of regrets and flattery and wounded voices howling, matter transformed into slow notes, my aching tiredness, waking up late, night falling and stirring up delusional minds, a plea for forgiveness, a struggle for stillness. Perfect stillness, the magnificent confusion of souls vanquished by a three-minute song: that's 45rpm. And they have to dance alone, because I want to watch them frantically whirling, I want the goal in life to be reduced to an elegant tap to end the piece and wait for them to put on a reasonable song. *Rumba* is when you can't go on.

I considered the various stages of the *rumba*: exhaustion, madness, senselessness, young guys destroying their futures over a single night of debauchery. And in the moment when they lost their last shred of dignity in the eyes of their beloved, they'd scream that hymn to pill-popping 'Bollocks!' only to collapse in a corner half an hour later, consumed by a remorse they can do nothing about, but one they were happy to find, to feel, not realizing it just makes the exhaustion worse. The party organizers politely try to wake one of them up and he opens one eye and spews insults at everyone. So they give him a kick up the ass, get the fuck out of here kid, and like his parents he's probably thinking, 'Life's not worth shit,' and he stumbles a few feet, he's about to shout that he's better than all that and then slumps down next to a lamp post, thinking, 'I'm going to devote my life to the rush, chaos will be my master. But first I need to catch some Zs.' The dark shadows of consciousness, the Boy from the South waking up to wind and weather, sniffed and snuffled by stray dogs, dressed in the new suit his *mamá* brought him from San Andrés at great personal cost. He'll wake up, humming, having briefly nurtured the idea that he's been left out in the sun to burn. How many times has he thought about and postponed that moment when he wakes up, the horror that he can't forget, the shame of what he's done? 'They're pouring boiling soup over my chest and my face.' With this thought he opens his eyes: looming over his vicious headache is a pale, sickly sky; grease bubbles from his forehead and trickles down his cheeks, snaking its way into the collar of his shirt, and he can't work out how since his shirt is still buttoned, since he slept like this, choked by his collar and his damned tie. He leapt to his feet thinking maybe the world might look different if he confronted it head on. It was worse, since a vertical position means facing the world, facing the abyss. And then he ran, because when a man is in pain (as I'd later learn) he races away from his mind. His girlfriend's house is only two blocks from here. He pounds on the freshly painted door like a lunatic, waking everyone up (they've only just gone to sleep) and over and over begs his girlfriend to forgive him. 'I was drunk, you know how it is, it could happen to anyone.' His girlfriend, Blanquita, who's been torn from pleasant slumber to be confronted by his fetid apologies, gets her brothers to kick him out. His Sunday has got off to a bad start. He needs to keep running.

I indulged myself with these fantasies, already focused on the supreme challenge: I would forever be the centre and the reason for the *rumba*, not its victim. I would be the spirit of harmony and endless pleasure. I was the soul that gives rise to the *rumba*, its lover, the one who'd always win out, always in control, always in demand, overwhelmed by healthy exhaustion, sleeping the few short hours of the just, lulling myself with plans for the next *rumba*, the one tonight, the one where I'll perfect my system. I wasn't going to fritter away the *rumba*: I planned to wreathe it with crowns, with kingdoms of recklessness, my skin flushed with the red glow of night, my hair a wild enchanted flower, a weed that dazzles, confuses, bewilders and brings sleep to the unwary. My hair would grow free and strong, and with every step take on a dazzling lustre that came from the very roots of my soul. My soul would grow like a field of daisies on the scorched lawn of the wild *rumba*, forbidden territory: anyone who picked one of my flowers to fill himself with energy for the *bomba* would certainly face the consequences.

Music that knows me, music that inspires me, fans me or shelters me, the pact is sealed. I am your distributor, the one who throws open the doors, carves out the path, spreading the news through the valleys of your harmony, your strange joy, the fleet-footed messenger who never rests, entrusted with a terrible mission; enfold me in your arms when I feel weak, hide me, shelter me till I recover, bring me new rhythms to restore me, send me out into the streets refreshed, into an afternoon like a necklace of coloured beads. Let my airs perplex and mislead: I flaunt your airs and blur them until they're the tragic heart of those who know me, of those who see and can never forget me. For the dead.

The *rumba* at the Parque de las Piedras was the last I went to with Rubén. I didn't want him around me any more, this bird of ill omen: I abandoned him to his fate, and it didn't turn out well. You see, I'd noticed this lanky beanpole of a guy with Indian hair and a jutting chin; he had lips like Jagger and a showy way of dressing and of walking. I danced with him twice, taught him complicated steps and weird salsas, and he wound up embarrassed and confused by my stance and my swagger, so he stumbled over to a wall to catch his breath, greedily gulping some *aguardiente* and getting away from his friends. I was laughing at him and turned my back. During the third dance he suggested, '*Pelada*, how d'you fancy a day of sun, salsa and stimulation tomorrow, since Sunday in this city is unbearable?'

'I never say no to nothing,' I said without looking at him, already thinking I wasn't even going to help Rubén pack away his equipment tonight.

The guy lost control of his fancy footwork. I stepped aside and waited. He came back, twirled me around. We didn't talk any more. I knew he was going over and over my words in his head: how could this long string of negatives add up to a tremendous 'Yes'?

When the song was over, he headed back to his spot by the wall, but someone else had taken it. He deliberately shoved the other guy and started a fight. Since the other guy was alone and had no friends to back him up, they had no trouble kicking his ass.

Then all his friends came over and patted Bárbaro – that was his name – on the shoulder and told him to chill out. His response to their advice was to neck more *aguardiente*. He could have asked anyone, checked my references, everyone would have told him, 'You wanna be careful with that *pelada*, she's a live wire,' but he didn't ask anything. He carried on drinking and – when I let him – stared into my eyes. I laughed to think that if the music wasn't so loud, so wild, he might have come over, kissed my hand and quietly told me the plans he had for me, brushed a speck from my eye with a corner of his handkerchief, blown tenderly into my face, crossed his legs, told me his life story and sensitively asked me about mine, and we might have reached an amicable understanding. But we had to rely on the music and we had to shout above the pounding racket. I parked myself right in front of him and danced a couple of dances with some other *mancito* till I'd tired him out, and managed to drive Bárbaro half crazy. He started trembling and kicking the wall. His friend came over and calmed him down again. He shrugged that he was okay, everything was cool, and went on drinking and staring at me. Then he called two of his best friends over. He obviously said something to them about me, because the two of them, a gangly boy and this other guy who was old before his time, came over to where I was shimmying and whispered very politely in my ear, '*Señorita*, would you be so good as to go out into the park to exchange a few words with our good friend Bárbaro?'

I agreed and bongoed across the floor. Bongo gets my people moving.

I slipped out discreetly, but a couple of kids noticed and made comments about the girlfriend of the guy spinning the tunes. I had no regrets about Rubén: he'd already done his vomiting, so I'd done my duty. I stepped out into the glorious moonlight, the moon that follows me whenever for an instant I forsake my music.

Bárbaro was out in the park surrounded by *barrio* kids, not one of them of them older than twelve, all toking on a fuck-off Barquisimeto. So the guy came up to me and all the kids traipsed after him and stood together, staring at us wide-eyed. Surprisingly, Bárbaro managed to walk in a straight line (first time I see him zigzag, I'll turn my back, fuck him), and when he spoke, out of his mouth came the scent of magnolias. I thanked him for his impeccable manners, fluttering my eyelashes and laying my cheek on his chest. He sighed (as did the kids), laid his right hand on my head, and I could hear the hammering heart from which he took his orders. 'Just looking at you is so cool, *pelada*. I want to show you my kingdom, but it's not of this world. My citadel is far away on the nearest plain to the high mountains where the guava trees and poisonous black nightshade grow. There we will never lack for salsa, or for 'shroom-munching gringos – a tribe, I can say in all modesty, I specialize in hunting.'

It was about six in the morning by the time Rubén came out, with a face that looked like it had never seen the sun. I stared at him from the park, my face flushed, drinking in the colours of my new paramour, who had slipped his hand around my waist while the kids standing behind us, wide-eyed and wild in this hour of abandonment, passed around another Barbuco, what they called a Wake 'n' Bake, the spliff that lifts the veil and prepares you for the slings and arrows of the day, and I thought, 'Do these kids have the same energy I've got?'

Rubén moved with slug-like slowness, single-handedly dragging out his massive speakers and the complicated array of amplifiers with a tangle of cables trailing behind. He obviously didn't feel too hot knowing I was weighing up and memorizing his every move only to forget them a few hours later in the name of my new companion. Bárbaro looked at him with a twisted smile. Just as well Rubén had his hands full, because otherwise he wouldn't have known where to look. His legs weren't working at a normal rhythm, he was bound to take a spill and I wouldn't be able to stop myself laughing at him: the kids might have managed to – after all they still had some respect for the guy who'd brought the music.

In the end, Rubén compared his black mood with the luminous daylight all around and, more wretched than ever, gave a limp wave and said goodbye. He could barely manage to look me in the eye. I smiled at him the way that, in ancient times, noble, hard-working sailors' wives would smile as their husbands sailed off to their deaths.

He climbed into a taxi, forlorn and forsaken, knowing I was in classy company. I didn't want to watch him leave, didn't want his sad face engraved on my memory, a jagged line puncturing my mornings. And I never saw him again. Later I heard he killed himself, having got into the bad habit of banging his head against the wall.

Let no one exist unless I give my permission, my consent; let them crumble to dust as the reader turns the page. A character cannot exist unless I bestow my favours; if I spurn him, he has no reason to exist, *nada*. What's so special about my melody? Knowing that others go astray while I run on through the Parque de las Piedras, freer than any girl can be, my hair streaming behind me, stealing all the best colours from the anthuriums and the morning chrysanthemums, with Bárbaro behind me, cooling himself in the wake left by my body, and the kids revelling in the clearness of the air, knowing that they never had a childhood (by the time they turned ten, they'd discovered music, drugs, doubt, misery, mistrust and lovelessness) while our youth would last forever. Oh, the radiant flushed pink of my complexion: here they could stagnate, grow stunted, never to be productive, immortal in their indolence, longing only to talk like grown-ups and watch resignedly as colour drained from their faces, leaving behind the yellowish, wooden features of those who've swerved from their true path. I was transmitting to them the song that had struck me that night, a song that had pierced my perfect oneness, '*Change your trip or your dress will rip,*' and we formed a line in diminishing order according to inner intensity and height, and I was thinking about their little skulls, probably damaged and punctured with air holes, their fontanelles reopened from too many hallucinogens, with bronchial tubes in their brains and atrophied holes in their suspect hearts.

But what was I doing thinking about this at such a time! Bárbaro had just invited me to take a trip into the deep south, far beyond the Río Pance, in the foothills of the *cordillera*. Xamundí, now there was a place where they appreciated salsa, a harmonious region; how can I envision you, place where I am not, how could you let yourself be so suddenly discovered? I shut myself within you in this discovery and you rejected me, region choked by the thousand shades of green. Goddess of the desert, you would not listen to my song.

I should point out that Bárbaro had no problems getting by, not one. He lived in an artist's studio but he didn't work with leather or clay or anything at all. I think one of his cousins owned the studio; Bárbaro had saved his life in La Bocana, so he let him live there. They looked on him fondly, and on me with hungry little eyes, but I didn't care. 'She's my *pelada*, and they respect her,' Bárbaro said. They plied me with necklaces, with bags and blouses made by native women, and in this curious garb, I took on the scent and the flavour of the earth, I redoubled, retripled my ardour because my beloved and I were living south of Pance. Doing what? Mugging gringos. This was how Bárbaro made his living, and he liked action.

As soon as we stepped off a *Blanco y Negra* – the black-and-white bus that heads south – and felt the first lash of the blazing sun in the vast emptiness, he felt an overwhelming thirst for violence, a thirst he had to slake: blonde *gringas* – not blonde like me, because my hair is like ripe mango while theirs was the colour of sun-scorched wheat, of pale flax. I have to say I also felt a burning rage to see how many dumb gringos came to our country in search of the seven deadly sins, in an attempt to 'find themselves'. The very sight of them had me itching to thump them, but anyone seeing us circle our prey saw only a cute couple, me all smiles and swaying hips, sometimes stumbling across the stony ground, and inevitably some gringo would fall over himself to help me up: '*Señorita.*'

And me: '*Ay, qué pena.*'

And Bárbaro: 'What a polite young man! Where are you from?'

'America,' curtly.

'America? But isn't this America right here? Unless you're talking about Club América FC? Are you taking the piss?'

I was the only one to laugh, a sound like a series of delightful sneezes. But the gringo would be stone-faced, bewildered, and he'd turn down the volume on his cassette player.

'Don't do that! Rock has be listened to at full blast,' Bárbaro protested and, *bang*, his hand was already on the volume knob, his fingers silken, his smile tremendous beneath this accursed sun. 'Am I right?'

'Yeah,' the gringo admitted and by now he was glancing around him, but there was no point because I was doing the same thing, making sure there was no one about: this boy was a long, long way from home, completely lost and almost certainly alone in the death-like stillness of one o'clock in the afternoon.

But Bárbaro did not explode just yet. He'd get the boy to agree to everything he said, and the gringo would say, 'Oh, yeah, I love Colombia, the countryside's so beautiful, the people are so cool (pretty little *peladas* to be taught the mysteries of mainlining), and the dope and coke are so cheap.'

'Ah, yes, *las peladas*,' Bárbaro would say. 'Especially the ones who get the hots for any gringo.'

'Um . . . my name's Dino.'

'And what are you doing alone all the way out here, Dino? Don't you know this place is dodgy, I mean really dodgy. It can be dangerous round here, you know. A lot of delinquents.'

'No way. Everyone I've met here is so laid-back. And I often come out here. I always find 'shrooms, and no one ever gives me a dirty look, because I'm all about peace and love.'

'Really? Well I know a lot of people who don't like seeing all these gringos around, you know? Found a lot of mushrooms then?'

'Yeah, loads of them, especially Golden Tops.'

'All inside your skull?'

'*Boom!* Yeah, all up in my brain.'

'You must have a brain like a sieve. Don't you feel ashamed that the cows are looking at you, with their rumens, reticulums, omasums and abomasums, thinking: "Shit-Eating Biped"?'

'What?'

'How would you react if my pretty *pelada* put a hand on your tape recorder?'

Half understanding, assuming we were asking him to lend us the machine, he was about to graciously give it to me when, with a savage jerk – *crack* – I snapped his will to be polite and – *whack* – turned down the volume and in the sudden silence and the lowing of the River, his eyes, racing against the clock to understand, could see no way out but abject terror.

He might have made a run for it if Bárbaro hadn't slammed an elbow into his nose, a knee into his belly, a fist into his temple and laid him out flat. Then, the flash of a knife: 'We're going to kill you, gringo.'

'Nooooo!'

'Oh, yes.'

'What do you want? The tape recorder? Money? I've got loads of cash.'

He tried to get to his feet but another punch and he was on the ground again, blood pooling on the dry grass.

'Don't you dare get up while we're here. Turn out your pockets, but do it down there, where you belong – ' Bárbaro was enjoying this – 'paying due respect to us as the true masters of this land.'

And immediately the gringo stuffed his hands in his pockets and pulled out a wad of notes so thick he couldn't close his fist around it, plus three metres of nose candy and acid, and Bárbaro said, 'You dumb gringo, what the fuck are you doing going around loaded like that?' Another whack for being so pig-ignorant.

And the gringo started sobbing: 'What more do you want?'

I was already pocketing the stash, everything except the acid, which I tossed into the River, and as I did so, I pictured some unsuspecting swimmer opening his mouth wide to suck in air after a long dive and swallowing three of the fourteen tabs, and the heavens themselves would tremble . . .

'Take off the natty shirt,' Bárbaro ordered. 'And the Levi's.'

The gringo couldn't get his head round the enormity of the offence; couldn't manage to strip to order. 'First, you have to take off your shoes, you dumb fucking gringo.' Then, puzzled, holding them out between thumb and forefinger, Bárbaro muttered disgustedly,

'Who the fuck would want shit like this? They must be at least size 48,' and, *zzzzzusss*, into the River. 'Now you can strip off those pathetic boxer shorts, kid, and stand there with your balls hanging out; maybe that'll teach you something about how tough life is in this country.'

We didn't leave him there bawling in the field. We dragged him to the River. A couple of days later we read an article about a gringo suffering from heatstroke – or off his face on drugs – wandering naked looking for the road to Cali, who'd run into a couple of football teams and the twenty-two players had humiliated, used and abused him. 'Though still in a fragile mental state, he will fly back to Miami today where his parents are waiting with open arms.'

We walked away happy, skipping along, and got completely blitzed at the first beer and fried-food stall we could find. And as the sun sank behind the mountains, we were reborn with the new-minted night and tumbled into the Parque de las Piedras to recount our feats.

Ah, those days will never come again! But it doesn't matter: they trail behind, they're the sole pleasure of my melodies. Pity I have no one now to share my siestas with. Pity that I'm so alone. But the night swells, spirits rise, it is glorious, and I carry on with my story, and if I should die tomorrow I don't want anyone to weep for me. I hope I finish before the dawn, because it would be too confusing to have to face the day without exposing myself to the darkness in which, as always, I sparkle and flash, just like in the old song Tico and Carlos Phileas and all the other guys took turns dancing to with me at parties long ago, *Little star, why have you lost your curious spell? Here on earth from the distance we hear your sad wail*; we were such kids – pay no mind to me, reader, don't believe me if I speak of sorrows. As my pen scutters across the page, I imagine the distant, feeble river renewing itself, silvering over the stones. A river is ageless, and though it may dawdle here on its travels, it is not the end. Reader, follow me joyfully. I've shaken off such thoughts as 'What will become of me?' I have marshalled my strength, have found long-forgotten words, so many words, a jumble of words by a dancer who put me through *blue-funk blues* before I could get him to fall into step.

When not mugging gringos, our life was utterly peaceable. We listened to cassettes in the park and when we went for a drive, tuning to the signals of a hundred radio stations, we'd imagine ourselves tracing lines of sound through the warm air. Nobody complained that our speciality was robbing gringos, and none of the gringos could come looking for revenge. We never robbed a 'neighbour', as Bárbaro called our fellow countrymen.

Back now to Parque de las Piedras, but this to recount a farewell. It must have been 7 a.m. on the first Monday of last December that, shining and stylish, we were preparing to set off on our next trip. The *barrio* kids had got up early – unusual, what with them being noctambulation junkies – to wish us well, get stoned and say good-bye.

The sky was murky, milk-coloured, harbouring both moon and sun at opposite extremes. Three feet above the ground, rising or falling – I don't know which – was a blanket of reddish mist and as I walked I felt my skin resist this strange, prickly, itchy air. But Bárbaro was clearly awestruck by the promise of the day, which he casually described as 'incredible'. He was not wrong, as the reader will shortly judge.

I got to my feet, standing on the soft grass, prepared for anything, though feeling slightly nervous. Each of us is an abandoned nest where the marauding bird of sorrow seeks refuge. Sorrow and danger: this was what I foresaw, what I feared. As though two mountaineers (reduced to the scale of the black man's knees that long ago I looked out at through the windows of my parents' house) were colliding inside me with every step I took through this carpet of dusky, reddish air.

We walked in silence along Calle Quince, past the Departmental Hospital. I tied up my hair with a Spanish scarf and beneath the counterpoint of sun and moon and milk-white sky I looked stunning.

With great care we boarded the Transur bus and, seeing all the other passengers were black, I felt a strange unease, a sort of racist reverie, and even as I say this I apologize. I felt as though we were travelling in a black cloud. Could it be that the events that took place later that day were punishment for this thought? But the darkling *morochos* looked at us, smiling, completely relaxed by the undulating heat sucked in by the moving bus and creating little eddies between the heads and necks of the passengers. And I didn't feel too good when, like an incantation, three different radios all started playing the same song:

Ala-lolé-lolé lalá-lo-loló lololala-lalalalalá oiga mi socio oiga mi cumbilá que voy en cama-caló alala-lele-lee lolo-lolá epílame pa los ancoros como le giro este butín gua-guancó ala-lolé l-o-o-lá oiga mi socio oiga mi cumbilá le voy a encamacaló le-e-lo-lá ala- lo-lo loló epílame pa los ancoros como le giro este butín gua-guan-có cuando mi mene era un chiquitín y ya empezaba a rodar pachitum jamercoyando y no me pudo tirar pallá pallá oye-ló ala-le-loo lololololo-lololá y el niche que facha rumba aunque niña bien tullida cuando varan a la pira lo altare la araché el niche que facha rumba e-e-e-e-e cuandoro si que le encoje lo altare la araché ay qué niña bien tullida lo altare la araché y-y-y-y-y-y que ina que ina la noche lo altare la araché al niche que facha rumba lo altare la araché el niche que facha rumba e-e-e-e-e-e-e chinfanchum jamercoyando lo altare la araché mira cómo nos mira cómo nos mira cómo nos coge la noche lo altare la araché e-e-e-e caína caína nos coge la noche lo altare la araché e-e! el niche que facha rumba pero melé pero melé nos coge la noche lo altare la ara-ché ey caína nos coge la noche lo altare la araché yevere caín yevere caín yevere caína la noche lo altare la araché aunque niña bien tullida lo altare la araché pero caína caína nos coge la noche lo altare la araché mira macochó mira macochó mira macochó ma-co-chó lo altare la araché el negro el negro que monta coche lo altare la araché.[57]

And the judder of the bus and the hum of the air, boiling fit to burst, and the wheels as they sank (but they couldn't be sinking, since we were moving) into tarmac like molasses and every metal surface sizzling like a frying pan. And the blacks sweating ebony and platinum, collars of pearls, white shirts that looked like they were stained with mud around the armpits and the back, their noses glistening; they were relaxed and happy, chugging forward since this way there was no drowsiness, this way they wouldn't succumb to the embrace of the heat, and in this weather was the justification of their race, in this and in the fields, still lush green despite the harsh and treacherous sun. They were all smiling at the song as though it communicated some secret message of revolution and tragedy. As for me, the song's insistence on *la noche* – the night – made me feel at odds with the world, especially as our day of youthful transgressions was just beginning. And just then images flooded back of mornings waking up through venetian blinds and I felt a sudden surge of joy; but one that wasn't insolent, it didn't make me move or pull faces, it was simply a feeling of anticipation. A joy at meeting the new day face on as we drove through the valley while, back in the city, my parents would only now be waking up, examining their new wrinkles, standing motionless under the spray of a scalding shower.

The bus zoomed through the valley at top speed, but Bárbaro's excitement sped faster, overtaking the bus. 'A good takedown,' he said, 'a fat gringo, with glasses, with good hair and better threads.'

In our wake, we left the modern suburbs, the schools for rich kids, the derelict mills – the relics of rice fever, fields of plum trees, of sugar cane and bitter guavas, but even in the midst of these calm, darksome people, Bárbaro's fury swelled. He'd found no other way of dealing with the world. Ever since primary school, his first instinct was to follow the mob. He was adopted as a mascot by the toughest gangs, back in the days of Edgar Piedrahíta,[58] of Frank and El Mompirita; he was there the night the El Águila gang killed that poor long-haired bastard at the 'Centro' of my '6os: he'd known these people, hung out with them. And now that the gang culture had waned, his violence had resurfaced to be unleashed on gringos: I had no problem with this, it was expedient, a service to society; there on the bus I wrapped my arms around him. There wasn't a breath of wind and the belching exhalations of the carburettor blasted us full in the face.

When the bus arrived in Xamundí, all the *morochos* got off and instinctively we followed them so we wouldn't be abandoned by the music. *No one tells me that I got here first, that I've got the cash, that I'm whiter than you.* We walked slowly down the aisle of the bus, careful not to touch the white-hot metal, stepped down on to the red earth of Xamundí, into air that was fierier still, into the shriek of birds driven mad by the shimmering pool that the sky had become.

The *morochos* disappeared towards the Parque Central, famous for its cracked, dried-up fountain. And Bárbaro made a deal with a German to take us in his jeep to a place called 'Yeah? That way'. Offered him twenty pesos. 'Yeah? That way' is a spa town and dance hall on the banks of the Río Xamundí from where it's possible, preferably on foot, to get to the rivers El Jordan, El Turbio, El Estrellón, El Claro, El Bueno, El Zumbón, El Cojecoje, El Renegado,[59] each feeding into a beautiful, treacherous pool that, from what I've heard, gives form and life to small valleys which people say are verdant and beautiful. For the moment I'll reserve judgement.

We were walking north-east along a path dappled by acacias, looking for the Valle del Renegado – Renegade's Valley. The long stroll through the shadows revived our spirits, but left us unprepared for the vision that awaited us: suddenly, as I crossed the bridge and found myself face to face with the valley, I wanted to turn away from the dazzling glare, from the scant, strangely orderly vegetation. But Bárbaro grabbed my shoulder and forced me to look.

The Valle del Renegado was circular, with a slight depression towards the south-east, which might have been a track, a path leading into the next valley. Beneath both moon and sun, the grassland – perhaps because of the abundance of poppies – looked like a swarm of deranged dragonflies squandering their diurnal energy. Meanwhile the river that gave the valley its name was particularly turbulent and the roar as it crashed against the black rocks and the red mud banks made it seem as though the meadows were shifting without moving forward, like a sickening sluice of waves. I've got some weird ideas in this little head of mine. The true inhabitants of this place were thorny, sickly shrubs. In a moment of panic it occurred to me that if we couldn't withstand the sun's glare, the only possibility of sheltering in the shade would be a two-kilometre race against rapidly advancing heat-stroke to the magnificent young ceiba tree thirsting (the very sight of it made me feel parched) on the nearest rocky outcrop, where everything was very different: there was cool vegetation, a paradise for birds, all the fruits of the vibrant tropics. Hills that were anchored to the valley by roots of deep red earth, like bleeding wounds, that gradually extended like a vast starched petticoat to form a rocky outcrop, a devourer of souls and aeroplanes, the first mountain rampart on the difficult road to the sea, crowned by a peak shaped like the head of a condor, beak and all. A peak like a beak? The intense, vivid blue made it seem sharper, gave it a sense of rage, of urgency. Was I hallucinating? No, the mountain in its grandeur was stirring from its slumber, but for now it dozed, its wings folded over its breast.

Having my gaze perched at such dizzy heights began to exhaust me. I can say that I reacted with a perfect straight line, a vertical glance down towards the shrub that grew in the very centre of the valley, reddish and larger than the others; as old as time itself, it presided over the orderly, concentric furrows in which the others were planted. Oh, the pointless neatness of this scorched vegetation! I had dared to lower my gaze from the beak of the condor to the centre of the earth upon which I trod. Something shuddered, or perhaps the earth quaked, because my heart or his was trembling. *Changó ta vení. Changó is coming.*[60] God of cunning and vengeance, seditious god, deliver me not into danger, lend me your sword and with it I will vanquish.

As my eyes moved in that straight line, tracing a meridional incision through the mountains, I saw, at the far end of a chain of hills like breasts, the famous half-ruined house of Don Julián Acosta,[61] a tormented oral poet who, having achieved a certain renown in the city, had opted for a life of asceticism (and later, alcoholism) in the mountains; famous because his door was open to every weary walker, every lost hiker. Until one night he emerged from that very door like a soul possessed by the devil and disappeared into the mountains beneath a raging moon. The house remained uninhabited (it's said) because people were afraid of it. I thought, just to be contrary, that we might 'have ourselves a little climb' if the day was going to be as long as the tardy position of the sun implied. It should be noted that Don Julián's house was perched on what was known as 'Ninth Hill', the last step: a lone breast, and flat besides.

In the valley, dominated by the largest bush, almost unmoving in their contented rumination, were fourteen black-and-white cows. Cowpats were abundant, fresh and flourishing. And around the beasts, following an obsessive circular route, never taking their eyes off the ground, crouching from time to time to pick speckled mushrooms, was a pair of gringos.

And so there we headed.

What had happened? Why, why this sudden fear? The body of a tiny woman as young as I, but naked, ravaged and clinging to my body. And I was running. I was fleeing through this wretched land and she, though weaker, fled, climbing up my body. What had happened? A knife sheathed in blood. Was there a body lying next to the bush, a body already dead and rotting in the sun? And on what did they walk, my bare feet?[62] Human teeth, ivory-looking teeth.[63] Why did she not stop weeping over me; when would Bárbaro stop? Why did the sun not ascend the heavens, why was time suspended? Why were we not running better?

'Clock, don't mark the hours.' I thought just now as I was writing: 'I have no reason to hide anything. My conscience is a suspended veil.'

'Hola!' we called in chorus, offering our sweetest, our most dazzling smiles.

The gringo guy turned out to be exactly as Bárbaro had hoped and his girlfriend was pretty, a babe, from the moment I set eyes on her. Not exactly a *gringa*, as she explained: 'Puerto Rican.' She lived in Miami, spoke perfect Spanish, and so we redoubled, retripled our smiles like crazed crows. They showed no fear because, as she put it, 'we had appeared as one more extension of space', and she gave me a thin, bold smile that said, 'Sorry if I ramble when we're talking, I'm pretty much off my face,' and I stared intently, fondly, into her eyes and after a while, as a joke, I swung my head in a circle to watch as her pupils gradually dilated – oh, the poor little green of your eyes.

And now she was running over my body. Escaping from herself into me? I was running too, I wanted to lose myself, but we were both running in vain. To truly escape would mean ripping our heads off.

Faced with such a harvest, 'bonanza', Bárbaro felt ready for a 'onefellswoop' and he started talking about 'shrooms, which made him angry. Had they eaten many? 'Seven each.'

'That's the base,' said Bárbaro. 'The masterly, magical number.' And he was thinking, 'Too bad, gringos, I'm going to fuck up your trip, you're in for a bad ride.' And he said, 'Cool, isn't it? Feeling like you've got no bones, no legs, everything falling away, constantly peaking.' And he was thinking, 'Shouldn't have strayed so far past the bridge and the woods. But right here we're going to be bosom buddies. Ah, the memories of my attacks. Aaargh, but I don't want to go back to the city to the same comedown. I'd rather take a one-way trip. No one will hear them if they scream for help.' And he said, 'Best thing about it is they're free, am I right? I'll bet you've only spent about twenty of our paltry pesos to get here and now here you are, stuffing your faces, out of your heads in the middle of paradise.' And he thought, 'Paradise lost, as far as it goes,' and then said so.

The gringo caught on, but didn't know how to react. Bárbaro's eyes had misted over. Knowing the kicking and punching was about to start, I reached out to the girl, and I smiled – a pretty smile, I think – running my fingers through two beads of sweat, one at the root of her hair, the other just above the swell of her small breasts. She felt the transfiguration of pleasurable feelings and brazenly reached out and clutched my hand; she looked as though she were trying to flay her lips (which were chapped) the way she bit them, the slut. I hoped that Bárbaro wouldn't launch into the violence just yet.

Because he was saying, 'A pure, uncultivated product, vegetal even, and worst of all, it's free. You know, you were right to get here early. Later in the day the whole area is crawling with witless hordes of mushroom-eaters. They get here at four in the morning so they can lick the sap from the tree bark, all dressed in white and wearing faggoty shit. What really fucks me off about these people is their gutless laziness.'

The pretty *pelada*, María Iata Bayó her name was, slipped a hand into her ethnic bag (exactly the same as mine, we'd already commented on the coincidence) and said to me, 'I bet you can't guess what we've got here,' with an accent like she was from Bogotá, and she showed me a couple of mushrooms, their stalks entwined – they looked so sweet, so tender. 'Look,' she said, 'a male and a female'; the male clearly had a little prick, while the bell-shaped female was the colour of flesh, and Bárbaro became angrier and his eyes began to quiver and he said, 'They come in couples so they can be gobbled up, united together against the Swinish Amoeba.'

And the girl said, 'Why don't we eat the two of them?'

And I laughed, picturing the scene: the two of us hurling ourselves on Bárbaro and the fat gringo under the sex-transmuting effects of the brutal 45rpm, teeth bared, sinking into the rich, sweet, thick fat beneath the sun.

To justify my laughter, I accepted: we separated male from female. I wrung the neck of the male. The mushroom tasted of clammy, fragrant earth and I felt the painful furrow it left as I swallowed. She must have realized this was my first time (can you believe that, gentle reader?) and took a flask of ice-cold lemon juice from her bag. So I went on chewing little 'shrooms, washing them down with this intense juicy freshness. I ate more than a dozen, I lost count, and all this time Bárbaro was looking at me reproachfully. Finally I shrugged in a gesture of independence, a 'So what?' Then, brusquely, he turned his back on me and took maybe three steps towards the large bush, crouched down over some fresh cow dung and came back all smiles, with another little couple in his hand. He looked at me greedily, cleaned the root of the mushrooms and swallowed the female whole. He offered me the male and I ate it very slowly, carefully observing the black stripe, the strange pulp, the speckled gills and the spaces between them, my focus and gaze increasingly microscopic. I felt the girl's hand alight on my shoulder then fall away. Thinking about it objectively, her warm hand had emerged from my mane of hair. And my skin does not baulk at a challenge.

'Sexy little *pelada*,' said Bárbaro crudely. 'Not something you could say about the fat tub of lard she came mushroom hunting with.' And he licked his fingers, black with pure psilocybin.

I flashed the fat guy a look. I enjoyed seeing him as the words rolled and collided in his head; the penny finally dropped and his eyes grew wide like a fish on scorching sands. His girl didn't look at him and, weirdly, she gave a soft laugh. Was she on our side? And what side was that? I had no time to find an answer and she had no time to give one, because Bárbaro whipped out his knife and tossed it to me. And right then, María Iata threw a punch that hit me right in the face. I found myself on the ground and I happily dropped the knife and hurled myself at her like a she-wolf, gave her a swift elbow to the jaw, played a military tattoo with my feet on her shins and her belly. Bárbaro passed me the knife, and I hadn't finished with the girl yet, but I heard: 'Let's get her to strip for our degenerate pleasure. Like in *Man of the West*.'[64]

So many lines of sight meeting. The fat guy opened his eyes wide and that earned him a headbutt right between those vacant eyeballs. 'Don't you open your eyes at me, fuckhead,' said Bárbaro, now a ball of fury, pounding him into the ground until I began to think it was high time I said, 'Stop it now.' Then he turned towards us. The gringo managed to shield himself, throwing himself face down on the ground where he huddled, a quivering mass of melancholy staring at the infinite green stretching out before him, at every jagged, ragged blade of grass in the vastness of the valley: would he be searching in the distance for something he had mislaid, for some new magic mushroom?

'Listen up,' said Bárbaro. Because María was waiting, breathing very slowly. Faced with such dazzling beauty lying helpless now before me, my smile twisted and became pitiless and I made little jabs with the knife where earlier I'd run my finger through two identical beads of sweat. They might have been sweeter that the first, I did not taste them. But the point of the blade was hot against my fingers and I flushed away her pearl of sweat with razor-sharp gentleness and, with an artless movement of her shoulders, she welcomed this caress.

She was about to take off her striped 'Lady Manhattan' blouse. Knowing she intended to unbutton it in a slow, sexy fashion, I became impatient and slashed off the row of buttons to speed things up a bit. The blouse fell open – and how! – revealing a beautiful expanse of cinnamon skin, perfect ribs and a chest like a boy's.

My mouth must have fallen open because she smiled mockingly, justifiably, proudly. Then Bárbaro, for no reason, without even looking down, very aahhh – *ictus interruptus* – lashed out with his heel at the coccyx, at the neck of the lump of lard who, by my reckoning, probably thought he'd been safely forgotten. The *crack!* echoed around the valley but the fat gringo accepted the heel embedded in his flesh without a whimper.

Bárbaro looked at us lewdly. Thinking this was funny, I made a gesture that said 'slowly, slowly': María Bayó had lost and that frightened her. She ran one hand over her face and then the other, and closed her eyes as though to hold back tears.

'No, don't do that,' I said, moved, filled with joyful tenderness, and rushing over to her, I stroked her pretty head.

'Do I have to get undressed?' she whispered in my ear like a naughty girl.

'Yes,' said Bárbaro, taking the knife from me.

At this she cracked, took her arms from around me, unbuttoned her jeans and let them fall so I could see. She seemed almost relieved as she slipped off her pants.

I stepped away from her and rejoined my friend in the deep silence of her beauty. A silence Bárbaro broke with a sudden *whack!* that made the body sprawled on the grass shudder.

In that moment I felt weary as I realized that violence blooms when led on by beauty. The pure exhilaration of brute violence, the kind that nothing can satisfy. I felt a fleeting terror at this thought, but prepared myself to accept whatever happened. Let's teeter over hell itself. If you fall it's because you've filled yourself to bursting with remorse.

In that moment, we kick-started our destiny again. If I moved closer to this naked body and stroked it, if I kissed and sucked this skin, these mounds and hollows, the convexities and concavities, wouldn't every action produce a mirror image, an equal and horrifying reaction in the other body that lay sprawled, ugly, incapable of fighting, at our feet? But could that body even think? Could it feel pain? It was as though already it could not.

'Turn him over, yeah?' I said to Bárbaro and he did so with his feet. All right, the gringo's face was covered in grass and itch mites[65] and foul earth, his features were flushed purple with effort like those of any mute, but as Bárbaro turned him over, he suddenly opened his eyes and they moved blankly over our bodies (I felt unappreciated), then up towards the mountain, before his gaze finally settled on the beak of the condor.

Bárbaro enjoyed the sight of this body. He licked his lips, brought his hands to his face, rubbing it, stimulating it, took a deep breath and simply waited for the two of us to perform the deadly ritual of beauty.

I asked for permission to take María Iata a few metres away: we did not want to have to listen to the whimpering of that mess of bones swathed in bruised and battered flesh. Bárbaro agreed, smiling but a little wary. 'But don't go hiding behind a bush,' he warned. 'I need to be able to see you, otherwise what's the point.'

So we chose a patch of waste ground within the vast immensity of wasteland in which we found ourselves. María Iata Bayó wrapped her arms around me gently, without complaining, without crying, making a soft sound like a *brzzzzzzzz* which alarmed me because at first I thought it came from inside my head. But it was simply that I was breathing the same air and could inhabit that same skin, the furious fricative sound of possible and imminent communion. We stared at each other, separated only by a millimetre: the tiny points of red in her eyes so green, the moistness of my lips, the twigs of strawberry tree in my hair and our dilated pores like dried-up swimming pools and licking, *ouuuuuuf*, in a wild deranged desire that made everything around us a reason for our lust, for ourselves, summoning lifeboats as we drowned in every pore, sucking ruin from the maelstrom of our veins, drunk on the scent of downy hair, robbed of words, all perception of the world reduced to this single act, everything is mine, every fold of flesh and every languid frizzy hair, the cheekbones flushed with pleasure, knowing, perhaps, that faced with another barrage of phosphorus, the brain would have to look away from you and think of something else, the mind fleeing because it cannot resist, the fingernails buried in every fold of flesh, the tip of the tongue exploring places that neither she nor I knew existed, both of us so pink and so whorled inside, but I was the more powerful: I pinned her to the ground, stroked her, opened her, penetrated her and cursed her: 'You'll never be a good girl now, because you'll forever be haunted by the memory of this playful swallow, this seven-phallused snail, this bitter, *coclí*[66] feather I've got inside you.'

Oh, Camilo José Cela, who freed himself from his shackles at the age of fifty.[67]

I got to my feet, still bathed in her – tremendously proud, obviously, because of the powers that welled in me – and I walked back recklessly towards Bárbaro. Barely had I taken three steps when I heard her whimpering from behind me, begging me not to leave her. But I wasn't prepared for what was I was about to see.

The gringo was bolt upright, but for his head, which was slumped on one shoulder. Sitting in a pool of his own blood. The knife had been planted in his navel. And I didn't miss a thing: I noticed that all around his shoes were various small white things, freakish shapes and bloody roots. Probably while I was counting María's eyelashes one by one, my friend had pulled out every tooth in his head.

I didn't try to understand. I simply thought I had to get her away from here so she wouldn't see this. But even as I turned, her howl hit me full in the face. Terrified, I answered with a howl of my own and a 'Fuck!' And I shook her by the shoulders and, after a long while (during which the sun didn't move a millimetre in the sky), she seemed to become calm and detached. But as soon as I let her go, she screamed again, without form, without purpose, without thought of duration. I grabbed her forcefully by the hand and dragged her away. Feeling herself being led, she became calm again. And so we walked, with great courage, to where Bárbaro sat.

He was sitting in the perfect position of a mystic, focusing all his powers on the largest bush.

What was he trying to do? There was no point wondering: he began to grind his teeth, covered his ears as though he didn't want to hear the murmur of the whirring going on in his brain. Except that as he shielded himself from all sound, he set two parallel lines buzzing in my head, one much shriller than the other. María must have felt it too because she broke away from me and collapsed on the ground. I turned my head and rolled my eyes, but hell itself had taken up residence in my entrails. I tried to move closer to Bárbaro, but it was worse. When I retreated, the storm and the intestinal inferno began to subside. Bárbaro's skin was cracked like an ancient clay jug, like the skin of Monsieur Valdemar,[68] and still he didn't take his eyes from the bush. And it seemed to me that the bush began to quiver (there was not a breath of wind), the leaves began to rustle, the branches to move.

Was it possible? Whatever was happening, Bárbaro's hair stood on end (who has ever seen a long Indian mane stand completely on end?), and as his face began to suck in the hollows of his cheeks, his hair grew tauter and, with the noise of a sharpened knife, flew off into the arid air and rained down, curling again, likes ashes from some distant volcano.

Again the bush quivered. Do you understand me when I say that Bárbaro was wasting all the vital energy of his seventeen years on a simple attempt to move this bush by force of will? Could it be that he was confronting something so small? Deep inside me, the flesh and the mud of this valley crackled; María Iata had already buried her face in the ground. Bárbaro sent up a curse to the heavens but clung fast to the earth as though before and behind him a hurricane was struggling to unseat him. The bush veered from pale red to flame black, shook its branches wildly and moved forward several centimetres. Another tremor and it folded in on itself the better to draw itself up and charge like a enraged boar straight at Bárbaro. I did not baulk. Bárbaro managed to give a yell of triumph before realizing the plant was not going to stop at his feet – in fact it was already upon him, it knocked him over and, with a bound, planted itself in his belly. My friend threw his arms and his legs wide and went completely limp, rivers of pleasure murmuring as his entrails gave up their sap to feed the plant, causing it to bring forth heavy, pink moonflowers that (many years later, people would say) brought intoxication and illumination.

I said, I thundered, 'That's enough, he's shrivelled away, I won't look any more,' and I imagined what it would be like, taking the meek and gentle María Bayó by the hand, to run all the way to the ceiba tree behind us and from there into the mountain to hide her nakedness in the shadows and the stillness of the silver trumpet trees. I thought, 'We'll run until our spirit runs free and when it returns, wind-blown and revitalized, we'll stop and eat some juicy lemons, faces puckered with calm concern. Then we'll climb these hills like 8½[69] pairs of breasts, constantly looking over our shoulders, crushing the rough colour of the air in the luminosity of the valley.' And I concluded: 'We will be safe there, and the house on the Ninth Hill will once again have hosts.'

I took time to think about this as I turned and held out my hand to María Bayó. But I'd misjudged the extent of her fear. Not only did she scratch my hand, she clambered up my arm till she was hanging from the tree of my body. I steeled my flesh, a glorious sensation, and with her astride me I took the first step, thinking, 'You will not cross the mountains on a man's back but riding pillion on a white dove.' I was fleeing and she was fleeing my body. But I never took the second step towards the mountains.

My knee didn't reduce the angle of advance of this desiccated air, which snarled in its dryness. The pores of María Iata opened to their fullest, then closed as though someone had stuck spikes into them. From her elevated position, she had a better view of the mountains. But how could I look at the peak, at the beak of the condor as it narrowed its eyes, then yawned and ruffled its feathers? The whole mountain flourished green again. María sank her nails, her teeth into my shoulders. The condor stretched its neck – *oooooooooooh* – a clamour in our heads, a beating of wings and it took flight, taking with it the whole mountain! Blossoming with the colours of *mamey* sapote and Madras thorn, jacaranda, cascarilla, fig and agave, the young ceiba tree where I'd hoped to feel the first hint of shade, wingleaf soapberry, pigeon wood and the loathsome *timbo blanco*, strangler figs and gliricidia, serried rows of wild cane and swaying walls of guadua bamboo, my havens of tranquillity, my unfinished trails, my rickety pathways, dazzling guava trees, the noble guava, the Cattley guava, the perfume guava, the para guava and the naranjilla, the devil's fig, kindly birch trees, the seminarian's *chilca*, cedar trees and whorish pines, carob trees, banks of Buritica, bandits' hideouts, yellow *ipê*, black trumpet trees with their poisonous berries and Juan Ladrillo[70] hiding behind a wild mulberry tree, turning over in his mind the compelling reasons upon which he was to found, between swampland and deadly brushwood and facing an accursed sea, the port of Buenaventura; Pascual de Andagoya, having captured him and sent him in chains to the powerful lord Don Felipe, Prince of the Spains and the Etceteras; Sebastián de Belalcázar compelling seven families to live in the aforementioned port, which seven died within seven months from despondency, mosquitoes and black slime, to be replaced by seven other families . . . And I thought I saw the ocean coming towards us, but I pulled myself together and controlled my fantasies: behind us the rest of the mountains held firm, so womanly and selfassured, as though happily watching the ascension of their sister into the heavens, and the condor flitted monstrously through kilometres of warm air; the castor oil plant wilted and the charcoal trees grew pale, the star apple retaliated with its sweetness and the breadfruit with its wholesome fibre; there was a vast, resplendent display of ripening strawberry trees, plums, gooseberries, custard apples, Jerusalem cherries, chilli peppers, Cambray pineapples, lemons in seventy different colours, soursops, bananas, plantains and Chinese plums, tamarinds, sapodillas, pomegranates, bitter oranges, dragon fruits, gru gru palms and peach palms.

The mountain also robbed us of the house on the Ninth Hill. It was not like people said, that the house was haunted: someone lived there. I don't know whether the reader will remember Hectór Pie-drahíta Lovecraft,[71] a precociously intelligent young boy who, some-time around 1969, managed to devote himself equally (earning both fortune and posthumous fame, as attested by the various cults of different and conflicting Dadaist ramifications that have sprung up around the figure of Hectór P. Lovecraft, and in particular it must be said around *Mare Tenebrum*,[72] his novel, an adaptation of H. James, so 'white' and so depraved) to the theatre, the plastic arts, fiction and his famously contemptuous articles about cinema, which were entirely in keeping with his personal behaviour as a direct (and astonishingly diligent) carrier of 'cinesyphilis', as he called 'the Span-ish disease'.[73] Four years later (a rather disturbing period, since it's not known what he did beyond bullfighting with automobiles) he disappeared. Muckrakers hinted at all manner of wretched and degrading deaths, but in fact he was here, clinging bow-legged to a sturdy pine overgrown with choking ivy and bastard fern, when the shockwave hit him and he was carried off in this flight across the heavens.

In the presence of all this, we were like sleepwalkers. But every *mimmosa* must find its patch of earth so, with great care, I set María down on the ground and her legs (so brave she was, so divine) sup-ported her, firm and keen-eyed.

The condor wheeled in the sky, a little astonished by the immensity and the monotony of the landscape over which it flew, and it looked down at us on this spent earth, heads aflame and spliced together, buttocks hovering over the looming wonder, small personal hurricanes. With a joyous somersault, the condor planted its beak in the verticality of the slope. After that we didn't see it again.

The sun and moon also cartwheeled and mother sun remained in the east sapodilling from her cradle. Was night about to engulf us?

From Don Julián's cabin twelve sheets of official paper fluttered down. They had traced 130 long 'S's and nine 'Z's in the air when we collected them in the circle of devastation left by the departed mountain and we realized that they were handwritten documents. They contained declarations, short notes that each bore a date, written by well-known people. Here below I will divulge the contents of those I have closest to hand, since very soon I'll be swallowed by the night born of my story, and I don't want all this to be hushed by oblivion.

8 January 1966

Having withstood the hardships of the long trek – humidity, jungle and exhaustion and a small bear that crossed our path – we reached the summit of the mountain and Señor Julián Acosta's house. Here we blissfully admired the beauties of the landscape and spent our nights playing dice.

Carlos Valencia Tejada / Roberto Calvache / Eduardo de Francisco

5 April 1966

The roughest gang and the toughest man in Kali were here.

Marquetalia Republic[74]

Nane / Hugo F. Porras / Armando Rodríguez / Almeiro Salazar / Alvaro Gomez, 'The Phenomenal Fino' / Chiminango

4 July 1963

'THE TRIANGLE'

Diego Ortega / José Fernando Mejía / Henry Ossa (Barranquilla) / Rodrigo Ortega / Helmer Collazos ('Judas') / Leonel Moreno

7 January 1964

'The Anchors' [T-shirt with a drawing of an anchor and the name of the gang. Supported by the Vampires, the Nazis, Smoke Gets in Your Eyes and the Triangle.]

Leader: Javier H. Jaramillo

Nadim Taborda / Jorge Lemos / Julián Llanos / Luis XX / Lalo / Piter / Zamorano / Corso / Piquiña

There are a hundred of us. Bretaña district. Anyone who wants to join the gang should go to Number 9-02, Calle Veinticuatro. Ask for Javier (aka Terror). Thanks.

24 August 1966

ADEVAD gang: we drink, we hunt, we dance, we pray.

9 February 1964

The Death's Head gang was here. Had a cool time. We came by helicopter. Landed on the lawn. People at Don Julián's place were very polite. They served us rabbit meat tougher than a bandsman's beat.

26 December 1963

Left at 6 a.m. Arrived at 12.30 p.m. (six hours).

27 December 1963

The light aircraft left at 10 a.m. Arrived at 1.40 p.m.

Ernesto Gutíerrez (Thickhead), Francisco Mejía (Tough Guy), Daniel Perea (Gunslinger). Thanks to Señor Julián Acosta for sharing his lively company and his comfortable cabin which we used as a stopover while conquering the peak of this difficult and bewitching mountain, the tragic scene of the death of Major Fabricio Cabrera.

We invite all those who read this to discover and enjoy the delights offered by this magnificent landscape.

1968

We arrived on 10 April at 9 p.m. Having filled our bellies, we went to bed. Another rather sultry night. Before we arrived, we spent about six hours a mere two kilometres from here.

Today we plan to carry on climbing and exploring.

Fernando Barrios / Alfonso Llanos

The Cliffs of Kali, February 1964

The Gang of Fifty from the *barrio* Evaristo García stayed here, and a member of the Salomia gang. *Viva Cuba!* Long live the Russian Union 'USSR' – *Yankees out of Panama and Colombia.*

[There are drawings of skulls and crossbones, hammers and sickles, swastikas, snakes and knives.]

17 August 1965

Julián,

With your horse possessed of blood and speed, and adhering strictly to your advice about drugs, I cantered over the peaks of these mountains in a record time of four hours. A wild, whip-hungry steed!

Ulpiano Montes

March 26 – Holy Thursday

Señor Julián,

Those of us bound by a friendship which dates back many years have been disgusted to see the careless way some of your visitors have treated your furniture and chattels. We believe that living amid such magnificent scenery, your customary bad habits have led you to open your doors to philistinism. We hope that this place, which is visited by people from such diverse walks of life, both social and intellectual, may one day be restored to the atmosphere of former days, one that we are grieved to note has disappeared.

Armando Escobar / Reinaldo Paz Saa / Heliodoro Escobar

2 October 1964

Here I spent another day of my sojourn in this world.
Rodrigo Cabal H.

21 January 1968

Next time I'll come with Daniel Perea, Nelson Parra, Camilo and Julio.
Pablito

Julián, we came to meet you but sadly did not have that pleasure. Greetings from the friends you have not met.
Omaira Calero / Rosario Bueno

Was night about to engulf us? To soothe our sorrows, I put María Iata's clothes back on her. I brushed her hair gently and carefully. And walking in silence, we recommenced the circle of achievements. The Andean lapwings would attract other birds of prey to the corpses of Bárbaro and the gringo. Serenely, the two of us stood gazing at the river into which we could not bring ourselves to plunge our battered heads.

On the way back, I felt proud: behind me was one mountain fewer. Fresh, fertile pastures rolled away since the Valle del Renegado had grown by my presence. Cattle stared at us, surprised to see two beautiful bipeds make use of the flowers of their excrement.

Scrawny guava trees and scorched poppies. Beneath the one, upon the other we walked. The boundlessness of the land on the western horizon, the distinctive state of mind brought on by the scents of night drawing in.

What mushrooms do to you is dry up every last particle of food in order to create a huge bubble in your stomach, from which come spurts of psilocybin. But I remained peaceful, reconciled. María Iata had a terrible tic in her jaw and neck. As she was complaining of feeling 'disorientated and dopey', she stumbled over the rocks. How many burned-out neurones? And always spending your time staring at the ground looking for mushrooms, hunkering down to eat shit, produces a feeling of resignation towards everything, which in itself is bad for our people.

How must we look, from the second mountain? Backs straight, facing the long road home, happy to be alive but reluctant to go back?

As we crossed the bridge, we encountered three white campers, red as lobsters, who were singing:

> *Rain and snow rain and snow rain and snow*
> *Rain and snow rain and snow rain and snow*
> *Rain and snow rain and snow rain and snow*
> *Rain and snow rain and snow rain and snow*
> *Rain and snow rain and snow rain and snow*
> *Rain and snow rain and snow rain and snow*
> *Rain and snow rain and snow rain and snow*
> *Rain and snow rain and snow rain and snow*
> *Rain and snow rain and snow rain and snow*
> *Rain and snow rain and snow rain and snow*
> *Rain and snow rain and snow rain and snow*
> *Rain and snow rain and snow rain and snow*
> *Rain and snow rain and snow rain and snow*

Rain and snow rain and snow rain and snow
Rain and snow rain and snow rain and snow
Rain and snow rain and snow rain and snow
Rain and snow rain and snow rain and snow
Rain and snow rain and snow rain and snow
Rain and snow rain and snow rain and snow
Rain and snow rain and snow rain and snow
Rain and snow rain and snow rain and snow
Rain and snow rain and snow rain and snow
Rain and snow rain and snow rain and snow
Rain and snow rain and snow rain and snow
Rain and snow rain and snow rain and snow
Rain and snow rain and snow rain and snow
Rain and snow rain and snow rain and snow
Rain and snow rain and snow rain and snow[75]

It made me hungry for a hot place and some cool music, 'Corazón de melón',[76] as we headed back on the bus towards the city in a dense somnambulistic silence. María's spirits sank further in the embrace of the green and concrete fog: this to offer the reader a glimpse of the adventures of city children in *papá*'s jungle.

I helped her as much as I could. On the corner of Avenida Sexta and Calle Quince I found her a taxi and flashed her messages of strength with little smiles and one last (masterly) hand on her ass. I said goodbye to her, all friendly and bright. Far from my south now, watching her go I knew that from here on she would be plagued by sleepless nights or by dreams of a single plain yellow backcloth. On the first jet the next morning, she went back to her adoptive country. She was where she needed to be: why should we shoulder the problems of others? I'd already warned her the USA would kill her in the end. She couldn't mould herself to studying or to life on the street. She shuts herself away, toying with the idea of seizing the day and spattering her brains against these walls she stares at. And feeling that the far side of her seclusion is lapped night and day by the treacly sea of Miami . . . shit the colour of shampoo.

*

Far from my south. How was I going to explain the death of their friend to the kids? All day they sense my presence but do not seek me out. If I allowed myself one last trip, one last great flight, I would land on them in one of those late afternoons the colour of mamey apples that make you want to bite into them. But I don't go, flower of twilight. And I yearn, oh yearn, for someone to take care of me, to give me affection and a little attention before I sleep: little girls who've had a hard day are lulled to sleep, that's the law of life – they sleep on cool, fresh sheets, snuggled in a blanket. A pat on the head, a gently plumped pillow, good night, my darling; and when they turn out the light, I wouldn't be afraid because at an earlier stage in my life I used to fall asleep drawing up a favourable balance sheet of the day's events.

Ahhhh, my gentle reader already knows that I'd deserve a slap around the head if I let this sadness descend on me. This paradoxical sadness, this fickle sadness, *ay ay ay*, don't let it touch me.

I refused to show up at my parents' house. From that day I saw them only one last time. Cruel vanished childhoods: it's like asking for green mango from the ripe. I could no longer go either north or south, so scaling mountains was impossible . . . And so all that was left was to turn firmly towards the dazzling and revolutionary east. Oh, the countless *rumbas*, the distant borders whence they blow! I heard a distant mayhem of potent melodies. Night closed in and lingering in my mind were the lyrics I'd heard on that terrible expedition I transcribed. Deliberately repeating 'S's and 'Z's, I set off in search of music. May the sun of peace and joy forever illuminate you. May the night, when you engulf it, smile on you: this is what I wish for you. As for me, I have the power to conquer. I walked and as you walk through this city you realize that the things that remain are close by, and it was close by that I found a happening street-corner *rumba* where they welcomed me and where I stayed looking for young guys, rich *papitos* who'd give me something pink, something soft, without having to touch first, for my silken hands, my sinuous curves, this crossroads where they split the rocks of women and grind the heads of men, I am a rock, *sway, Miki, sway, Miki, it's for the saints, Miki.* From where I said goodbye to María Iata to where I live now is barely twelve blocks, meaning that I had only to cross the River to get to this crucifixion of corners.

I didn't show up tired. I stood on the corner and the tough guys gave me respect. A shoeshine boy with a face on him like a worm, his skin rolled and rumpled over his stick-thin skeleton, offered to shine my boots for free and I accepted, and while he was polishing leather, I boogied to the beats blasting full volume from six different shops, so I had to fuse them, create a single throbbing pulse; that's how music is, it has no use for bars or shuttered windows: still it trickles out. From Los Violines came the supplication 'Arrepentida', from Fujiyama, 'Si la ven', from the bakery opposite, 'La canción del viajero', from El Nuevo Día, the hard salsa of 'Alafia cumayé', and they say that in Natalí they were playing 'La voz de la juventud'. But I'd have had to cross the street and walk another block to hear it; a lot of people headed there, a lot of people stayed, but standing here on the corner where I'm telling my story, some said that at the Picapiedra – the Rocksplitter – they were belting out 'Here Comes Richie Ray', don't miss the big *rumba* about to go down there, so that's the place I chose, I have three Marías inside me. I hugged the walls until I found the entrance, which a fat man was blocking with his short stubby legs; he stared at me, trying in vain to recognize me. As soon as I turned to him, glanced at him fleetingly, he lowered his legs and allowed me into the long, narrow stairwell; they were still at the first third of the song and I thought to myself, 'I've arrived,' and in my memory I fixed every square inch of the doorway that, from this night on, would lead me every night to this same music.

At the bottom of the stairs there was a bend and then the bar, lined with real men; to the left was the dance floor, *jala jala*, where a woman with the longest legs and the skimpiest shorts was pounding out the beat on her thighs – I sing only for myself and for Yemaya; and everyone thought it was all kinds of weird that I sat at a table by myself – 'Iqui con iqui', bold as brass – and ordered a beer, and the customers warily approached my table, checking me out, *and I'm playing the jala jala just for you, Puerto Rico is calling me*. After the seventh beer I threw myself on to the dance floor and all the tension built by my presence was shattered, of course, *saoco and bring on the beat*; the guys gathered around me, and when the music stopped and I stood there, the only thing this one skinny guy who'd been staring at me could think to say was, '*Pelada*, how much you charge?'

I stared back, turned on my heel and he followed me to my table; I sat down, looked at him again, picked up the glass of beer in front of me and said, 'Three hundred and you pay for the room.' That's what I'm worth, top of the range. They all bitch, but they all come flocking just the same.

We left. Like an explorer, he led me to a room with tiles on the walls. He undressed me slowly, parted my legs: I let him press his repulsive face against mine, for the dead; he tried to put it in me but the great maestro couldn't work out how. I had to slide my hand down to slip it in me. He was talking about the sort of pictures they paint on buses when I suddenly used my insides and blew him up like a bellows. He must have felt a shard of ice, a creeping coldness, a swelling . . . he tried to pull his prick out but by now it had blown up like a melon. He completely exploded inside me, the shreds of his skin like lashes from a whip. That, to me, was living.

I ran out of there screaming and caterwauling: 'My john's just snuffed it on me.' *Richie Ray just got up to get down, and that's something everyone knows.*

That night, I wanted to sleep and sleep, so I went back to the hotel. I woke to a horrible, sweltering Sunday morning and went to visit my folks. I remember the whole scene in a sort of photographic blur, a *gauze*, they call it. *Mamá* opened the door to me and gave me a brief hug. They were both up and dressed. They invited me to stay for breakfast, and every plate I touched clanged loudly against the glass-topped table, but they had no problem, except when my *papá* choked and coughed and spewed *café con leche* all over my shirt. By now they were well used to me not being around and they didn't miss me, although they'd have been pissed off if they knew what I got up to at night. They realized I'd just come to get some clothes. When I told them I'd seen a little apartment, they agreed to shell out for the rent without even asking me where it was.

'You're very young,' they said. 'You'll learn.'

Astounded, I told them I agreed.

I went up to my room. The venetian blinds were closed and covered in dust. Out of sheer perversity, I opened them and looked down at the park dappled with droplets of dew, the sweat of the trees and the mountains, pockets of life. The mirror was missing.

They suggested I stay for lunch and maybe even a siesta, but I didn't want to: I couldn't have survived a Sunday afternoon in that house.

I left, knowing I had my whole life ahead of me. And I'm not done living it by a long shot.

Though I don't plan on moving from here, I like to imagine there are better places than this frenzy on the corner of Cuarta and Calle Quince, that it's only out of pathological abulia that I don't go looking, the fact that I'm no longer capable of moving in a horizontal direction, now that the *rumba* is pounding, because since I got here, I don't walk anywhere any more, I've got the *rumba* twenty paces from here – even when I'm in bed I can hear it. I hear rumours that things are better, more modern on Avenida Octava, at the Séptimo Cielo and the Cabo E, but look at it this way: I'd have to walk four blocks down Calle Quince and along Octava, way past Calle Veinticinco, past the cemetery. No, I'm not moving any more. These days I'm a bit freaked out at the thought of constantly looking for new directions when in the end there's only one beat. And it's Richie's rhythm, nothing else. They come to me, the *papitos* seek me out because they know I'm down here on Calle Quince, and I get them going with my little mounds and my sweet luscious locks, I pinch them sweetly, pretend they hurt me; I'm better than they are and if they so desire, I guide them in their first steps through the outer limits of this jungle.

How does a former student at Belalcázar Secondary School wind up working as a whore? I get other visits that are less pleasant. Recently, it was the Cricket, the Marxist, who came to get smashed, to drown his heartbreak, prattling on about the thousand and one failings of the bourgeoisie (the *pelada* he's in love with lives in the heart of *El Nortecito*), and I just nodded at everything he said and suggested – only half joking – going and doing some damage, and he was patting me on the back until the silence came and he realized where he was, who he was with, how it would look, and made a first attempt to stand up. No cigar. Sitting there, powerless, he told me he had to go to the toilet. I took him by the elbow and helped him to his feet. He stood there with duck eyes, swaying in the middle of the empty dance floor. When they're drunk, it's like men have their eyes closed: for as long as you don't move them, they resist; shake them up a little and suddenly they're more composed. I'm the opposite: get a drink or two inside me and I'm head over heels and pounding to a *rumba*. The Cricket moved his legs apart to get a better foothold on terrain that offered none, then he looked round to find the toilets, and I pointed them out: whether what caused him to bloat was the slow, precise movement of my lovely arm, the actual distance to the toilets indicated by my arm, or whether my gesture, my outstretched arm, made the distance seem greater, I don't know. Whatever it was, he gave up on the idea, *sad is his song*. He trekked back the short distance to tell me he was leaving. Oh, how terrible it must be for a man to suddenly discover he's in the midst of such debauchery, to realize that he's failing in his duty but incapable of going to find it because the moment he moves he looks pathetic. I walked him to the door, as was my duty, but didn't help him down the stairs, I didn't even stay to watch. If he'd rolled down the stairs like a sack of potatoes, I wouldn't have stayed to watch.

It was one evening, naturally, staring out at the six layers of mountains, that I decided that it was impossible, that to leave this place would be to cause myself intolerable pain because of the distance, even assuming that having left I'd come back: the road back to the place where you belong is never-ending. I've no reason to live anywhere but here where I have my heart, my *rumba*, the land I love. The *papitos* see me, although they don't really get me, my sophisticated air, the way I look straight ahead, but they never ask questions: they know that I appeared one evening and some night I'll leave them telling each other stories about the *pelada* who was like a princess but crazy, absolutely crazy about music.

My dreams these days are weightless. I've come home having listened to pure pleasure, come home still wide awake, simply because it's four in the morning, the hour when, by law, everyone has to be in bed. I go back to my room where I have a vision of Saint Barbara and another of Janis Joplin clinging to a bottle of booze, because *in me a sun is born and I don't find my love.* I go to bed reciting lyrics but I don't sleep, I don't dream; in me I feel a hammering that beats out a rhythm, I struggle to recite the lyrics and I cover my ears and grit my teeth so as not to hear them, not to speak them, to make it clear that I'm in pain, and all the while in my head are recent flickering images of me agreeing to dance, all smiles, awkward, drinking in the newest, the best *rumba*. I spend the mornings buying fabric for dresses, looking at myself in the mirror, making plans to head south and spend the day cheering up the kids. But I don't go there any more, I don't cross the River any more. I stay on my street, the one that brings me music. More often than not, the guys that come here are from the north, because up there everything's gone silent, so they come here for a bit of excitement, they come for my conversation.

Hey you, make your childhood more intense by loading up on adult experiences. Couple corruption to the freshness of your youth. Rappel down the possibilities of precocity. You'll pay the price: by nineteen all you'll be left with are tired eyes, emotions spent, strength sapped. By then, a gentle, pre-planned death will seem welcome. Get in ahead of death, make a date with it. No one loves an ageing teenager. You alone know you've confused the squandered years and the thoughtful years in a furious whirlwind of activity. Living simultaneously forwards and in reverse.

When you finally explode in the midst of your friends, what will you do? Will you fall asleep, slack-jawed, right in front of the ones who've always admired your energy? Will you say goodbye, stumbling off, leaving people to bitch about you behind your back? Will you explode and splatter everyone around? Why seek out friendship in moments of humiliation? Cultivate your addiction to solitary vices.

It was strange feeling that this was going to become an everyday occurrence, this walking past a record shop and stopping, dumbfounded, whenever I hear the beat of drums, people saying, 'Can I help you?' and me, open-mouthed, astonished: 'No, I'm fine, thanks.' At first, I even thought about setting up a record shop. I would have been acclaimed, the *pelada* with all the salsa back at her place. But what place? The rented room I live in with a toilet and a mirror? I never was much good at collecting things anyway, I lack the self-restraint, I'd end up lending out all the vinyl, and besides, I thought, 'If I collect records, I'll end up listening to them myself. I'll turn into a melancholy shadow, and from there it's only a short step to tango.' But I would have been respected all the more, people with records are always respected. Not that people disrespect me, because I whisper in their ears the lyrics of every bolero, good and bad, because I explain even the stuff that can't be understood, the slightest turn, the faintest call that leads to *salsa dura*.

I cash my parents' cheque every Friday. They've redoubled their generosity. And every Friday I rob some guy: one of those fat guys who venture into these streets. And every guy who's heard of me I leave with his own little wound, so the next day they can tell everyone at school what they survived. Since I don't want the other girls wondering how I come up with all the cash, given what I do, I don't go strutting around all *cuchí cuchá*: the girls all know I love them.

The birds sing and in the trees (far from here, on the other side of the River), I imagine them swaying in the twilight, then I imagine every leaf making the raw sound of trumpets that is the call of the jungle that caught me in its spell. I know I'm a pioneer, a lone explorer, and that some day, in spite of myself, I'll come up with the theory that books lie, movies exhaust, let's burn them all and leave nothing but music. If I head that way, it's because that's the way we're headed. We're living the most important moment in the history of humanity, and this is the first time so much has been asked of its children. Looking into their faces, into the gaping mouths or the rings around their eyes – in my humble opinion, these kids, *mis amigos*, have succeeded. *We are the plaintive note whimpered by the violin. They laughed at boogaloo, and just look at them now.*

Hey you, don't baulk at a challenge. And don't become part of any clique. Never let them label you or pigeonhole you.

Let no one know your name, let no one give you shelter.[77]

Ignore the trappings of fame. Leave something of yourself behind and die in peace, trusting a few close friends. Let no one turn you into a grown-up, a respectable man. Never stop being a child, even when you've got eyes in the back of your head and your teeth are starting to fall out. Your parents gave birth to you. Let them support you forever, and fob them off with empty promises. Who gives a fuck? Never save for the future. Never let yourself become someone serious. Make heedlessness and fickleness your rules of conduct. Refuse all truces, make your home amid ruins, excess and trembling.

The world is yours. You are entitled to everything: charge the earth for it.

Never allow yourself to feel satisfied.

Learn never to lose your vision, never to succumb to the shortsightedness of those who live in cities. Arm yourself with dreams so that you never lose your vision.

Forget that some day you might ever attain what people call 'normal sexuality', and never hope that love will bring you peace. Sex is an act of the shadows and falling in love a union of torments. Never expect that you will one day come to understand the opposite sex. There is nothing more different or less inclined to reconciliation. Listen: practise fear, rape, struggle, violence, perversion and the anal route if you believe that satisfaction depends on tightness and a dominant position. If you prefer to withdraw from all sexual congress, so much the better.

For the hatred instilled in you by the censor, there is no better cure than murder.

For shyness: self-destruction.

The rhythms of solitude are best acquired in cinemas; learn to shun cinemas.

Never succumb to remorse or to the pettiness of social climbing. Better to fall, to become an outcast; to end a long, undistinguished career in dreary dissolution.

To harden your skull, practise beating it against brick walls.

There is no moment more intense, more agonizing than a man waking at dawn. Complicate and draw out this moment, waste away within it. You will slowly die and, bellowing, learn to face each new day.

It's sensible to listen to music before breakfast.

Listen: conceal oblivion. Learn to stoically contemplate each beginning. If you are tempted by evil, give in: you'll end up spinning on the same axis.

Eat everything that's harmful to the liver – green mango, mush-rooms and salt with everything – and learn to wake up with the worms. Become a ceiba tree, providing food for parasites.

Hey you: never worry. Die before your parents to spare them the ghastly sight of your old age. And look for me wherever all is grey and no one suffers. We are legion. Tell no one this.

I bet no one can hear how much the screech of every heel, the smash on head of every bottle, the plea of every collapsing drunk, *the beat of every bembé*, how everything, everything calls to me, just as everything belongs to me and the *rumba* calls me. If I'd never known this wild and savage sound, I'd be a sordid soul lost in the jungle. But now they call to me, they howl for me. They say people come from distant cities to meet me and squander garbage. Photos of me are published in the scandal sheets and I laugh, imagining the scandal-ized faces the pigs would make; were it not for the fact that I no longer have the strength, I'd join them, go out and chant slogans, smash windows, but what use are fantasies when those parts of the city are so remote now, they're not part of my stamping ground any more? I suppose the Marxists must have seen the photos and thought, 'Just look how low the bourgeoisie can sink.'

It's so sleazy but it's so good.[78] I don't mind serving as a scapegoat, I am beyond all judgement and in every photo I look divine, I look fabulous. Strength, I have. I have given myself a name –

LIVEFOREVER[79]

– propitious because to walk trustingly hand in hand with the night does not mean he shelters you, the coachman who comes and stops, *the black coachman with the brightly coloured saddle.*[80] I will carry on, because the *rumba* is not what it was yesterday, no one can name it – savour it? – because the *rumba* is not what it was yesterday, no one can tame it. You: find the way then lose your way, rumba on till you're rumba'd out.[81] Toss it all into the cauldron where you'll brew the salsa of your confusion. Now I'm going, leaving a trickle of ink on this manuscript. *There's a fire at number 23.*[82]

María del Carmen Huerta (A.C.[83])
Los Ángeles – Cali
March 1973–December 1974

Discography

That the author, in writing this book, has made use of the following songs[84] will be obvious to the observant reader. I have done my best to list the best version (all stemming from one ancient African melody) and the label (including bootlegs). But I've heard most of the music she mentions through open doors, on radios or on buses. Consequently, as the list progresses, the information is scarcer. Songs marked with an asterisk are cheesy *caballerías* of no interest whatever.

Rosario Wurlitzer[85]

'¡Qué viva la música!', Ray Barretto (Fania)
'Cabo E', Richie Ray/Bobby Cruz (Alegre)
'Si te contaran', Ray/Cruz (Fonseca)
'Here Comes Richie Ray', Ray/Cruz (Alegre)
'Guaguancó triste', Ray/Cruz (Vaya)
'Guaguancó raro', Ray/Cruz (Alegre)
'White Room', Cream (Phillips)
'Moonlight Mile', Rolling Stones (RSR)
'Ruby Tuesday', Rolling Stones (London)
*'Llegó borracho el borracho'
'Salt of the Earth', Rolling Stones (London)
'She's a Rainbow', Rolling Stones (London)
'Loving Cup', Rolling Stones (RSR)
'Amparo Arrebato', Ray/Cruz (Alegre)
'Toma y dame', Ray/Cruz (UA)
'Bailadores', Nelson y sus Estrellas (PON)
'Bembé en casa de Pinki', Ray/Cruz (Vaya)

157

'A jugar bembé', Ray/Cruz (UA)

'Piraña', Wille Colón (Fania)

'Lo altara la araché', Ray/Cruz (Alegre)

'Sonido bestial', Ray/ Cruz (Vaya)

'Te conozco bacalao', Willie Colón (Fania)

'Feria en M.', Ray/Cruz (UA)

'El diferente', Ray/Cruz (UA)

'Convergencia', Johnny Pacheco (Fania)

'Agúzate', Ray/ Cruz (Alegre)

*'Sufrir . . .'

'El Guarataro', Ray/Cruz (UA)

'Ay compay', Ray/Cruz (UA)

'Bomba en Navidad', Ray/Cruz (Vaya)

'Bomba camará', Ray/Cruz (Alegre)

'Yo soy Babalú', Ray/Cruz (Alegre)

'Adasa', Ray/Cruz (Alegre)

'Agallú', Ray/Cruz (Alegre)

'El hijo de Obatala', Ray Barretto (Melser)

'Iqui con iqui', Ray/Cruz (Alegre)

'La música brava', Andy Harlow (Melser)

'Ponte duro', Robertico Roena, Fania '73 (Live) (Fania)

'Ricardo y Chaparro', Ray/Cruz (UA)

'On with the Show', Rolling Stones (London)

'Play with Fire', Rolling Stones (London)

'The Last Time', Rolling Stones (London)

'Heartbreaker', Rolling Stones (RSR)

'It's Only Rock 'n' Roll (But I Like It)', Rolling Stones (RSR)

'I Got the Blues', Rolling Stones (RSR)

'Richie's jala jala', Ray/Cruz (Alegre)

'Colombia's Boogaloo', Ray/Cruz (Alegre)

'Pa chismoso tu', Ray/ Cruz (Fonseca)

'Che che colé', Willie Colón (Fania)

'Quien lo tumbe', Larry Harlow (Fania)

'Que se rían', Ray/Cruz (Alegre)

'Colorín colorao', Ray/Cruz (Alegre)

'Lluvia', Ray/Cruz (Vaya)

'Lluvia con nieve', Mon Rivera (Alegre)

'Ahora vengo yo', Ray/Cruz, Fania '73 (Live) (Fania)

'Traigo de todo', Ray/Cruz (Alegre)

'Guasasa', Larry Harlow (Fania)

'Mambo jazz', Ray/Cruz (Fonseca)

'Suavito', Ray/Cruz (Fonseca)

'Comején', Ray/Cruz (Fonseca)

'Qué bella es la Navidad', Ray/Cruz (Fonseca)

'Micaela se botó', Pete Rodríguez (Alegre)

'Se casa la rumba', Larry Harlow (Fania)

'El paso de Encarnación', Larry Harlow (Fania)

'Vengo virao', Larry Harlow (Fania)

'Tiembla', El Gran Combo (Melser)

'Anacaona', Cheo Feliciano, Fania '73 (Live) (Fania)

'Tengo poder', La Conspiración (Fania)

'Si la ven', Willie Colón (Fania)

'La voz de la juventud', La Conspiración (Fania)

'El día que nací yo', La Conspiración (Fania)

'Alafia cumayé', Ray/Cruz

'La peregrina', Ray/Cruz

'El Abakuá', Ray/Cruz

'Trumpet Man II', Ray/Cruz

'The House of the Rising Sun', Animals

'Canto a Borinquen', Willie Colón

'Salsa y control', LeBrón Brothers

'Bongó loco', LeBrón Brothers

'Monte adentro', Monguito con Fania '72 (Live) (Fania)

'Seis tumbao', La Protesta

'San Miguel', La Protesta

'¿Mi guaguancó?', Ray/Cruz

'¿A mí qué?', Típica Novel

'La ley', Sexteto Juventud

'La canción del viajero', Nelson y sus Estrellas

*'El gavilán pollero'

*'Vanidad'

*'La vida no vale nada'

*'Yo perdí el corazon (¿Qué será de mí?)'
'Pachanga que no cansa', Manolín Morel
'Oye lo que te conviene', Eddie Palmieri
'Changa con pachanga', Randy Carlos
'Charanga revuelta con pachanga', Randy Carlos
'Con la punta del pie, Teresa', Cortijo y su Combo
'Pal 23', Ray Pérez

Unidentified lyrics from unknown songs:[86]

'¿Quieres más bugalú?'
'Sambumbia y saoco en el bugalú'
'Cómete ese piano, Richie'

Notes

The following notes deal with some of the more curious allusions in Caicedo's novel. A list of the lyrics that run like a thread through the story, inflecting dialogue and suffusing María's narrative, can be found in the 'List of Song Lyrics' (p. 171), while a (more) complete list of the songs, together with the singers, can be found in the 'List of Songs' (p. 177).

1   *Babalú*: Babalú is the spirit of the earth and an Orisha, or god, in the Yoruba pantheon. Salsa lyrics routinely use Yoruba words relating to Santería, a system of beliefs combining the Yoruba religion with Roman Catholic and Native American traditions.

2   *Jeanette MacDonald . . . Indian Love Call*: Jeanette MacDonald and Nelson Eddy were the quintessential 1930s Hollywood musical couple, most famous for the song 'Indian Love Call', from the 1936 film of the musical *Rose-Marie*, which became their signature song.

3   *John Gavin*: Mexican-American actor (b. 1931) who played Sam Loomis in Alfred Hitchcock's *Psycho* (1960).

4   *The Underdogs*: Los de abajo, a novel by Mariano Azuela about the Mexican Revolution (1910–20). Published in 1915, it was translated into English as *The Underdogs*.

5   *cover of a John Lennon album . . . bottom left corner*: Probably a reference to the cloud on the cover of *The Plastic Ono Band: Live Peace in Toronto 1969*.

6   *The People Next Door*: A Canadian film made in 1970 about how a teenage girl descends from drug addiction to being committed to a mental ward. It was released in Colombia as *Viaje hacia el delirio*.

7   *charanga*: Salsa-style music played by a big brass band.

8   *Cavorite*: A fictional anti-gravity substance that would allow flight –
     'discovered' by Mr Cavor in H. G. Wells's novel *The First Men in the
     Moon* (1901).

9   *"A Mile of Moonlight"*: 'Moonlight Mile'; the song title is deliberately
     mistranslated here to convey the awkwardness of Ricardo's translation.
     For the sections from the song that follow, however, I have used the
     original lyrics, as – despite his protestations – Ricardo's translation is
     entirely faithful.

10   *The garden of Marienbad*: Referring to the avant-garde 1961 French film
     L'Année dernière à Marienbad (*Last Year in Marienbad*) with its geometrical
     château garden that provides a striking setting for certain scenes in the
     film.

11   *Nadaístas*: Literally, 'Nothingists', a 1960s literary movement in
     Colombia which verbally challenged/desecrated Colombian society.

12   *House of Usher . . . Corpses walled up behind mirrors*: The first of a
     number of references to the writings of Edgar Allan Poe, whose
     work influenced Caicedo. Here the reference is to the burying alive
     of Madeline in a vault in Poe's short story 'The Fall of the House of
     Usher' (1839).

13   *Keith Richard*: Richards spelled his name without the 's' during the
     1960s.

14   *Bacillus*: The first of many words (all beginning with 'B') that Caicedo
     uses to refer to a spliff. 'Bacillus', being a rod-shaped type of bacteria,
     resembles the shape of a joint.

15   *La Pasionaria*: Literally, 'passionflower', another nickname of Caicedo's
     for marijuana.

16   *guaguancó*: A subgenre of Cuban rumba, a complex rhythmic music
     and dance style.

17   *'Take It and Give Me'*: Title in English of the song 'Toma y dame'.

18   *bembé*: A feast in Yoruba mythology and hence, in salsa (which draws
     heavily on it – see note 1), a style of music. See also note 46.

19   *butín, butero tabique y afuero*: Lyrics from 'Tin Marín' roughly translatable
     as 'eeny meeny miny moe'.

20   *on the tips . . . of your toes*: Lyrics from and a reference to the title in
     English of 'Con la punta del pie, Teresa'.

21   *López Tarso*: Mexican film and stage actor Ignacio López Tarso (b. 1925).

22 *'Get Sharp!'*: Title in English of the song 'Agúzate'.

23 *'Changó, bestow . . . they gave me more drink'*: Referring to the poem 'Corta Changó, con tu espada' ('Cut, Changó, with Your Sword') by Cuban poet Severo Sarduy (1937–93), which calls on Changó, the Yoruba god of fire, thunder and lightning.

24 *King (Richie) Ray*: Ricardo 'Richie' Ray (Richard Maldonado Morales – born in Brooklyn, New York, in 1945, of Puerto Rican parentage) is a virtuoso pianist, singer, music arranger and composer. He is most famous as one half of the duo Richie Ray & Bobby Cruz, considered to be the foremost exponents of *salsa brava*. Ray met Bobby Cruz (Roberto Cruz Feliciano – born in Hormigueros, Puerto Rico, in 1937) in 1957 and played bass in his band. Though he gained admission to the Julliard School of Music in 1963, Ray left after a year and he and Cruz formed a group. They signed to Fonseca Records and in 1964 released *Ricardo Ray Arrives/Comején*. The albums recorded for Fania Records, *Agúzate* (1970) and *El bestial sonido de Richie Ray y Bobby Cruz* (1971), which marked the transition between virtuoso boogaloo to freewheeling salsa, are considered landmarks. The duo were hugely successful in Colombia in the late 1960s and their sound greatly influenced Colombian salsa.

25 *Ray Barretto*: Born to Puerto Rican parents and raised in Spanish Harlem, New York, Ray Barretto (1929–2006) was a Grammy Award-winning Latin jazz percussionist. He played congas with Charlie Parker and later with Tito Puente, and his highly individual style made him a regular with jazz combos. He released his first solo record, *El Watusi*, in 1961 and joined the Fania record label in 1967. Aside from his successful solo career, Barretto played congas on albums by the Rolling Stones and the Bee Gees.

26 *Larry Harlow*: American producer and salsa pianist (b. 1939) who studied music in Cuba before the revolution. Harlow has played with many of the greats of salsa and recorded and produced dozens of albums in his own right for the Fania label.

27 *Alirio and His Rhythm Boys*: Alirio y sus Muchachos de Ritmo.

28 *saoco*: In salsa, *saoco* means to have rhythm in your blood.

29 *Obatala, Obatala who owns all heads*: According to the Yoruba people, Obatala is the creator of human bodies, and the owner of all *ori* or heads. See also note 1.

30 *Monguito*: Monguito 'El Unico', a Cuban salsa singer (d. 2006).

31 *The Abakuá . . . waiting for the signal*: Paraphrase of lyrics from 'El Abakuá' containing a recitation in the tribal dialect of the Efik. Abakuá is an Afro-Cuban fraternity or secret society.

32 *Enkame*: A chant whose precise meaning is known only to members of the Abakuá – see previous note.

33 *Parque Panameriquenque*: A nickname for the Parque Panamericano in Cali.

34 *the key ritual*: Part of the rite of Santería (see note 1) in which colours (green, in this instance) are invested with certain powers.

35 *jala jala*: Jala literally means to be drunk, or to be up for anything, but here it refers to a specific dance rhythm (*jala jala*) and the dance associated with it.

36 *Like a whole bunch of peace*: His name, 'Paces', sounds like the plural of peace (*paz*).

37 *Miki Vimari, Mike Collazos [sic], Russell Farnsworth and Pancho Cristal*: After their initial success with Fonseca, Richie Ray & Bobby Cruz signed to Alegre, where the famous Pancho Cristal was assigned to produce their new recordings. Among the musicians who worked on the seminal albums *Jala jala y boogaloo*, volumes 1 and 2 (1967 and 1968), and *El bestial sonido de Ricardo Ray y Bobby Cruz* (1971) were Miki Vimari (lead and backing vocals), Mike Collazo (timbales) and Russell 'Skee' Farnsworth (bass guitar).

38 *Don Rufián*: Rufián means a tough or a thug.

39 *Guaguancó bizarro*: Literally, 'Bizarre guaguancó', referring to a type of Cuban dance music related to salsa; in this case it also alludes to the song title 'Guaguancó raro'.

40 *El Viti*: Santiago Martín (b. 1938), aka 'El Viti', a famous Spanish bull-fighter.

41 *El Cordobés*: Manuel Benítez Pérez (b. 1936), aka 'El Cordobés', a Spanish toreador.

42 *Marracachafa*: Invented term for weed/marijuana.

43 *mango biche*: Literally, 'green mango', a powerful strain of Colombian marijuana.

44 *punto rojo*: Literally, 'red dot', another strong variety of Colombian marijiuana.

45 *Red Birds*: In Spanish, 'seis de Secos', referring to Seconal (barbiturates).

46 *sacatión manantión . . . sacatión manantión mojé*: Lyrics from 'El Abakuá' in Ñáñiga, one of the ritual languages of the Abakuá secret society (see note 31), thought to have originated from the religious worship of the Orishas (see note 1) during a *bembé* or celebration of the spirits.

47 *'I Invite You to Get Down and Boogaloo'*: Title in English of 'Te invito a echar un pie'.

48 *Hello, hello – okay – everybody happy*: The address from the stage is all in English in the original text and is probably a paraphrase of what was said at the actual concert.

49 *"El galiván pollero"*: 'The Chicken Hawk', a terrible song by Pedro Infante whose lyrics run (in translation): 'The chicken hawk took my chicken, / The chicken I love most. / Pour me another drink there, barkeep; / Without my chicken, I'll be toast.'

50 *Chow down on that piano, Richie*: Words shouted just before the song 'Viva Richie Ray!' on the album *Comején*.

51 *Yemayá*: Also known as Yemanja, Yemayá is an Orisha (see note 1), a goddess of motherhood and the ocean.

52 *Cándido*: Cándido de Guerra Camero (b. 1921), Cuban-born percussionist credited with being one of the first musicians to use congas in jazz.

53 *pass me the cauldron, Macoró*: These are (deliberately?) misheard lyrics from the salsa 'Agallú': the actual refrain is 'Give me the Ocha, my love', the reference to 'Ocha' ('La Regla *Ocha'*) being another term for 'Santería', initiation into which invokes the guidance of the Orishas – see note 1.

54 *'Suffering is My Lot in Life'*: Title in English of the song 'Sufrir me tocó a mí en esta vida'.

55 *pum catapum viva Changó*: The spoken introduction to 'Cabo E'.

56 *the Christmas bomba*: The title and lyrics in English from 'Bomba en Navidad'. A *bomba* is a kind of dance.

57 *Ala-lolé-lolé . . . lo altare la araché*: A freeform salsa scat from 'Lo atara la araché', written by Hugo González in an Afro-Cuban dialect and consequently incomprehensible to Spanish speakers, leading Caicedo to mistranscribe the recurring lyric 'lo altara la araché' as 'le coge la noche' ('night has taken him').

58 *Edgar Piedrahíta*: Another allusion to Edgar Allan Poe – see note 12.

59 *El Jordan . . . El Renegado*: The names of local rivers: El Turbio, 'Muddy'; El Estrellón, 'Starry'; El Claro, 'Clear/Limpid'; El Bueno, 'Good'; El Zumbón, 'Mocker'; El Cojecoje, 'Gimp'; El Renegado, 'Renegade'.

60 *Changó ta vení. Changó is coming*: An invocation of the Yoruba god Changó (see note 23), from the traditional song 'Changó ta vení': 'Changó is coming / with a machete in his hand / and the earth will tremble.' Famously performed by Justi Barreto.

61 *Don Julián Acosta*: According to his sister, Rosario, Caicedo is referring here to a real person who lived as a hermit on the Pico de Loro. Caicedo apparently visited the deserted house where he 'borrowed' the notes left by visitors and included some of them in the novel.

62 *And on what did they walk, my bare feet*: Possibly alluding to the last lines of Pasolini's *Theorem* (1968), 'Ah, my *bare feet*, walking on the desert sands . . . '; Caicedo was a cinephile and a great admirer of the work of the controversial Italian film director and poet Pier Paolo Pasolini (1922–75).

63 *Human teeth, ivory-looking teeth*: Referring to Edgar Allan Poe's short horror story 'Berenice' (1835), in which the narrator is obsessed with 'the white and glistening, and ghastly teeth of Berenice', his ailing fiancée. On being told that she is dead and buried, he has a blackout and wakes to discover she has been found alive in the plundered grave; knocking over a box on his desk, what tumble out and roll across the floor are 'thirty-two small, white and ivory-looking substances', while he himself is covered in mud and blood.

64 *Man of the West*: A 1958 western starring Gary Cooper and Julie London, in which the heroine (London) is forced to strip while her protector is held at knife point.

65 *itch mites*: In Spanish, *yaibíes*; *yabí* is a Colombian term for a type of insect (*Sarcoptes scabiei*) that lives in the grass, causing an itch if you come in contact with it.

66 *seven-phallused snail . . . coclí*: *Coclí* is a common name peculiar to Colombia for the Buff-necked Ibis. For 'seven-phallused snail', see the next note.

67 *Camilo José Cela . . . at the age of fifty*: Camilo José Cela (1916–2002), a Spanish novelist and short-story writer associated with the Generation

of '36 movement (a group of writers working at the time of the Spanish Civil War); he's mentioned here because at the age of fifty he published *Oficio de tinieblas 5* (*Tenebrae 5*), a book written in a radically different style from his previous work: it explores themes of sexuality, including bestiality, and in fact mentions the 'seven-phallused snail' cited earlier – see previous note.

68 *Barbáro's skin . . . like the skin of Monsieur Valdemar*: 'Señor Valdemar' in the original text; Caicedo is referring to a line in Edgar Allan Poe's story 'The Facts in the Case of M. Valdemar' (1845) describing Valdemar at the point of death: 'the emaciation was so extreme that the skin had been broken through by the cheek-bones.'

69 *8½*: Referring to the film *8½* (1963) directed by Federico Fellini.

70 *Juan Ladrillo*: Juan Ladrillero (*c*.1490–1559), Spanish explorer and the founder of Buenaventura – what follows is a potted history of the city.

71 *Hectór Piedrahíta Lovecraft*: As with his mention of 'Edgar Piedrahíta' (Edgar Allan Poe) earlier (see note 58), Caicedo is referring to H. P. (Howard Philips) Lovecraft (1890–1937), pioneering American writer of horror and fantasy whose 'Cthulhu Mythos' story cycle was an early influence on Caicedo.

72 *Mare Tenebrum*: A reference to the mythical *Mare Tenebrarum* (Sea of Darkness), described by the mysterious Nubian geographer Ptolemy Hephaestion and frequently mentioned in the works of Edgar Allan Poe.

73 *'the Spanish disease'*: Syphilis was so called because congenital syphilis ran in the Spanish royal family.

74 *Marquetalia Republic*: One of the enclaves in rural Colombia which communist peasant guerrillas held during the aftermath of the decade-long period of civil war (approximately 1948–58) known as 'La Violencia'.

75 *Rain and snow . . . rain and snow*: The title (and indeed the only lyrics) of 'Lluvia con nieve' ('Rain and Snow'), a largely instrumental piece of salsa written and recorded in 1964 by Mon Rivera, nickname of Efraín Rivera Castillo (1925–78), band leader, singer, composer and multi-instrumentalist who pioneered the trombone front-line in Latin American music. The 'snow' in the title is cocaine.

76 'Corazón de melón': Title of the song by Las Hermanas Benítez from the 1958 film Sube y baja (Get Up and Get Down).

77 Let no one . . . give you shelter: Caicedo is playing with the lyrics of 'El día que nací yo': 'Let no one dry your tears / Let no one give you shelter'.

78 It's so sleazy but it's so good: Alluding to the epigraph to the novel (see p. vi) – lyrics from 'Cabo E'.

79 LIVEFOREVER: In Spanish, 'Siempreviva', a succulent perennial from the genus Sempervivum whose common names include 'pinwheel' and 'house leek' as well as 'liveforever'.

80 the black coachman with the brightly coloured saddle: Probably a reference to lyrics which appear both in the song 'A Eleguá' and in some versions of 'Iqui con iqui'. Eleguá (also known as Eshu or Èṣù) is an Orisha (see note 1) and one of the most well-known deities of the religion – the god of fortune and death and a protector of travellers.

81 rumba on till you're rumba'd out: In Spanish, 'enrumbaté y después derrúmbate'; enrumbarse means 'to find the way' and derrumbarse 'to collapse, fall, crash', while the inclusion of rumba in both verbs gives the sense of partying on until you're partied out.

82 There's a fire at number 23: Lyrics from and the title in English of the song 'Hay fuego en el 23' by Arsenio Rodríguez (known by the nickname El Ciego Maravilloso, 'The Marvellous Blind Man') and covered by the group La Sonora Ponceña. The lyrics refer to an actual fire when Arsenio was living at 23 East 110 Street, in Manhattan. The song was written on the pavement while watching the blaze, and the words 'There's a fire at number 23' came to mean 'pay attention, this is important'.

83 A.C.: Andrés Caicedo.

84 That the author . . . has made use of the following songs: This is not an exhaustive list of all the songs in the book; some do not appear here and the list given does not follow the narrative chronologically.

85 Rosario Wurlitzer: The name Rosario is a nod to Andrés's sister Rosario Caicedo; Wurlitzer is a reference to the famous jukebox manufacturer.

86 Unidentified lyrics from unknown songs: The first two lines are lyrics from 'Iqui con iqui'; for 'Cómete ese piano, Richie' ('Chow down on that piano, Richie'), see note 50.

List of Song Lyrics

Song lyrics, italicized in the main text, are listed below in the order in which they are quoted in the novel, along with a page reference and the title of the song (in the original language) from which they are taken. In places Caicedo seems to have misheard lyrics, or amended them slightly to fit his narrative. Where lyrics have been paraphrased or misquoted by Caicedo, this is indicated in brackets after the quotation. Please see the 'List of Songs' on p. 177 for the names of singers.

Page	Lyrics	Song Title
p. 6	*Babalú walks with me*	'Yo soy Babalú'
p. 15	*Vanity, because of you I lost*	'Vanidad'
p. 22	*In the faraway mountains there's a horseman who's riding; he's alone in this world and for death he is biding*	'El jinete'
p. 29	*Peace and goodwill over my land*	'Guaguancó triste'
pp. 36–7	*When the wind blows and the rain feels cold . . . Down the road, down the road*	'Moonlight Mile'
p. 64	*this could be the last time*	'The Last Time'
p. 67	*Heartbreaker! Painmaker!*	'Doo Doo Doo Doo Doo (Heartbreaker)'
p. 76	*I can hear within me echoes of a cry*	'Guaguancó triste'
	This little girl is so famous, they know her all over the world. She entraps men like a spider, they'll do anything for this girl	'Amparo Arrebato'

171

p. 105	*go back to your school, little girl, because you can't handle me*	'Guaguancó raro'
p. 106	*You want more boogaloo? Who says no, who?*	'Iqui con iqui'
p. 108	*'cos I'll bring you a little of everything*	'Traigo de todo'
p. 110	*Comfort me, Adasa, give me your blessing*	'Adasa'
	pass me the cauldron, Macoró (misquotation)	'Agallú'
	a rolling stone, flotsam from a shipwreck, a suffering soul wandering alone	'Convergencia'
p. 111	*Ay, move like you, Ay, move like you, Ay, move like you*	'Agallú'
p. 112	*in the modern style*	'Mambo jazz'
p. 113	*get hard, bongo*	'Ponte duro'
	pum catapum viva Changó	'Cabo E'
p. 114	*the Christmas bomba*	'Bomba en Navidad'
	because, mamá, we got salsa	'¿Qué bella es la Navidad?'
	Tulia Fonseca, Tulia Fonseca (misquotation)	
p. 120	*Change your trip or your dress will rip*	'El paso de Encarnación'
p. 124	*Little star, why have you lost your curious spell? Here on earth from the distance we hear your sad wail*	'Lucerito'
p. 125	*blue-funk blues*	'Penas penitas'
p. 126	*Ala-lolé-lolé . . . lo altare la araché*	'Lo atara la araché'
p. 128	*No one tells me that I got here first, that I've got the cash, that I'm whiter than you*	'Bomba camará'
p. 129	*Changó ta vení. Changó is coming*	'Changó ta vení'
p. 130	*Clock, don't mark the hours*	'El reloj'

List of Songs

Below are listed the titles of all the songs referred to in the novel, including all those in the Discography (p. 157), and the artists who composed/sang them.

'A Eleguá' – traditional
'A jugar bembé' – Richie Ray & Bobby Cruz
'¿A mí qué?' – Típica Novel
'Adasa' – Richie Ray & Bobby Cruz
'Ae cumayé' – Richie Ray & Bobby Cruz
'Agallú' – Richie Ray & Bobby Cruz
'Agúzate' – Richie Ray & Bobby Cruz
'Ahora vengo yo' – Richie Ray & Bobby Cruz
'Alafia cumayé' – Ray Barretto
'Amparo Arrebato' – Richie Ray & Bobby Cruz
'Anacaona' – Cheo Feliciano
'Arrepentida' (composed by Osmar da Fonseca) – Orquesta Los Satélites
'¡Ay compay!' – Richie Ray & Bobby Cruz
'Bailadores' – Nelson y sus Estrellas
'Bembé en casa de Pinki' – Richie Ray & Bobby Cruz
'Bomba camará' – Richie Ray & Bobby Cruz
'Bomba en Navidad' – Richie Ray & Bobby Cruz
'Bongó loco' – LeBrón Brothers
'Cabo E' – Richie Ray & Bobby Cruz
'Canto a Borinquen' – Willie Colón and Héctor Lavoe
'Changa con pachanga' – Randy Carlos
'Changó ta vení' – Justi Barreto
'Charanga revuelta con pachanga' – Randy Carlos

'Che che colé' – Willie Colón and Héctor Lavoe
'Colombia's Boogaloo' – Richie Ray & Bobby Cruz
'Colorín colorao' – Richie Ray & Bobby Cruz
'Comején' – Richie Ray & Bobby Cruz
'Con la punta del pie, Teresa' – Cortijo y su Combo
'Convergencia' – Johnny Pacheco and Pete 'Conde' Rodriguez
'Corazón de melón' – Las Hermanas Benítez
'Doo Doo Doo Doo Doo (Heartbreaker)' – Rolling Stones
'El Abakuá' – Richie Ray & Bobby Cruz
'El día que nací yo' – Orquesta La Conspiración
'El diferente' – Richie Ray & Bobby Cruz
'El galiván pollero' – Pedro Infante
'El Guarataro' – Richie Ray & Bobby Cruz
'El hijo de Obatala' – Ray Barretto
'El jinete' – José Alfredo Jiménez
'El paso de Encarnación' – Larry Harlow
'El reloj' – Roberto Cantoral
'Feria en M.' – Richie Ray & Bobby Cruz
'Guaguancó raro' – Richie Ray & Bobby Cruz
'Guaguancó triste' (composed by Rubén Blades) – Richie Ray & Bobby Cruz
'Guasasa' – Larry Harlow
'Hay fuego en el 23' – Arsenio Rodríguez
'Heartbreaker' – Rolling Stones
'Here Comes Richie Ray' – Richie Ray & Bobby Cruz
'Here Comes the Sun' – Beatles
'The House of the Rising Sun' – Animals
'I Got the Blues' – Rolling Stones
'Indian Love Call' – Jeannette MacDonald and Nelson Eddy
'Iqui con iqui' – Richie Ray & Bobby Cruz
'It's Only Rock 'n' Roll (But I Like It)' – Rolling Stones
'La canción del viajero' – Nelson y sus Estrellas
'La ley' – Sexteto Juventud
'La música brava' – Andy Harlow
'La peregrina' – Richie Ray & Bobby Cruz
'La vida no vale nada' – Pablo Milanés

'La voz de la juventud' – Orquesta La Conspiración
'The Last Time' – Rolling Stones
'Llegó borracho el borracho' – José Alfredo Jiménez
'Lluvia' – Richie Ray & Bobby Cruz
'Lluvia con nieve' – Mon Rivera
'Lo atara la araché' – Richie Ray & Bobby Cruz
'Loving Cup' – Rolling Stones
'Lucerito' – Los Temerarios
'Mambo jazz' – Richie Ray & Bobby Cruz
'¿Mi guaguancó?' – Richie Ray & Bobby Cruz
'Micaela se botó' – Pete Rodríguez
'Mira la lluvia caer' – Richie Ray & Bobby Cruz
'Monte adentro' – Monguito con Fania
'Moonlight Mile' – Rolling Stones
'On with the Show' – Rolling Stones
'Oye lo que te conviene' – Eddie Palmieri
'Pa chismoso tu' – Richie Ray & Bobby Cruz
'Pachanga que no cansa' – Manolín Morel
'Pal 23' – Ray Pérez
'Penas penitas' – Mambo Nuevo
'Piraña' – Willie Colón and Héctor Lavoe
'Play with Fire' – Rolling Stones
'Ponte duro' – Roberto Roena con Fania
'¿Qué bella es la Navidad?' – Richie Ray & Bobby Cruz
'Que se rían' – Richie Ray & Bobby Cruz
'¡Qué viva la música!' – Ray Barretto
'Quien lo tumbe' – Larry Harlow
'Ricardo y Chaparro' – Richie Ray & Bobby Cruz
'Richie's jala jala' – Richie Ray & Bobby Cruz
'Ruby Tuesday' – Rolling Stones
'Salsa y control' – LeBrón Brothers
'Salt of the Earth' – Rolling Stones
'San Miguel' – La Protesta
'Se casa la rumba' – Larry Harlow
'Seis tumbao' – La Protesta
'She's a Rainbow' – Rolling Stones

'Si la ven' – Willie Colón and Héctor Lavoe

'Si te contaran' – Luis Frank Arias and Guillermo Rubalcaba

'¡Sonido bestial!' – Richie Ray & Bobby Cruz

'Suavito' – Richie Ray & Bobby Cruz

'Sufrir me tocó a mí en esta vida' – Los Solitaros

'Te conozco bacalao' – Willie Colón

'Te invito a echar un pie' – Ray Pérez

'Tengo poder' – La Conspiración

'Tiembla' – El Gran Combo

'Tin Marin' – Richie Ray & Bobby Cruz

'Toma y dame' – Richie Ray & Bobby Cruz

'Traigo de todo' – Richie Ray & Bobby Cruz

'Trumpet Man II' – Richie Ray & Bobby Cruz

'Vanidad' – Los Tres Ases

'Vengo virao' – Larry Harlow

'White Room' – Cream

'Yo perdí el corazon (¿Qué será de mí?)' – Antonio Cartagena

'Yo soy Babalú' – Richie Ray & Bobby Cruz

PENGUIN MODERN CLASSICS

LOLITA
VLADIMIR NABOKOV

With an Afterword by Craig Raine

'Lolita, light of my life, fire of my loins. My sin, my soul.'

Poet and pervert Humbert Humbert becomes obsessed by twelve-year-old Lolita and seeks to possess her, first carnally and then artistically, out of love, 'to fix once and for all the perilous magic of nymphets'. This seduction is one of many dimensions in Nabokov's dizzying masterpiece, which is suffused with a savage humour and rich, elaborate verbal textures.

'*Lolita* is a comedy, subversive yet divine... you read *Lolita* sprawling limply in your chair, ravished, overcome, nodding scandalized assent'
Martin Amis, *Observer*

Penguin Modern Classics

THE GREAT GATSBY
F. SCOTT FITZGERALD

'A classic, perhaps the supreme American novel'
John Carey, *Sunday Times*, Books of the Century

In *The Great Gatsby*, Fitzgerald brilliantly captures both the disillusion of post-war America and the moral failure of a society obsessed with wealth and status. But he does more than render the essence of a particular time and place, for in chronicling Gatsby's tragic pursuit of his dream, Fitzgerald re-creates the universal conflict between illusion and reality.

'Fitzgerald confronts no less a problem than what might be involved, what might be at stake, in trying to see, and *write*, America itself. *The Great Gatsby* is, I believe, the most perfectly crafted work of fiction to come out of America'
Tony Tanner

'It must be one of the most perfect novels ever written. Technique and tact and moral sensibility are as finely tuned as in any of Turgenev's great novels, and yet it is as American as Hollywood' John McGahern, *Irish Times*

With an Introduction and Notes by Tony Tanner

PENGUIN MODERN CLASSICS

FICTIONS
JORGE LUIS BORGES

'One of the most memorable artists of our age' Mario Vargas Llosa

Jorge Luis Borges's *Fictions* introduced an entirely new voice into world literature. It is here we find the astonishing accounts of Funes, the man who can forget *nothing*; the French poet who recreated Don Quixote word for word; the fatal lottery in Babylon; the mysterious planet of Tlön; and the library containing every possible book in the whole universe. Here too are the philosophical detective stories and haunting tales of Irish revolutionaries, gaucho knife fights and dreams within dreams, which proved so influential (and yet impossible to imitate). This collection was eventually to bring Borges international fame; over fifty years later, it remains endlessly intriguing.

'Hurley's efforts at retranslating Borges are not anything but heroic. His versions are clear, elegant, crystalline' Ilan Stavans, *The Times Literary Supplement*

Translated with an Afterword by Andrew Hurley

PENGUIN MODERN CLASSICS

ON THE ROAD
JACK KEROUAC

'A paean to what Kerouac described as "the ragged and ecstatic joy of pure being"'
Sunday Times

On The Road swings to the rhythms of 1950s underground America, jazz,
sex, generosity, chill dawns and drugs, with Sal Paradise and his hero Dean
Moriarty, traveller and mystic, the living epitome of Beat. Now recognized as a
modern classic, its American Dream is nearer that of Walt Whitman than F. Scott
Fitzgerald's, and the narrative goes racing towards the sunset with unforgettable
exuberance, poignancy and autobiographical passion.

With an Introduction by Ann Charters

PENGUIN MODERN CLASSICS

NEAR TO THE WILDHEART
CLARICE LISPECTOR

'A genius' Colm Tóibín, *Guardian*

Clarice Lispector's sensational, prize-winning debut novel *Near to the Wild Heart* was published when she was twenty-three and earned her the name 'Hurricane Clarice'. It tells the story of Joana, from her wild, creative childhood, as the 'little egg' who writes poems for her father, through her marriage to the faithless Otávio and on to her decision to make her own way in the world. As Joana, endlessly mutable, moves through different emotional states, different inner lives and different truths, this impressionistic, dreamlike and fiercely intelligent novel asks if any of us ever really know who we are.

'Brilliant ... Lispector should be on the shelf with Kafka and Joyce' *Los Angeles Times*

Translated by Alison Entrekin edited by Benjamin Moser

Penguin Modern Classics

WE HAVE ALWAYS LIVED IN THE CASTLE
SHIRLEY JACKSON

With an Afterword by Joyce Carol Oates

'A marvellous elucidation of life … a story full of craft and full of mystery'
The New York Times Book Review

Living in the Blackwood family home with only her sister Constance and her
Uncle Julian for company, Merricat just wants to preserve their delicate way of
life. But ever since Constance was acquitted of murdering the rest of the family,
the world isn't leaving the Blackwoods alone. And when Cousin Charles arrives,
armed with overtures of friendship and a desperate need to get into the safe,
Merricat must do everything in her power to protect the remaining family.

In her final novel, Shirley Jackson displays a mastery of suspense, family
relationships and black comedy.

PENGUIN MODERN CLASSICS

THE WILD BOYS
WILLIAM S. BURROUGHS

'Burroughs's boldest experiment and, perhaps, finest achievement'
Los Angeles Times

In this funny, nightmarish masterpiece of imaginative excess, grotesque characters engage in acts of violent one-upmanship, boundless riches mangle a corner of Africa into a Bacchanalian utopia, and technology, flesh and violence fuse with and undo each other. A fragmentary, freewheeling novel, it sees wild boys engage in vigorous, ritualistic sex and drug taking, as well as pranksterish guerrilla warfare and open combat with a confused and outmatched army. *The Wild Boys* shows why Burroughs is a writer unlike any other, able to make captivating the explicit and horrific.

'An ethereally beautiful book' *Rolling Stone*

Contemporary ... Provocative ... Outrageous ...
Prophetic ... Groundbreaking ... Funny ... Disturbing ...
Different ... Moving ... Revolutionary ... Inspiring ...
Subversive ... Life-changing ...

What makes a modern classic?

At Penguin Classics our mission has always been to make the best
books ever written available to everyone. And that also means
constantly redefining and refreshing exactly what makes a 'classic'.
That's where Modern Classics come in. Since 1961 they have been an
organic, ever-growing and ever-evolving list of books from the last
hundred (or so) years that we believe will continue to be read over and
over again.

They could be books that have inspired political dissent, such as
Animal Farm. Some, like *Lolita* or *A Clockwork Orange*, may have
caused shock and outrage. Many have led to great films, from *In Cold
Blood* to *One Flew Over the Cuckoo's Nest*. They have broken down
barriers – whether social, sexual, or, in the case of *Ulysses*, the
boundaries of language itself. And they might – like *Goldfinger* or
Scoop – just be pure classic escapism. Whatever the reason, Penguin
Modern Classics continue to inspire, entertain and enlighten millions
of readers everywhere.

'No publisher has had more influence on reading habits than Penguin'
Independent

'Penguins provided a crash course in world literature'
Guardian

The best books ever written

PENGUIN  CLASSICS

SINCE 1946